HARD LABOUR

BILL BATEMAN

ODYSSEY
BOOKS

Published by Odyssey Books in 2017

www.odysseybooks.com.au

National Library of Australia
Cataloguing-in-Publication entry

Author: Bill Bateman
Title: Hard Labour / Bill Bateman
ISBN: 978-1-922200-74-7 (pbk)
ISBN: 978-1-922200-75-4 (ebook)

Cover design by Elijah Toten

To Carmel, Zoe and Sally.
For their love, tolerance and support.

1

Dr Vincent Hanrahan woke the second his phone started ringing. It was a habit he'd developed over the years so the subsequent raucous sound wouldn't wake his sleeping partner ... back when he had a sleeping partner.

He glanced at the clock on his bedside table: four-ten am.

'I hope she's bloody well ready this time,' he muttered sleepily, groping around for his jangling mobile. This was Vince's version of the standard prayer of the Obstetrician who'd been called in several times during a long labour. Each time the phone rang, he hoped it would be that fat lady singing.

The patient, a young idealistic first-timer, had started out with high hopes of a natural, drug-free birth. Instead, it had been brutal and soul destroying, so her birth plan, as well as her confidence, lay in tatters on the labour ward floor.

'Hanrahan,' Vince muttered, hoping for the best but fearing a stalemate with maternal distress or a compromised baby. The tone of the midwife's voice would reveal all.

'Good morning, Doctor.' The salutation was at once loud and familiar but upbeat and cheerful. A good sign. 'Better get yourself up here if you want to catch this one, matey. Your girl's pushing and the head's on view.'

This was music to Vince's ears. No Mozart symphony was ever as sweet. He rolled out of bed and pulled on his clothes.

Ten minutes later he pushed open the doors of the birth room at the Warrnambool Base Hospital and inspected the tableaux within. Normally, the patient would be on the bed, attended by a couple of midwives with the partner at the top end. Sometimes, he would arrive in the lull between contractions and everything would be eerily quiet; the nurses checking the baby's heartbeat and the anxious father-to-be offering sips of iced water to the resting woman, with the soothing beep-beep-beep of the foetal monitor in the background.

Or else it would be all action with a cacophony of the characteristic sounds of labour. The patient, red-faced and pushing, straining and shouting or sobbing and laughing simultaneously, like an over-tired toddler; the partner gripping the sweaty hand, making reassuring noises but looking bewildered; the midwives providing counter-traction with experienced hips and exhorting the labourer for that last big effort. Other times Vince would arrive too late and be greeted by the tell-tale sound of a baby crying. Smiles all round.

This time he stood blinking under the blazing birth room lights, gobsmacked and incredulous at the scene he beheld. For an instant he thought he must be in the wrong ward. His patient lay on the birth mat on the floor, surrounded by a group of figures momentarily frozen like an impressionist painting. Protruding from the mother's slack mouth was a rubber tube connected to a cylinder on a trolley; leads were attached to stickers on her chest. A doctor, wielding large white paddles, stared at the monitor on the resuscitation crash trolley—a foreign vehicle in this midwifery terrain. A nurse clutched a black ventilation bag, a young intern was looking intently at the digital display on the blood pressure machine, and in the corner at the head of the king-size bed stood an ashen-faced youth holding a tightly wrapped bundle revealing a glimpse of a wet pink head at one end.

Suddenly the doctor looked up from the monitor and shouted: 'Stand clear!'

All sprang back as he applied the paddles to the girl's chest and watched her limp body twitch convulsively. He barked an order to a nurse who turned up a dial on the trolley, then he did it all again. At once all the players in this macabre drama paused and looked at the monitor and were then galvanised back into action. The intern pushed forcefully on the girl's chest, the nurse began squeezing the black bag, and the senior doctor stared at the screen.

'Bugger it,' he said. 'She's still in VF.'

Everyone seemed transfixed by the erratic, irregular green tracing. Even a mug Obstetrician like Vince recognised the pattern—Ventricular Fibrillation; the girl's heart was producing minimal output, certainly insufficient to perfuse her brain. There was a critical point at which the team realised the CPR, ventilation, drugs and defibrillation had all failed. However, they would all persevere with their tasks until the most senior person called a halt. It was obvious this time had come—everyone was looking to the boss to make that call.

The doctor grimaced, put down the paddles, took a deep breath, and gently shook his head.

The team quickly removed the tube, unhooked the patient from the monitor, disposed of all the spent syringes, packed their gear back onto the trolley, and retreated into the dark corridors of the hospital.

Vince turned to the skinny young man who stood like a statue in the corner, still clutching the swaddled babe and staring in disbelief at the motionless form on the birthing mat. Abruptly, he stepped forward, stumbled. Vince lunged, catching the falling newborn as the man crumpled onto the prostrate figure of the dead girl.

2

Vince handed the baby over to the shocked midwives and walked out into the corridor where the head of the resuscitation team was busily washing his hands at a scrub basin. Danh 'Danny' Nguyen had been in the same year as Vince at medical school and they had roomed together during their first year in college. Danny had only been in Australia two years before he'd blitzed Year Twelve at Melbourne High and romped into Medicine at Melbourne University. He'd done part of his specialist-physician training in Warrnambool, fallen in love with a local girl and settled there, much to the displeasure of his extended Vietnamese family in Melbourne.

'Shit, Ox, I'm sorry,' he said, using Vince's old Newman college football nickname. 'We just couldn't get her going. First arrest I've ever seen on the mid floor, mate. I think I'll leave the next part to you.'

Vince was suddenly very much awake. 'Thanks, Danny. You're probably a bit more used to the death bit. I'm more of a birth man myself.' He shook his head. 'So, what's the story?'

Danny shrugged as he dried his hands. 'There was a Code Blue for the labour ward. Apparently, she'd just delivered then suddenly went flat. They couldn't get a blood pressure reading or pulse so they hit the buzzer.'

'What do you reckon happened, mate?' Vince asked, frowning. 'She was young and healthy.'

'I don't know. Your guess is as good as mine. The midwives say she didn't have a post-partum bleed, so I guess she must have had a pulmonary embolus or an amniotic fluid embolism or something. Cerebral haemorrhage maybe. She didn't have any past cardiac history, did she?'

Vince shook his head. 'No, nothing. Shit, Danny, she was only twenty-three. No history of anything in the past and nothing amiss antenatally.'

The sound of a wailing baby came from the adjacent special care nursery, where Vince and Danny could see the night staff attending to their tiny patients—doing observations, tube feeding, giving antibiotics and checking blood sugars. They watched silently for a minute or two.

'Well,' said Danny eventually, 'we'll just have to wait for Sarah Bell to give us the answer. I'd better get back to ICU. It's more my home ground than this place. And Ox,' he added with a chuckle, 'you've got a big blob of that shitty meconium stuff on your shirt. I knew there was a good reason I didn't go in for Obstetrics.'

Vince tried to wipe off the sticky black mess and only succeeded in spreading it further. His old Prof used to say that meconium had the same tenacity as Lady Macbeth's dammed spot.

'Ninety-five per cent of the time it's all happy days.'

'Yeah, it's the other five per cent I could never stand.'

'You and me both, mate,' Vince muttered, taking a deep breath and returning to the Birth Unit.

* * *

The midwives had the baby on the trolley and were doing what midwives do after a birth; up until now they hadn't had the opportunity. The long umbilical cord was still dangling with the attached forceps swinging like a pendulum and the baby was still covered with greasy, blood-stained vernix. The nurses were visibly upset as they went about their business: shortening the cord, putting on a name band and placing the baby in a warm wrap.

'How's the bub?' asked Vince quietly.

'She's fine, Doc. Good Apgars,' answered the senior night midwife in a subdued tone, completely different to the buoyant one of her early morning phone call of less than thirty minutes ago.

'I'll check her out later, Richo.' He turned his attention to the other side of the room, where the new father was still lying on the birthing mat with his dead girlfriend folded in his arms, her tangled mane of blond hair hanging like a hessian curtain and her nose stud catching the overhead lights and sparkling like the first night star. The boy's skinny body was shaking with convulsive sobbing.

Vince squatted and put one hand on the narrow shoulder and the other on Polly Cotter's hand, which was flopping limply across her lover's lap. 'Emu, I am really sorry about this,' he said slowly, searching for the right words, 'but I think you must have worked out what's happened here.'

The youth suddenly stopped sobbing and turned to face Vince. His long hollow face, framed by jet-black dreadlocks, reminded Vince of a Goya painting he and Lydia had admired at the Prado a lifetime ago.

'Polly is dead, Emu, and … and at this stage I don't know why.'

He paused and forced himself to meet the boy's bewildered gaze. 'It's really rare for someone to die in childbirth these days, mate, so something very unusual must have happened. We'll just have to wait until the post mortem to find out. The doctors and nurses tried every-thing but there was just nothing else they could do.'

Emu Quick's pallid face, scarcely more vascular than that of his girlfriend, whose lifeless body he gently lay back down on the blood-stained drapes covering the birth mat, suddenly crumpled into tears again. Then he slowly stood, shaking his head.

'You must have some bloody idea, Doc. Twenty-three-year-old chicks don't just fucken die havin' babies!'

The words hit Vince like a sledgehammer and forced him to think out loud.

'She could've had a big haemorrhage, mate, just after she had the baby or maybe a problem with her heart. Sometimes an air bubble can develop in the water around the baby, then enter the mother's blood stream and block off a big artery. Or a blood clot can form in a leg vein and travel to the lungs.'

The boy's dark eyes seemed to bore right through Vince and he could see his lame explanation was going nowhere. Words wouldn't work and he knew he should try to reach out to the shocked youth in some way, but he just couldn't. Not anymore.

'Look, mate, I'm really sorry but I don't have the answer. Polly is dead and we'll soon find out why. Your mum and your sister are out in the Nurses Station, why don't you go home with them? The midwives will look after the baby and we'll have another talk when I know more.'

After Emu gave Polly a final embrace and sobbed his last goodbyes, Vince walked him out to the waiting family. The two women jumped up from their chairs expectantly.

'What's goin' on, Aaron?' asked Emu's mum, her voice tremulous and anxious. 'We heard the little one cryin' but they wouldn't let us go in.'

Emu shrugged and shook his head, tears again streaming from his eyes.

His sister, Gabrielle, put her arm around him and looked at Vince. 'We seen all youse runnin' in and out, Dr Vince. Is something wrong with the baby?'

'Polly collapsed just after giving birth,' said Vince quietly. 'I'm sorry to have to tell you both that, unfortunately, she has passed away. The baby is fine,' he added as a lame afterthought. *Beautifully done, dickhead.*

He left them to their grief; there was no point attempting another feeble explanation.

Vince spent several minutes writing a detailed account of the proceedings in Polly's notes—he'd learnt the importance of good records the hard way. Whatever he wrote now would be subjected to intense scrutiny later. He returned to the birth room, already restored to its usual orderly state by the grim-faced nurses, ready for the cleaners who would arrive when morning came. Even Polly had been tidied up and laid out on the birthing bed—her head on a large pillow, closed eyes facing the ceiling, a rolled white towel tucked under her chin and her body a small but symmetrical shape under the bedclothes. It seemed that if all traces of death could be removed, then it was as if it hadn't happened at all.

He went into the nursery to do his routine neonatal baby check. The night supervisor, Pat Richardson, was preparing a bottle of formula—a stark reminder of what had happened.

'Another one of yours came in the middle of all that, Vince,' Pat informed him. 'Lisa Cabresi, a few days over, multi three, contracting since midnight, membranes intact and not much happening on the CTG, so we put her to bed and she's sound asleep now.'

On it goes, thought Vince.

The baby was in good condition and he passed her back into the safekeeping of the sombre midwives. He recorded the details of his examination and headed downstairs and out of the hospital into the cold darkness of pre-dawn. It was just before five as he got into his car; too late to go back to bed and too early to be up.

Vince often found himself wide-awake in the early hours after a bit of labour-ward action and usually went out for a run or surf depending on the swell and his mood. These nocturnal activities made him tired and even grumpier than usual by mid-afternoon, but it was worth it for the luxury of a couple of solitary hours in the ocean.

These days he preferred his own company to the clamour of the maddening crowd. He figured Thomas Hardy was right on the money whereas John Donne had it all wrong. Vince was quite content to be an island. Not only that, but after the events of tonight, he knew there would be rough seas ahead and he needed some time in the wind and waves to clear his head.

Sitting there in the hospital car park, surrounded by darkness, Vince suddenly had a vivid vision of *another* dead woman in *another* labour ward and was instantly reminded of the reason for his banishment to the bush. He immediately felt that familiar tightness in his chest and escalating sense of panic, and fought to slow down his breathing as he'd been taught.

He fired up the engine of his ancient Volvo station wagon, Benny, and pulled out, heading south through the dark town, turning left onto Merri Street, which ran along above the main beach, and parked in behind the sand dunes at his favourite surfing spot, the Flume.

Vince clambered up onto the sand hill behind the car park to check out the surf. As always it was lighter at the beach and judging from the sound of the waves and what he could see and feel, there seemed to be a good offshore breeze and a decent swell. Being winter there was no one else around and Vince was happy to put up with the cold in return for the solitude.

He plodded and slid back down the hill to the car park, lifted

Benny's tailgate and pulled his gear out onto the cold, damp sand, shivering inside as he recalled that pale, lifeless body on the floor.

Clad in his old Rip Curl steamer wetsuit, he paddled out through the surf just as the sun started its ascent over the breakwater and the heavy black curtain began to lift. He felt that familiar stinging salty slap in the face as he rode up and over the freezing white water.

3

After his early morning surf, Vince ducked home and fed his perpetually hungry dog, Deefer. He'd recently moved from a depressing sixties-style unit on the highway to a small house in South Warrnambool, an unfashionable part of town near the beach, his modest dwelling close to the large textile factory that had provided employment for generations of his neighbours. Vince reckoned the area was the town's best-kept secret, but unfortunately some local developers agreed and rows of fisherman's cottages like his were slowly being replaced by boxy apartments for yuppies and empty nesters.

His new abode was within walking distance of the beach and the rent was cheap, but the twins, who'd visited last weekend, had been less than impressed with his choice.

'This place is so cold, Dad,' commented Tessa, 'and there's nowhere to sit down or put your stuff.'

'Yeah,' added Georgie. 'And the bathroom is gross! Living in this dump is like camping. It's *sooo* not like a real home.'

Christ, thought Vince, *they are fourteen-year-olds, what do they know?* 'Listen girls, I won't be here all that long, so there's no point getting too carried away with the *Home Beautiful* thing.'

'It was better the last time we came,' Georgie went on, 'when you were in that poxy flat. At least the toilet flushed properly.'

'Okay girls, I get the message,' he responded. 'Tell you what, I'll enter the joint in one of those TV makeover shows and get it zizzed up before your next visit.' *Which gives me plenty of time*, he observed darkly, as he dropped them off at the station on the Sunday night.

Deefer gobbled up her tucker but Vince couldn't come at any breakfast himself—his nerves were jangling too much, just like when he was drinking, and he quickly poured down a strong instant coffee before jumping in the shower. After rinsing off the salty ocean water he emerged cleaner and warmer, then stepped out onto the faded blue lino and glanced at himself in the cracked mirror on the back of the bathroom door.

The steamy image looking back was certainly no oil painting: freckly Wimmera skin, a completely chrome dome, and a dial only a mother could love. Big enough—over six foot two in the old, and solidly put together.

'You're built like a brick dunny, son,' his father used to tell him from the boundary line, 'so get in and bust a few packs open.'

So he did, and now had the crooked hooter, buggered knees and bent fingers to show for it. Lydia used to say his smile was his most attractive feature but Vince didn't do much smiling these days.

Forty minutes in the cold Southern Ocean had certainly cleaned out the cobwebs, but a nauseating sense of déjà vu remained and he knew that not even a tsunami would wash that away. He returned to the hospital with an unsettling feeling of dread.

Vince parked and walked up the ramp to the main entrance. The Warrnambool Base Hospital was an architectural hotchpotch of different styles and vintages, with the original redbrick building surrounded by two sixties-era cream brick wings and now a recent modern extension with sleek rendered walls, shiny metal panels and gleaming glass windows; mostly, as far as Vince could tell, to accommodate the ever expanding Administration Department.

He started his rounds as usual with the children's ward and finished on the midwifery floor, where, as well as the new baby, he had a thirty-one weeker with high blood pressure. His other overnight obstetric admission had proved to be a false alarm and been sent home, and he had two postnatal patients to visit.

In his previous life, Vince used to sit on the bed of each new mother and earnestly quiz her about after-pains, sore perineum and engorged breasts, and cluck-cluck over every newly hatched sprog. These days, he just raced through the ward and the staff knew they would have to virtually trip him up if they want him to attend to something.

After the round, he scribbled in the patients' progress notes and looked up at the Nurse Unit Manager. 'Barbara, could you arrange a little meeting for me with the staff that were on last night?'

'Well, Doctor Hanrahan, I hardly think a meeting is necessary at this stage,' answered Sister Barbara Craig. 'We will conduct our usual routine debriefing following a maternal or foetal death. Surely we should wait for the autopsy and Coroner's findings before any further discussion?' A frown creased her brow. 'The hospital insurers will expect a major incident report in due course. My staff from last night are naturally upset and are having a well-earned rest before the debriefing this afternoon.'

Lucky midwives. The nursing hierarchy obviously realised that it made good sense to provide counselling to staff after traumatic events. There was no such luxury for doctors. No doubt there had been many incidents, especially during his early days in the game, which had caused Vince significant psychological angst. Of course he hadn't realised this at the time; like most young doctors he thought he was bullet proof. And there was nothing a few glasses of red couldn't fix.

'Oh come on, Barbara, it's no big deal,' he responded impatiently. 'I'm the one carrying the can here and it would be useful to have a talk about Polly's labour to try to see what might've gone wrong. Call it quality assurance.'

She paused, considering his request. They went back a long way and he knew she would cooperate eventually—in her formal, prickly, old-school way. Barbara had been a charge nurse at the Royal Women's Hospital when Vince was a resident and she still treated him like the ignorant ingénue he was back then. Her reputation was that of a very good midwife, an excellent leader who didn't take shit from anyone.

When Vince first arrived in town, there was initially much gossip about the two of them getting together, but that was never going to happen. She was completely wrapped up in her job—twenty-four-seven; in fact, Vince wouldn't be surprised if she wore her uniform to bed. Besides which, she just did not press his buttons.

'Barb, I haven't got all day. Let's just make a time and get on with it.'

'Very well, Doctor,' she relented, with an air of condescension. 'Shall we say one o'clock here in the staff tea room?'

$$4$$

Vince pulled into the car park at the rear of the surgery and fumbled for his stethoscope from amongst the mess on the passenger seat. Benny was dark blue, twenty-five years old and was a fine example of that large and square Volvo-style of the late eighties—safe but definitely not stylish. It was all Vince could afford when he arrived last year, and he could fit his surfboard in Benny's capacious interior. He grabbed his bag and pushed open the back door.

The Timor Street Medical Centre had once been a stately sandstone house circa 1895 and sat grandly on the corner a block down from the hospital. Vince's predecessors had adapted the building over the years. The dining room at the front was now a reception area and the grand sitting room a waiting room. Vince had to admit the joint was classy enough, but the vagaries of GP clinic architecture were not his bag. As far as he was concerned it was always just another day at the salt mines. He was there under sufferance—a conscript. The Medical Board had deemed that he work in one of the town's general practices as well as be a faux-Obstetrician, so he had no choice in the matter. For now.

As soon as he opened the door, Vince was greeted by the usual barrage of familiar sounds: the continuous ringing of the phones, the babble of conversation from the waiting room, the voices of the staff making appointments and processing accounts, babies crying and consulting room doors opening and closing. He was met by a guard of honour—a phalanx of receptionists, each wielding a piece of paper and jockeying for position to gain his attention first.

'Mr Norton is waiting to pick up his referral for the dermatologist—'

'Sister O'Shea wants you to visit Mrs Nervo at lunchtime—'

'There's a man from the meat works with a cut hand and Rita thinks it will need a stitch—'

'Okay, okay, just give me a bloody chance, girls,' Vince barked as he resolutely headed past the throng of waiting punters to his room. He flopped down at his desk and tossed the messages onto yesterday's pile.

He'd learnt that this constant state of chaos was part and parcel of being a 'Geep', a term coined by his old uncle—a GP in a one-doctor town in the Mallee. Just like a Jeep was a 'general purpose vehicle for rough terrain', Uncle Phonse reckoned this was a good working definition for a GP. He also referred to patients as 'punters' on the basis that consulting a Geep was akin to backing a racehorse. Variable odds.

Before kicking off, Vince had a couple of important calls to make. The first was to the Coroner. He had absolutely no idea of the cause of Polly Cotter's death, so he couldn't fill in the death certificate, which automatically made it a Coroner's case—there would have to be a post mortem. He then rang the Victorian Medical Defence Association to speak with Bridget Ryan, a medical litigation lawyer and a contemporary of Vince's from uni days, who was the VMDA Claims Manager.

'Good to hear from you, Vince. You just can't seem to keep out of trouble, can you? I thought you'd be okay down there in the country. So was this girl a private patient?'

'No, Bridget, she was public.'

'Where was the antenatal care conducted? '

'At my rooms.' He was wondering where this was all going.

'Okay, unless something can be sheeted home to her antenatal course clinically, then it's a job for VMIA.'

More bloody acronyms. 'Come again?'

'Don't you guys keep up with the changing world of medical indemnity?'

Vince was in no mood for a medical insurance current affairs quiz. 'Bridget, with all due respect, I was hoping never to speak to you again.'

She sighed deeply. 'I never cease to be amazed how allegedly intelligent specialists seem unable to keep up to speed. Vince, listen and learn. Since 1998 the Victorian Managed Insurance Authority has covered all Victorian public hospitals. VMDA only apply to a doctor's activities in their rooms or involving private patients in hospital. This is definitely a job for the VMIA.' Bridget paused. 'You're not anticipating any litigation at this stage?'

'I certainly bloody hope not,' Vince answered, aware of a sudden burst of gastric tightening. 'I'm just being a good boy and reporting an adverse outcome, like I've been told.'

'About time too. I'll open a file on the matter and ring the VMIA and get them to contact you. Keep in touch. Regards to Lydia and the girls. Cheers.'

Regards to Lydia! Who's the one not keeping up? Vince took a deep breath, booted up his computer and called in his first patient, Mrs Aureline Dove. He had one important call yet to make, but it would just have to wait.

Mrs Dove was an absolute heart sinker—a GP's nightmare. She had some legitimate medical concerns but they were buried beneath a veritable avalanche of the psychosomatic and the neurotic.

After unloading her after only twenty-three minutes, probably a record, Vince was still confident that if he could rip the next one through he could get back on track, but he came up against another shocker—a middle-aged woman who casually tossed an unopened seven-page insurance medical form on his desk.

He picked up the phone and let the young receptionist have it with both barrels. 'Listen Suzie or Tracey or whoever you are, these bloody medicals need a double appointment and you've got to get the punters to fill in their part of the form first! Got it?'

He raced the alarmed patient rapidly through the process and herded her out the door—nineteen minutes flat, definitely a record. By this stage he was almost an hour behind, fast losing confidence and praying for a quickie like a pill script or blood pressure check.

His next patient was new; a pleasant looking man is his mid-sixties.

'What can I do for you, Mr Perkins?'

The bloke unravelled a long list from his pocket and said in a jocular voice, 'Doc, how long have you got?'

Bugger, thought Vince, *the game's up—the medical gods have turned against me!*

'Just excuse me, mate. I'll be back in a minute.' He marched out the door, through the busy waiting room, past the office staff and out into the tearoom, where he collapsed into an easy chair. 'Shit, shit, *shit!*'

Vince's boss, Dr Shirley Tiang, a tiny bird-like figure with an elfin face and dressed entirely in black, was sitting at the tearoom table with a coffee, doing some paperwork.

'Having a bloody bad day, eh Vince? You're buzzing around like a fart in a bottle, cobber.'

Shirley, a Malaysian Chinese, was in her late fifties and married to Gareth Jones, the local psychiatrist. She'd started the clinic from scratch several years back and built it up into a thriving concern, and Vince was grateful she'd taken him on. He knew he was a risk.

'Geez you're astute, Shirl,' he replied. 'I thought I was hiding it really well.'

'You're always Mr Grumpy anyways, champ,' she commented, head cocked and dangly earrings jangling. 'Makes it hard to tell.' Shirley reminded Vince of Puck from *A Midsummer Night's Dream*, but with more attitude.

On day one last year, Vince had sauntered in fifteen minutes late for his first meeting with his new employer. 'Hey sunshine,' he'd said to the receptionist, 'white with one sugar, and tell the boss I'm here.'

Shirley had come out of her room fuming, shrewd eyes flashing. 'Don't you dare keep me bloody well waiting, mate. Just cos you're a big shot fanny mechanic doesn't mean jackshit here.'

Jesus, he'd thought, *she's a bloody mad woman!* 'Settle, Dr Tiang. I'll soon get the hang of the joint. It's only general practice, how hard can it be?'

'I'll tell you nothing for something, buddy. You've got a lot to learn and if you don't pull your leg round here, I will drop you right back in the shits with the board!'

Hell, this is going to be a bloody long sentence.

Vince soon discovered Shirley had boundless energy, a good head for business and mostly female clientele—'tears and smears, mate'. And that she looked after her own.

He suppressed a yawn. 'Just running miles behind, Shirl, the usual thing.' He sighed. 'Oh yeah,' he went on, after staring at the wall for thirty seconds, 'there's also the small issue of a maternal death.'

Vince knew Shirley would've learnt of last night's events on her rounds that morning. Not much got past her and the sombre mood on the mid-floor had been palpable.

'I did hear something from a tiny bird on the grape line.'

Shirley loved to use Aussie sayings and slang but often butchered them, despite constant correcting by Vince and the other doctors. Her father had learnt his English while working in a factory in western Sydney and it was this rough mix of Sino-strine, swearing and collo-quialisms that she had grown up with. She also added frequent mala-propisms to this bizarre linguistic cocktail.

'What a bastard, eh? So what happened, bud? Give me the drums?'

After his talk with Bridget Ryan, Vince had tried to push last night's events from his mind, but they were still there—right at the front.

'It was Polly Cotter, Shirl. She had a long first stage with a posterior position, but then it all came good and she did the business but collapsed and arrested after the third stage. Danny and his troops just couldn't get her going, then it was thank you linesmen, thank you ballboys.'

Vince sat back in his chair pensively.

'How old was Polly, Vince? Only about bloody twenty?'

He nodded. 'Twenty-three.'

Shirley shook her head with disbelief, earrings chattering. 'Can't remember the last maternal death round here, bud. Be way back before my times. Bad shit for you.'

Vince shrugged. Nothing to say.

'She didn't have any relevant past histories, did she? Or antenatal problems?'

He shook his head.

'Maternal death, mate, rarer than chicken's teeth these days. It's a Coroner's case then?'

'Well I can hardly write the death certificate, can I, Doctor?' Vince responded impatiently. 'Unless you want me to make something up!'

He pushed back his chair and stood. 'Listen Shirley, I know the routine. I've rung the Coroner and reported the death to the medical defence people and now I'm just waiting for Sarah Bell to do the PM. Must've been a concealed bleed or a cardiac thing or a pulmonary embolus or some other such bloody bolt from the blue.' Vince pointed at his chest and shook his head. 'Nothing to do with me.'

The tearoom phone suddenly burst into sound. Shirley picked it up and listened for a few seconds.

'Vicki has resigned because you yelled at her and Mr Perkins is at the reception desk saying he can't wait any longer and is about to blow his heap.'

'Too bad,' Vince muttered, sitting back in his chair and looking at the new man's card, which was still in his hand. 'It says here he's retired, so what else does he have to do?'

Shirley put her ear to the phone for another minute. 'Apparently he works at the Red Cross shop and runs the Meals on Wheels and needs to get back home to check on his disabled wife. Shit, Rooned, the man's a *good doer!*'

One of Vince's old patients had dubbed him 'Rooned' after a character sharing his surname in a poem penned by Father John O'Brien—an Aussie bush poet from early last century. That particular Hanrahan was an eternal pessimist who constantly predicted ruination for the locals—'We'll all be rooned, said Hanrahan, before the season's out.' Shirley thought this was hilarious and habitually called Vince 'Rooned', especially when she thought he was being a wet blanket—like most of the time.

She turned her attention back to the phone. 'Tell him Dr Hanrahan is on his way, Lynne.'

'Shirl, you are better than any anti-depressant pills,' Vince responded, laughing for the first time that day, as he reluctantly headed back to his room. 'A good doer is someone who likes his tucker; you know, good on the tooth. This bloke's a do *gooder*!'

5

Eventually Vince got through his morning session then had a long phone discussion with the VMIA case manager Bridget Ryan had arranged. She must have worded the bloke up about Vince's past, because the case manager seemed wary to the point of being accusatory. *And he's supposed to be on my side*, thought Vince with a shudder.

He was all too aware he still hadn't rung the Australian Medical Board—the number of which he knew off by heart—but he told himself he was just too busy for the moment. Do it later. He was already running late for the meeting at the mid floor, so he bolted out the door, drove back to the hospital and sprinted up those familiar stairs.

'Sorry I'm late guys,' he said, wedging himself onto a stool next to the coffee machine in the midwives lounge. The three nurses from last night, and of course Barbara Craig—obviously there to bat for her staff—were all squeezed around the table, as well as Dr Petra Smit, the hospital resident who had been covering the mid floor last night.

Petra was a local girl who'd done her internship at the Royal Melbourne Hospital last year and had apparently struggled to cope with the demands of the job. She had then unexpectedly returned home and was now a second year resident at the Warrnambool Hospital. Suddenly she knew everything. The roster included regular GP sessions at the Timor Street practice, which Shirley regarded as a good way of identifying potential future recruits, but definitely not in Petra's case.

'That sheila is lazy as sins,' she'd told Vince after Petra's first week. 'Wouldn't work in an iron kidney!'

The midwife who'd been assigned to Polly last night was Louise Bourboulis, a thirty-four-year-old mother of three who looked uncharacteristically tired and pale. The night shift Nurse Unit Manager, Pat Richardson, a large cheerful middle-aged woman with a ruddy pleasant face, had also been involved in the labour, as well as Rita Findlay. Rita was one of the practice nurses at the Timor Street Clinic and did occasional shifts on the mid floor to keep her hand in.

Vince had met Rita and her husband Allan a few months after his arrival in Warrnambool, at the mid floor Christmas party. He hadn't been feeling especially festive but went along because he knew how important it was to stay on the right side of the midwives. He and Allan, a Deakin University academic, had quickly found they had a lot in common including surfing, the Geelong football club, and their senses of humour—although Vince's was mostly in recession. Allan was to become the closest thing he had to a friend in the town, which suited Vince fine. He'd be gone soon enough.

Seeing Rita reminded Vince that Polly Cotter had been working in Allan's department at the university and helping him set up Abgrow, his precious new abalone farm.

'Have you told Allan about Polly yet, Rita?' Vince asked quietly, while the others were loading up on coffee.

'Yes, I just spoke to him a few minutes ago,' Rita answered, her voice flat with fatigue. 'He was in Melbourne last night accepting a gong at a big aquaculture award presentation and he's coming home on tonight's train. He was supervising Polly for her PhD, which is, I mean *was*, about abalone breeding. She'd been doing a lot of the work for Abgrow. He's really upset.' She paused. 'They were *very* close.'

Vince detected a hint of extra topspin in the last phrase. *Probably just sleep deprivation playing with my mind.*

Barbara waited till Vince and Rita stopped chatting, cleared her throat and put on her 'let's get on with it' look.

'So what's this, Vince?' said Pat, arms akimbo, in her customary forthright manner. 'The Inquisition?'

'No, Richo,' Vince responded. 'It's not a matter of pointing the finger, I just want to have a chat about Polly's labour. Any maternal death needs close scrutiny.' *Ain't that the truth.*

'I have the partogram printout here, Doctor,' said Barbara. 'Perhaps you would be the best person to start off, Louise?'

Louise scanned the chart that detailed the progress of Polly's labour: observations, nature and frequency of contractions, and drugs given. Everything relevant to the labour was supposed to be recorded.

'Well, according to the changeover from the late shift,' she said slowly, 'Emu rang about eight and said Polly thought her waters had broken during the morning, but she wasn't contracting. Cos she was a primip and not due for a week, Pete told her to stay put and ring back in two hours. So he called back after we came on, and she was having fifteen-minutelys, so I told him to bring her in. We did her obs and an amnicator was positive for liquor, and the trace showed regular contractions. So I rang Dr Hanrahan, told him her waters had broken and that she was in early labour, and put her to bed in the low risk birth room.'

'So on admission her obs were all okay?' Vince asked, keen to cut to the chase.

'Blood Pressure 110/65, temp 36.5 and urine NAD,' Lou read off the chart. 'But then after an hour or so her contractions stopped all together, so at ten-thirty I rang you to come and assess her.' She peered closely at the page. 'The sooner we start using computerised partograms the better.'

'Let me translate, Lou,' Vince said, holding out his hand for the partogram. 'I did a vaginal examination and she was only three centimetres dilated and the foetal heart looked okay on the tracings, so I got young Petra here to put up a drip and give her some synto to get things moving.'

'I wondered about that at the time, Dr Hanrahan,' said Petra Smit promptly. 'She wasn't due for a week. I assumed you would just wait and see if she came into labour by herself before intervening with drugs.'

'Come on, Petra,' Vince responded impatiently. 'Her bloody membranes had been ruptured for twelve hours. At thirty-nine weeks do you think there's any point in exposing the baby to the risk of intra-uterine infection by just sitting on your hands once the membranes have gone?'

Petra sat back in sullen silence, arms and legs angrily crossed. With her pencil thin figure, heavy makeup and impatient, fidgety demeanour, Vince felt she had 'urban specialist' or 'wife of same' written all over her.

'Be that as it may, Dr Hanrahan,' said Barbara, eager to stick to the main game, 'if patients in the low risk birth room require IVs, they should be moved to one of the normal labour wards. By definition, they have ceased to be low risk.'

She was talking to Vince, but looking at Pat. 'This is clearly detailed in the regulations governing the use of the room.'

Vince could see Pat seething and about to explode, so he hurriedly cut in. 'Mea culpa, mea culpa,' he said, fist over his heart. 'I told Richo it was okay. Polly just needed a bit of tickle with the synto, so it was hardly worth shifting the whole shooting match up the corridor.'

As far as Vince was concerned, birth room or not, when the shit hit the fan, it was on with the lights, off with the music, out with the bystanders and in with the technology. Sometimes this made him unpopular but it kept him out of trouble. Most of the time.

Having made her point, Barbara looked at Louise, eyebrows raised quizzically.

'Okay,' said Lou, 'the labour got going with the syntocinon drip and Polly started contracting well. She was doing okay with the gas but then she became distressed and we gave her pethidine, one hundred milligrams at eleven. The foetal heart was good and she was resting well between contractions.'

'Then about midnight, she really started to struggle,' added Pat, looking at the partogram. 'A lot of back pain, and it was smelling like posterior to me, so we rang the doc again.'

Vince retrieved the chart. 'I reassessed her at a quarter past two and she certainly had a posterior position with a high head and only five centimetres dilated. I considered an epidural but her pelvis seemed pretty roomy so I hoped she would rotate spontaneously. We turned up the synto and hoped for the best.'

He glanced at Petra, but she passed no comment.

'She laboured on pretty fast after that,' said Louise, 'and the head seemed to be coming down. We gave her more peth at two-forty-five and she really seemed to crack on.'

Rita chimed in. 'I came in for a short time at about half past three, while Lou was at tea,' she said. 'Polly was just starting to get a bit of an urge to push by the time Lou came back.'

Lou nodded her agreement. 'After a while, the urge got pretty strong, so we let her have a crack. As she was a primip, I didn't expect much, but after three good pushes, suddenly the head was on view, so I pressed the button.'

'When I came in and saw the state of play,' said Pat, 'I rang Vince and paged Dr Smit, and went back to give Lou a hand.'

'I came in too,' said Rita, with a wry smile. 'I know Pat's views on the birth room. I thought I could help with the hands-on while she did the paperwork.'

'Then everything seemed to go so fast,' said Louise. 'Polly gave one of those huge long pushes and suddenly the head was delivered and before we could see which way it was restituting, the baby just shot out with a big gush of clear fluid. Then we gave her the syntometrine straight into the drip.'

She took a deep breath and went on, speaking very quickly with a hysterical edge to her voice. 'So I clamped and cut the cord and gave the baby to Rita and waited for the third stage. Polly was so happy and she and Emu were laughing and crying and really excited. But she suddenly seemed to go flat, so I raised the foot of the bed, checked for a post partum haemorrhage, rubbed up her fundus, and called out to Pat. Then I pulled on the cord and the placenta delivered.'

By now, Louise was sobbing and Pat put a strong capable hand on hers.

'I did her obs,' said Pat. 'Couldn't get a blood pressure, she wasn't breathing and had no pulse, so I called a Code Blue, turned up the drip flat chat, gave her some oxygen, and Rita and I started CPR.'

'Then the crash team arrived,' Louise cut in, the words tumbling out like a waterfall. 'It was just like a bad dream, as if we weren't even there. Those resus people and all their stuff—they don't belong on the mid floor. Our girls don't die up here … and Emu just stood there with the baby, poor guy didn't know what the hell was going on, he just—'

'Well he wasn't Robinson Crusoe there, Lou,' said Pat, in her sensible maternal way, putting her arm around the distraught Louise. 'None of us knew what was happening. I think that's just about enough for you now. It's time we all pulled up stumps and went home. In the words of my son—shit happens. It certainly wasn't your fault, Louie. You did a great job, my love.'

They all sat in silence for a minute or so, Louise sobbing quietly.

'So, Doctor,' said Barbara, as she started gathering up her papers. 'Unless you have any specific questions, I think we should leave it at that. I don't wish to have my staff upset needlessly. They've been through enough already.'

Vince was now running very late and his lunch had consisted of two cups of hospital grade instant coffee. He certainly had questions but what he really needed was answers.

Petra Smit abruptly rose and walked off with a churlish toss of her well-groomed curls. Against his better judgment, Vince followed her out.

'You got a problem, Petra?'

She looked about ready to explode. 'I'm just sooo over being told what to do by a bunch of country hick doctors who think their way is the only way. I'm expected to be in ten different places at once, like … "Mr Carruthers wants you in theatre", "an old gomer down in ED needs an IV", "Dr Tiang's expecting you at the clinic", and on and on. I didn't come back here to be a slave!'

'Welcome to the world of medicine, Petra,' Vince responded. 'It is what it is. And if you hate working down here so much, why did you leave the Royal Melbourne?'

She paused and looked away, her manner suddenly more vulnerable. 'I needed to … well, I just got sick down there, that's all … and then Dad wanted me to come home.'

What was that really all about? Chronic Fatigue Syndrome or depression maybe? Pure bloody laziness, more like!

Petra quickly reverted to her usual churlish self. 'And for the hours I work at that clinic, the money that woman pays me is pitiful.'

Vince shook his head and pointed his finger at her. 'If it's all about money, Doctor Smit, you'd better head back to the big smoke and take up Orthopaedics, but until then—stop whingeing, princess, and suck it up!'

* * *

Vince dashed back to the clinic for his afternoon session and eventually rounded off the day with two phone calls. First a predictably unpleasant discussion with the Medical Board.

His current provisional registration allowed him to work in general practice, but only in a rural area of designated need, and to handle only low-risk obstetrics and even then under supervision, which meant he had to discuss every case with a board-appointed consultant from the Royal Women's Hospital. That person was Professor Lachlan McDonald, an experienced clinician and zealous administrator. As Shirley put it—'inflexible little prick and a brown arse licker!'

The two had been young Turks together during their specialist training; back then Vince had pipped McDonald for the prized Senior Registrar post in the Professorial Unit. They'd both moved on—Vince on and down, and McDonald on and up, but after all these years the newly minted Prof obviously still bore a grudge. As far as Vince and his mates were concerned, Lachlan McDonald had always had a bad case of 'little man' syndrome and although he was very much a 'Lachlan', they'd always called him 'Little Lachie'. As Vince punched in the man's number, he regretted for a moment that it had been more in derision than affection.

'A maternal death, Vincent, that's the last thing you need! The one thing you can't afford to have on your hands. You've got to realise that your professional future—'

'Lachlan, believe me,' Vince cut in ever so politely, suppressing an urge to tell McDonald to fuck off. 'I fully understand the implications. I'll send you a full report and a copy to the board, and after the PM I will certainly be in touch again. Good to chat, bye.'

6

Vince pushed open the hospital Pathology Lab doors and headed for the post mortem room. As usual he felt apprehensive in the sterile terrain. Starting the day cutting up dead people had never really appealed to him, so back in medical school he'd veered away from Pathology, instead choosing a specialty with live punters and mostly happy endings.

That's not to say the young Vincent Hanrahan didn't have a bit of time for aspiring pathologists. Especially one. Back in first year, Sarah Bell had been tall and willowy with a serene, almost mystical expression and Vince had immediately fallen for this ephemeral creature with the golden tresses. They shared a love of old movies, especially *Casablanca*, and Vince let his ginger hair grow and started reading Herman Hesse.

The relationship had peaked during a brief holiday on the NSW north coast, their version of 'we'll always have Paris', where Vince and Sarah had spent having sweaty sex, smoking dope and reading poetry to each other. They'd split up soon after, mostly due to the impending arrival of the Wimmera Football League finals (rather than the advancing German Army) and he'd then shaved off the beard and re-joined the mainstream.

They'd seen very little of each other during the intervening twenty-odd years, until on his first day in Warrnambool when Vince walked into the hospital Pathology department to chase up a result.

'Of all the labs in all the towns in all the world, you had to walk into mine,' said Sarah, giving him a hug. 'What are you doing here, Ricky?'

'Long story, Ilsa,' he responded, 'but both your obstetricians have shot through and I've been dispatched to fill the gap.'

'So you've taken over from Ravi and Cora.'

'Not really, Sarah. I'm the town's Clayton's obstetrician—doing the Caesars and complicated deliveries, but mostly general practice.'

The irony was that Sarah was now the conservative Benz-driving head of Pathology and Vince was the bohemian. Her long flaxen hair was now a Hilary Clinton-style silver helmet and the cheesecloth and denim had morphed into tailored suits and gold jewellery. Vince still found her attractive, but only in an aseptic sort of way—she'd always been more Grace Kelly than Ingrid Bergman. 'A classy chick,' was Shirley description, 'but no va va vooms!'

He entered the PM room and suppressed a shudder—the intense fluorescent overhead lights, polished concrete floor and large stainless steel sinks reminding him he was on foreign soil. Polly Cotter's body lay uncovered on the slab and a technician was suturing the large Y-shaped incision on the chest and abdomen, emphasising the chilling reality of her death.

'Morning, Vince,' said Sarah, pulling off her gloves, cap and gown and teasing her hair back into order. 'I don't know what to make of this one.' She nodded at the slab, paused and washed her hands. 'Usually with a postpartum death, it's just a case of "rounding up the usual suspects", which are haemorrhage, eclampsia, obstructed labour and sepsis, so …'

'But this was virtually bloody *intra*partum,' interrupted Vince impatiently. 'And she had no temp, BP was fine and the labour was not obstructed.'

'So,' continued Sarah, 'because it was so soon and sudden, I was looking for a cardiac cause, pulmonary embolus, cerebral bleed or amniotic fluid embolism, but your lady had none of the above. Did she a have a PPH, Vince?'

He shook his head, annoyed. 'Sarah, I'd have bloody well told you if she'd had a bleed! Only about two hundred mills all up—par for the course. Anyway, you tell me. Any sign of a concealed haemorrhage?'

Vince was only too aware that if a labouring woman bleeds behind the placenta, sometimes the blood can accumulate inside the uterus and shear the placenta off, causing the demise of the baby as well as a sudden deterioration in the condition of the mother. Double fatality.

Sarah shrugged her shoulders. 'No intrauterine blood clot and the placenta looked fine, and there is nothing to suggest blood loss was the cause of death anyway.'

She sat at her desk and began entering the details of the post-mortem into a laptop, seemingly satisfied she had performed her professional duty. A bit too satisfied for Vince's liking.

'So, what you're telling me,' he said impatiently, pointing at the inert form on the slab, 'is that Polly Cotter was a perfectly healthy young woman who had a baby and now happens to be dead. So much for the science of Pathology. Aren't you supposed to have the winning envelope, Doctor?'

Back in medical school they used to have a weekly conference about a patient who'd recently died. Each group, from the lowliest medical students through to the Professor of Medicine, would give an opinion about the likely diagnosis. Then, like the presenter opening the winning envelope at the Oscars, the pathologist would step up and give the post-mortem findings, and all would be revealed. As Vince and his mates loudly commented, it was all a bit late for that poor bastard anyway, but he realised Sarah loved the fact that the pathologist always had the final say. He also knew she liked to have the last word in her personal life too, and mostly did. Except for once.

She peered at him over her glasses. 'Settle down, Vince. Do you want me to invent a cause of death? I have some tissue blocks to look at with the microscope and we sampled some blood from her pulmonary vein to send off to the Victorian Institute of Forensic Medicine for chemistry and toxicology, so we might find an answer there.'

'And how long's that gunna take? Bloody weeks I'm guessing.'

'The VIFM stuff is usually a twenty-four-hour turnaround, Vince. Some of it takes longer. If they draw a blank, I will forward my report to the Coroner and there will have to be an inquest.'

The sound of that word hit Vince right in the guts. 'This just keeps getting better and better.'

'Have you gone through her notes, Vince? Sometimes nursing staff forget some of the clinical details, and even doctors can be prone to overlook important information, especially if their record keeping is a bit lax.'

Battling to control his temper, Vince looked hard at his surroundings and was struck by the orderliness around him—'a place for everything and everything in its place,' as his dad used to say. No chance of any paperwork going astray here.

'Listen, Dr Bell,' he retorted. 'I don't need any advice about the importance of good medical records. If you happened to be watching the national news last year, you'd know I've been reminded about that from a higher authority than you! But I have a maternal death on my hands and I need answers. So if you can't tell me something helpful, then get back to your slides and formalin and I'll return to the real world of live patients!'

Certainly when he was in private practice in the eastern suburbs of Melbourne, Vince had been a medical cowboy—an administrator's nightmare. He delivered over four hundred babies a year and raced between the fashionable hospitals in a large German car with an ego to match. He was a big hero, bringing new life into the world—too busy for that trivial paperwork crap!

But that was all in the past. Now he wrote everything down. In triplicate. Last night he'd gone through Polly's file with a fine-toothed comb. The partogram had been filled in appropriately by everyone involved; the nurses had dutifully recorded Polly's observations, and his own notes were clear and even legible. The record showed that at four-fifteen Polly Cotter had popped out the baby and then while the midwives were waiting for the placenta, she'd quietly died.

'Okay, Vince, okay, believe me I'm trying to help,' said Sarah, unfazed by his flare up. 'I know you regard pathologists as a necessary evil but you'd be lost without us. I just don't have any other answer for you right now.'

After a few minutes' silence, Vince took a deep breath, exhaling slowly. 'It just doesn't make sense. She was only twenty-three,' he said, his voice quieter but tighter. 'Something stinks about the whole thing.'

Sarah stared at him, *into* him. 'I think you're getting a bit paranoid.

Remember Occam's razor? A cock up is more likely than a conspiracy?' She paused as her printer shot out a copy of the post-mortem findings. 'Perhaps you've been spending too much time with the police. Or maybe you're just getting a little soft and caring in your old age.'

Vince let the first cryptic reference go through to the keeper, but he took a swing at the other one. 'I'm just covering my arse, because the Board is going to come after me. Sure, I don't like losing a patient but I did nothing wrong in the care of Polly Cotter. I need to find out what bloody well happened so no one can point the finger at me!'

7

Vince strode angrily from the room, his head buzzing. What was with that psychoanalysis? Sarah was a pathologist, not a bloody shrink. *Soft and caring—what a load of crap!* The compassionate approach hadn't served him too well in the past, so when he'd moved down to Warrnambool he'd dispensed with it all together—just like giving up sex. Or drinking.

The only exceptions to Vince's emotion-free zone were his kids. He still loved them unreservedly, but at a distance—three hours away up the Princes Highway. And of course, there was Lydia too, and they were just on a break, right? Otherwise he had no time for sentimentality. The occasional, evocative Paul Kelly song could test him out a bit, but that was more maudlin than meaningful. As for him being paranoid … shit, with a maternal death and no answer from the autopsy, he had plenty to be paranoid about.

And yes, he *had* been seeing a little of a certain local copper recently, but Senior Constable Elena Genovesi was just a mate, that's all. Sarah was getting her knickers all in a twist over nothing. Anyway, she was a snob; Elena wasn't cultured enough for the aesthetic Dr Bell, who preferred sushi to surfing and opera to Oprah. And her old feelings for him were dead and buried. *Surely.*

More importantly, despite Sarah's slicing, staining and spectrography, Vince was none the wiser about the cause of Polly's death. And like he said: he was looking after number one. He planned to see out his time in this remote backwater and then resume his old life back in Melbourne—professionally and personally—but this business threatened to upset the whole bloody thing. Bugger Polly Cotter!

Vince glanced at his watch; twenty to nine already. He knew he had a procedure booked at nine, so he quickly completed his hospital rounds.

Up on the mid floor, baby Indigo was doing well. The midwives had given her perfect Apgar scores at birth: ten out of ten at both one and five minutes. *Hell, if they had the same system for mothers, Polly would've got a ten then a zero.* Indigo had weighed in at a healthy 3201 grams and was feeding well on the bottle. She was also drop-dead cute and the nurses had already fallen in love with her.

As he strode out to the hospital car park, Vince noticed Emu Quick having a cigarette under the alcove to the side of the ramp leading up to the hospital entrance. A complete smoking ban had been imposed in the hospital and this was where the smokers now gathered. Patients in wheelchairs, some carrying drip poles and others already coughing and wheezing, crowded around the single ashtray like a group of refugees as the southerly gusted in from the ocean, forcing them to put their backs to the wind as they lit up.

Emu looked like he hadn't slept since the events of Tuesday night and was dishevelled, red-eyed and twitchy. With his jacket collar turned up and hands cupped around his rollie, he resembled a latter-day James Dean. Only hairier.

'How's it going, Emu?' asked Vince, pausing amongst the butts.

The youth just shrugged his thin shoulders.

'You look like you need a spell, mate,' said Vince, looking closely at Emu's pallid face. 'Why don't you head home for a sleep? The girls will look after Indigo.'

'Cut the bullshit, Doc,' said Emu impatiently. 'I know Polly's post-mortem was this morning and I don't want any bloody snow jobs. You doctors all cover for each other, I know how it fucken works. My old man reckons I should sue all you pricks.' He took a long drag on his smoke. 'So what did that pathology chick find?'

'Look, Emu,' Vince said, trying to sound convincing. 'I know you must be finding this really hard, mate, but the post-mortem results aren't through yet.' He patted Emu on the shoulder. 'Come in and see me next week and we'll talk about it, okay?'

Vince strode to his car. Well it wasn't really a lie, he reassured himself as he drove out of the car park and the pathetic figure of Emu faded from his rear vision mirror. We still don't know. But that word 'sue' had struck a chord. He realised the follow-up call to VMIA was now an urgent priority.

* * *

It was well after nine when he nosed Benny into his park at the rear of the clinic and raced into work. His patient was still sitting in the waiting room, fully dressed. The nurse, Kate O'Brien, was having a cup of tea and chatting to the receptionists.

'Good afternoon, Dr Hanrahan.'

'Morning, Sister,' he said. 'Enjoying your cuppa? Take your time, there's obviously no rush.'

Kate, who was in her mid-thirties, was an old scrub nurse of Vince's in his glory days at the Royal Women's and had come knocking on his door early this year looking for a job. Her husband had been killed in a car accident in Melbourne and she'd headed back to the country with her two children to be closer to her parents. Short and round, Kate had honey-blond hair and a permanent grin.

She casually beckoned the patient in. 'Okay Jeremy, why don't you wander in here, mate? The great man is ready to perform.'

Like many old friends, the two of them usually communicated via good-hearted banter, but today Vince was not in the mood. He strode across the waiting room, scooped up the surprised youth and marched him into the treatment room, his mother following in their wake.

Kate, obviously realising Vince was serious, hurriedly opened the surgical pack, turned on the operating light and passed him some gloves.

'Jesus, Kate!' he said, tossing them on the floor. 'Seven and a bloody half. You should know that by now!'

Jeremy was a fourteen-year-old basketballer, Lakers' cap on backwards and ears wired for sound, with an infected ingrown toenail. He needed a wedge resection—a procedure requiring application but not thought. *Beauty, I'm so over thinking.*

'Why is it always teenage boys who have these problems with their feet, Doctor?' asked Kate, drawing up the local anaesthetic.

'By the time they play sport ten times a week and wear these huge runners from dawn to dusk, their feet not only stink but become germ magnets. Isn't that right, Julie?'

Jeremy's mother nodded vigorously in agreement.

Vince got to work and concentrated solely on the job at hand until he'd finished twenty minutes later. Good therapy.

'Toenails, yuck!' commented Kate as she tidied up. 'It's a far cry from what you used to do back at the Women's, Vince—laparoscopic tubal surgery, gynae cancers, emergency Caesars and hysters. This is just minor stuff.'

Vince snorted. 'Well I'm certainly not planning on operating on toes for the rest of my life.' He pulled off his gloves with an angry snap, 'And Kate, notwithstanding your fascinating views about surgery, next time just make sure the bloody patient is ready to go when I come in. That clear?'

He raced back through the office, skilfully weaving past the receptionists, grabbed the morning's list and bumped straight into Shirley in the hallway.

She followed him into his room, bursting with curiosity. 'So, Vince, what happened with the post-mortem? What did your old fire have to say? Any hankys and pankys in the micro lab?'

Vince was used to Shirley's prurient interest in his dormant love life. 'Yeah, Shirl, we were really hard at it, Sarah cutting and weighing, and me watching and hoping.'

'So what was the cause of death, champ? Don't keep me on bloody skyhooks. She have a PPH or what?'

Vince grunted. 'If only, Shirl. Did you happen to read the most recent annual report of the Council on Obstetric Mortality and Morbidity?'

'Oh sure, Rooned. Real turn pager.'

'Well I spent half the night going through it. Five maternal deaths over sixty thousand births. One from blood loss after coagulopathy from amniotic fluid embolism; one due to haemorrhage after placental abruption; one from a spontaneous dissection of the subclavian artery; one suicide and one homicide. None considered to be medically preventable. And with Polly Cotter, you know what? None of the above. Zero, zilch, *nothing!*'

He wearily explained the post-mortem findings, or lack of them, to Shirley.

She frowned. 'Twenty-three-year-olds don't just die for nothing, champ.'

'*Really*, Shirl? Thanks for the insight.'

'You're on thin ice already with the Board, buddy. You need an answer.'

'Is that right? You're on the ball today.' Vince realised there was some self-interest involved for Shirley—even grumpy pricks such as himself were hard to replace in the bush.

'Well bud,' she said, as she continued towards her consulting room, 'just have to see what the forensic boffins in Melbourne come up with tomorrow, eh?'

Vince grimaced and hauled in his first punter, a newbie—a short dapper bloke, early forties, flash suit, flasher teeth and jet-black hair brushed straight back.

The man extended his hand. 'Jonathan Harkin, Jamiesons International Resources. You don't mind if I call you Vincent, Doctor?' Urbane English voice.

'Suit yourself, mate.'

'Vincent, we're down here laying the groundwork for some exploratory drilling off your beautiful coastline I play golf with Al Findlay and the good professor suggested I come to you for any medical needs.'

A bloody charm offensive, thought Vince. *Just what I need.* 'You're a bit of a golfer then, mate?'

Harkin flashed his dazzling choppers. *Certainly doesn't need a dentist.*

'Vincent, I work at sites all over the world and I've developed a system for quickly familiarising myself with the natives. Firstly, I become an avid reader of the local newspaper, that's the best way to find out about the absolute essence of a community—what makes it tick.'

Bit of knowledge about regional affairs would impress the locals no end, Vince reflected. Sounds like PR and Marketing 101.

'The next thing is to join the local golf club,' he went on, 'and meet the people who matter in the town. You know, Vincent, the movers and shakers.'

'Bit of networking, eh mate?'

'I'm not just out there for the ocean views and the smooth greens, Vincent.'

Smart strategy. 'So you really play golf to lobby the local conservative elite who actually run the joint.'

He nodded. 'Like the way you're thinking, Vincent. Capture their hearts and minds and you're nine tenths of the way there.'

'What about the other tenth?'

'Well, Vincent, I am a very persistent man. You see, I plan for this project to go ahead,' he added, 'one way or another.' He displayed his gleaming smile again. 'And my last golden rule is to employ a local girl to run my office. These lasses can be a valuable source of information.'

'And gossip?'

He nodded. 'Indeed, and they know who's who.'

'And who's *up* who, mate Harkin laughed. 'And they also know the best place to get my morning coffee, Vincent.'

Vince was impressed; this guy knew exactly what he was about, but Vince detected a jarring dissonance between his smooth charm and ruthless ambition. Turned out Harkin was off to Africa to 'scope out a new field' and needed some vaccinations.

The Englishman took off his Zegna suit jacket, undid a silver cufflink and rolled up the shirt sleeve to reveal a tattoo on his taut upper arm—a winged dagger and a banner proclaiming Who Dares Wins.

8

'Now, Toby, let's just have a look in the other ear and we'll see … shit, Toby!'

An unexpected kick to the scrotum at close range is enough to put any Geep off his game. Toby was a wild little tacker, so Vince had sat him on his mum's knee and told her to hold him tight. Then he got up close and personal, pinning the thrashing legs with his body as he did the business. He examined one ear then squatted back on his heels to allow room for her to swing Toby around, when the kid lashed out with one flailing boot and scored a direct hit.

Vince dropped his auriscope and went down like a sack of spuds. After a minute of silent but genuine suffering he was able to complete the examination.

'Toby just has a virus, Geraldine,' he muttered to the embarrassed mother, breathing deeply. 'Keep his fluids up; regular paracetamol for his fever. He should be okay by tomorrow.' *Bet I won't be though*, he thought, trying to ignore his aching balls. 'Bring him back if he gets any worse.'

Vince had learnt from Shirley that feverish kids like Toby could have anything from a simple virus all the way through to meningitis, so it was all a matter of clinical judgment. And a bit of a punt.

When he'd been sentenced to a stretch as a country general practitioner, Vince had expected it would be a doddle. Sure, he'd started out his medical life as a GP, but that was old history—been there, done that. Since then, hadn't he been a hot shot city specialist? FRACOG if you don't mind! But his first month in Geepland gave him newfound respect for the foot soldiers of the profession and the unpredictability of their game. Back in the big smoke, if a labour hit the skids, he had gassers and paedes on tap and could just bail and do a Caesar, but in rural general practice, there was no safety net.

Toby was Vince's last patient for the day. He looked at the mess on his desk, at least an hour of paper work and phone calls, but it was after seven and he was completely buggered. He sat back in the chair trying to accommodate his smarting scrotum and attempted to muster some energy.

His talk with VMIA earlier had been anything but reassuring. Dr Maurice Allen, an officious and ponderous Intensive Care Specialist and part-time Health Risks Consultant, had asked Vince copious questions about the clinical circumstances of the labour and the death, and requested a written account of the matter as well as a detailed report of the autopsy.

'Has there been any suggestion of legal action, Dr Hanrahan?'

Better tell him after what happened last time. 'Well, the boyfriend said in passing that people told him he should sue me, but I don't think he was serious.'

'Be that as it may,' Allen had responded promptly, sounding like Rumpole of the Bailey. 'Your timely notification of this adverse event is prudent and any potential action must be taken seriously. I shall raise a file, but we will not initiate an investigation at this point. However, we will seek some expert opinions and set aside some monetary reserves in case we receive a letter of demand or writ and have to proceed to mediation or court.'

Court! Right on cue, Vince had experienced that familiar jump in heart rate and churning in the guts. This guy had hit him right in his weak spot. Well, his *other* weak spot.

'I'm out of here,' Vince told the paper mountain in his too-hard basket. He turned off his computer, carefully got up and slowly walked out towards the office when he noticed Petra Smit striding past the front desk towards the door.

'Excuse me, Dr Smit,' Sharon, the receptionist, called out nervously.

'Did you get my message about that kiddie of Dr Shirley's who had the X-ray this afternoon?'

Petra grimaced and shook her head vigorously, hardly breaking stride. '*No way*, he's not my patient.'

'I know, but Dr Shirley had to go to the hospital for an emergency and Tess just wants to know if Alfie's broken his arm or not.'

Petra did an abrupt U-turn and faced the obviously intimidated Sharon face on. 'Why do you people expect me to do everything around here? I'm too busy with my own stuff, so get someone else to do it. Okay?'

She turned on her heels, slammed the front door, and seconds later her silver Alfa shot out of the car park, leaving the receptionist in tears and Vince and one of the other doctors, who'd come out to see what the fuss was about, standing in the office gobsmacked.

Hell, thought Vince, *even I don't make the staff actually cry!* 'What is with that girl, Prez?'

Dr Peter Menzies shook his head. 'Too busy,' he snorted, after glancing at the appointment list. 'She only saw four patients for the whole afternoon. Don't worry, Shaz, I'll do it.'

Peter was thirty-six years old with five children. He had been with Shirley from the start and was president of the swimming club, doctor for the Warrnambool football club, chair of the medical staff group, and he ran the church parish council. The Prez, as he was universally known, was little and wiry with an oval face, a lick of light brown hair and a permanently surprised expression.

Peter looked at Vince, who was creeping slowly along the hall, trying to avoid excessive scrotal swing. 'You look too tired to even stand up straight, Vince,' he added. 'Give me a bell if you want to discuss any of that stuff about Polly Cotter.'

'What's to talk about, Prez?' Vince responded, heading crab-like for the back door.

9

By the time Vince called in at the supermarket and wound his way back down the main drag, it was starting to get dark and Warrnambool was settling down for the night. After almost a year he knew his way around the streets but still felt like a stranger. All he'd known about the place was that it was on the south-west Victorian coast and over three hours west of Melbourne. Having grown up on a farm in the Wimmera, Vince was no stranger to the bush, but compared to tiny Minyip, Warrnambool was a bustling metropolis.

When he'd first driven into town last year, and passed the hardware shops, light furniture businesses and supermarkets flanking the highway, Vince had learnt from a large sign that it had a population of 32,878, all of whom promised a 'Warm Welcome to the Visitor'. 'SPE-SHILY IF YOU GOT BIG TITS' had been added underneath by a local graffiti artist. The sign also featured crests for Rotary, Apex and Probus, and a reminder that Warrnambool was the 'Home of the Nursery of the Southern Right Whale and Oddball.'

Service clubs, whales and a movie about a dog, he'd thought, *sounds just like my kinda town!* Right from the start he'd been determined not to settle in and regarded the place as a temporary stopover on the way back to civilisation.

Vince turned right at Merri Street circling the War Memorial roundabout, which featured an angel on a tall plinth holding a wreath that looked, when viewed from the side, to be sticking up from its groin. Naturally it had been dubbed the 'Masturbating Angel' by generations of local teenage boys—notorious experts at that particular art.

He took a left onto Wellington Street, crossed the railway line and drove down into South Warrnambool, crossed the Merri River, sped past the old Woollen Mills, turned right into Fay Street and pulled into his drive. Number Seven was a small sandstone cottage circa 1905 and one of a pair. On the 'For Lease' board, it had been described as: 'A quaint semi with all the charm of yesteryear. In need of a facelift.'

'Needs a bloody bomb under it more likely,' was Shirley's comment when she saw it. 'Better to buy a place, cobber.'

There were two reasonably-sized rooms off the narrow front hall, then a tiny sitting room and the small kitchen, bathroom and laundry in an asbestos lean-to at the rear. Back in yesteryear, they obviously didn't think kitchens and bathrooms were important. It was all a bit different to Vince and Lydia's forty-five square, Victorian, five-bedroom 'Italianate Villa' in Canterbury, complete with pool and tennis court.

The only really notable feature of Vince's new house was the startling, garish, external colour scheme. The whole of the rendered facade at the front, including the front door, was painted in red and white stripes a metre wide. Apparently the previous owner had been a lifelong fan of South Warrnambool, aka the Snappers, and when they'd recently won their first premiership in twenty years, he'd gone berserk with a roller and painted it in the club colours. The result was like a cross between an ice cream van and an old-fashioned barber's shop. Vince knew Shirley liked her employee doctors to purchase local real estate—it tied them to the town. Nothing like a mortgage to concentrate the mind.

'Listen, Shirl,' Vince had replied, 'I'm just passing through this particular bucolic paradise, definitely not in the market for home ownership down here.'

His current income was a fraction of what he'd been making in the city and he was still supporting Lydia and the twins in the way they'd become accustomed, so the Snapper House rental was all he could afford. Ironically, Lydia maintained that Vince's home and lifestyle were inappropriate for the teen girls and was reluctant to let them stay with him.

The limited space meant that when the girls did come down they had to share a bedroom. 'Just cos we're twins, Dad, doesn't mean we want to sleep together!' Not that they stayed very often; just a few days in the school holidays and the odd weekend along the way. They'd spent last Christmas, their first without Vince, at a friend's beach house at Portsea with the Beautiful People, whereas he had volunteered to be on call for the clinic, dined on reheated fried rice and watched a whole season of *Breaking Bad* between calls. Ho, ho bloody ho.

As he pulled up, Vince recognised the familiar figure of his neighbour Carmel Harrington out the front watering her garden. She reminded him of a Dickensian character—nearly as wide as she was tall with a dowager hump, a ruddy complexion and startlingly bright blue eyes capped off with a frizzy grey bouffant. Mrs H looked up from her task as Benny came chugging along the street and pulled into the cracked concrete drive next door.

'Hello, Dr Vince,' she called across the low picket fence. 'You're home late.' She watched Vince stiffly alight from Benny and creep slowly towards his front door, endeavouring to minimise any testicular tension.

'You look poorly. Got a pain in the tummy?'

'I'm fine thanks, Mrs Harrington.'

'I hear that Cotter girl died having the baby,' she said loudly as Vince pushed open his front door—he didn't bother to lock up down here at Warrnambool. Bit different to Canterbury. Nothing worth pinching anyway.

'I wonder what happened, Dr Vince,' asked Mrs Harrington, hoping for some 'horse's mouth' information to trump the neighbourhood speculation.

Vince was alert to her tactics and just shrugged.

Undaunted, she forged on. 'Knowing her family, I'd put it down to drink,' she commented while she hosed away. 'But you'd never know what those uni students get up to, all those drugs and that.'

Local goss was that Mrs H had talked her husband Paddy, once foreman at the Woollen Mills and a prodigious grog artist, into an early grave and her views on the moral decline of young people were well known to Vince.

'I better go in, Mrs H. I'm expecting a call from the hospital,' he said, lying shamelessly. Truth was, quite apart from his bruised balls, he was suddenly aware of an intense lassitude and desperately needed to collapse in a chair. And the last thing he wanted to talk about was Polly Cotter's death.

'Well make sure you have some proper tea, Dr Vince, with veggies and that, and don't worry about the dog neither. Kieran already fed her.'

When he finally made it inside, Vince dumped his groceries, grabbed a juice, shoved a packet of frozen peas down his jocks and collapsed in front of the box. He then stared at the news and current affairs shows for over an hour in a catatonic state. The talk was all about Queensland floods and the situation in Syria, but Vince's head was full of bewildering images of dead women and the strong urge for a stiff drink. Or three.

Eventually hunger got the better of him, so he dragged himself up, pulled out his trusty old wok and cooked one of his staple dishes: stir fried beef and peppers. *Bugger, forgot the peppers again.* He added a heap of noodles and a big slosh of soy sauce, and gulped it down standing in his tiny kitchen, then carefully balanced the dishes on the sink on last night's pile, took five steps and fell into bed.

Vince had found that one advantage of the Snapper house was that a few steps took you most places, with little chance of bumping into anything because there wasn't much there. The floors were a combination of bare boards and sea grass matting—just like in his and Lydia's first house in North Carlton—and the furniture consisted of a very old op-shop couch and an inverted milk crate TV table, with a rudimentary set of pots and pans and crockery in the kitchen. His only treasured possessions were his books, his Maton guitar gathering dust in a corner, and his prized collection of vinyl in the front room. And his poster of the Geelong 2011 Premiership Team on the dunny door.

He crashed heavily, only to wake an hour later, heart palpitating and mind racing. He dialled up the meditation track on his iPod and eventually nodded off again, dozing fitfully until the sound of his dog scratching at the back door woke him with a start.

'Oh shit, Deef,' he murmured, looking at his clock. 'Six bloody thirty. I just don't really feel like a run today, mate.'

The golden retriever was Vince's only memento from seventeen years of marriage. Lydia kept the house, the Landcruiser and the kids. Vince got the debt, deregistration and the dog. Deefer was a gorgeous animal but not even her best friends (everyone she met) would say she was bright. She'd bombed out badly at puppy school and, along with her natural stupidity, this lack of formal education made her a force to be reckoned with. However, she knew when she was hungry (all the time) and she knew when it was time for a run (ditto).

Vince rolled out of bed, rearranged the bedclothes in a desultory fashion and started pulling on his jogging gear—footy nicks, 'Bintang Bitter' T-shirt and old runners. He noticed a distinct dampness in the groin area and immediately thought he must have wet himself in the night. *Shit, now I'm incontinent!* He urgently pulled back the bedclothes and discovered a soggy mess of warm, wet peas, which had escaped from the packet and defrosted during the night.

'Must've forgotten to take them out of my jocks before I hit the bloody sack.' The peas seemed virtually cooked and he toyed with the idea of scraping them up and putting them in the fridge for tonight's dinner, but had second thoughts. As he told Mrs H, you can overdo the importance of vegetables.

He and Deefer walked down Stanley Street, crossed the Merri, then past the Deep Blue apartments and down to the Breakwater. After Vince paused to do up his shoelaces, they stepped onto the boardwalk adjacent to the Yacht Club and started trotting at their usual steady pace, which was in fact so slow that when the twins came to stay, they were usually too embarrassed to take part.

'Oh my God, Bins, those power-walking old ladies in their parachute tracksuits are actually faster than you guys!'

One mitigating factor was that Deef would have at least three poo stops in the initial stages of the run; suddenly just planting her paws and almost pulling Vince's arm out of its socket, typically right in front of the power-walking ladies, especially when he'd forgotten to bring plastic bags.

Today, due to his recent injury, Vince's initial jog was even slower than usual and he soon fell back to a wide-legged John Wayne gait. The track headed east along the main beach, up the hill to the lookout at Point Ritchie above the Hopkins River, and then down across the bridge to the whale-watching platform at Jap's beach—home to the serious surfers. It was about six kilometres each way but Vince and Deef usually just went to the lookout and back, which was a round trip of five.

They began the slow climb along the dunes above the beach, Deefer straining at the lead, impatient with the slow pace. Down below, there was a decent swell with a gentle off-shore breeze and about a dozen surfers out the back chasing waves. They then followed the path as it wound inland and inclined up to the lookout, surrounded on all sides by thick coastal scrub and a rolling sea of silver fronds.

During one early morning surf, Professor Allan Findlay had explained the expanse. 'That marram grass was originally introduced from South Africa to fight erosion, Vincenzo,' he'd said enthusiastically. 'Then it took off big time at the expense of the native flora, although there is still plenty of coastal pigface and New Zealand spinach lower down—see that stuff that looks like a thick carpet? And look up at those plants hugging onto those rocky cliffs above the river—that's cushion bush and sea berry saltbush. Isn't the coastal environment fascinating? And as for what's under the sea, don't get me started!'

However, Vince was no botanist and Allan's attempts to explain the more subtle aspects of the local flora fell on fallow ground. He preferred to enjoy the experience at a macro, sensory level and what he noticed mostly were the changing colours of the wide canvas, the thunderous sound of the waves down below, and the ever present gusty wind carrying that biting, salty smell.

Vince and Deefer paused at the lookout, ostensibly to take in the view but mostly for him to recover from the journey up. 'Sore knackers, mate,' he confided, leaning on the rail. 'Should've stayed in bed.'

It was a clear morning and Vince could see right across the river mouth to the big houses on the steep cliffs opposite and then back to the west along the coast with the saw tooth fringe of Norfolk pines all the way along to the breakwater with the town as a backdrop.

What usually nourished his soul was the mighty Southern Ocean, but this morning as he gazed at the heaving swell the magic just wasn't working and the indelible memory of the shrouded body on the slab and the spectre of the sword hanging above his head loomed larger than ever.

10

Vince donned his usual working garb—jeans, open necked shirt and ancient leather bomber jacket; swallowed some coffee and fed the beast. He then grabbed the newspaper and a handful of CDs, jumped into Benny and headed off across town at breakneck speed. By the time he parked in front of the Royal Hotel, ran down the side laneway and arrived at the studios of Breakers FM, it was exactly one minute to nine. The term 'studios' was overstating things a little; there was only one, and it was tiny and equipped with second-hand gear that had been begged, borrowed or stolen.

The red 'On Air' light was glowing, so Vince waited outside. Through the small window in the studio door he could see Allan in the guest chair, obviously waiting to take over the panel at the end of Heather Tancredi's breakfast program.

'Okay, that's just about it from me. Thanks for being my guests on "The Breakfast Show", stay tuned for Vince and Allan and 'Friday on My Mind'. It's now just on nine on this lovely morning, and you are listening to Breakers FM, 109.9 on your dial. I'll go out with "It's a Beautiful Day".'

Heather started the U2 track, turned off her mike, gathered up her CDs and notes, and quickly vacated the chair behind the panel.

'How's it goin', guys?'

'Just battling,' responded Allan, making no move in the direction of the presenter's chair, even though it was Vince's turn to anchor the show.

'Okay thanks, Heather,' said Vince, quickly donning the headphones, checking the audio levels and cueing up their intro tape. Running the program was the last thing he felt like doing but Allan seemed to be stuck to his chair.

'Just about ready to go, mate,' Vince said, as he faded Bono's soaring voice out and their intro track in, loaded up both players with fresh CDs, fished out the day's weather report then sat back and caught his breath for twenty seconds as the Easybeats sang them in: *I'm gunna have fun in the city, na na na na nana nana naa, to be with my girl she's so pretty, na na na na nana nana naa.'*

According to a large texta-scrawled sign on a piece of paper tacked to the wall, PRESENTERS MUST ARRIVE 15 MINS BEFORE THE START OF YOUR SHOW, but for Allan and Vince there was usually this mad last-minute rush. Occasionally, the eternally patient Heather had to put on another track and hang round till they burst in the door, but mostly they made it. Just.

Breakers FM was a local community radio station, and Allan and Vince had been doing a weekly show for several months—just playing their favourite tracks and shooting the breeze together. Allan had been presenting an environmental program for some years and after Vince came on as a guest a few times they decided to join forces and 'Friday on My Mind' was born.

Vince had also become an occasional guest at the Findlays' famous dinner parties, where he'd observed Allan at his best—captive audience, glass in hand, pontificating about everything from the world's best tenor and Geelong team selection to malt whiskies and the meaning of life. He'd done his PhD in Umbria and loved all things Italian, especially the Dolce Vita. (Italians really know how to live, Vincenzo!) Vince was a social hermit and reluctantly emerged from his cave for these soirees, drawn more by the promise of some good tucker than the dinner table repartee.

In time he became accustomed to Allan's fruity theatrical conversation style. With his halo of curly hair, close-clipped beard and specs perched on his nose, Allan looked the epitome of the middle-aged academic. That halo was rapidly turning grey but without a single follicle on his own cranium Vince was hardly in a position to criticise.

One Sunday last summer, after they'd been for a morning surf,

Allan had enthusiastically told Vince about his plan to set up a commercial abalone farm.

'Sounds like you're selling your soul, mate,' Vince had responded. 'Bit much for an old lefty, isn't it?' He liked to prick Allan's hubris from time to time.

'Vincenzo, a history lesson, if I may? I arrived in Warrnambool fifteen years ago as a new PhD and humble lecturer at the Local Institute of Advanced Education. Then when the Institute was upgraded to the exalted status of a university in the early nineties, I was given the Chair in Marine Science and soon became Head of Department.'

'Congratulations, Professor.'

Allan had ignored Vince's sarcasm. 'After that I trod water professionally for some time, Vincenzo, content, but with a pervading sense of *ennui*. Then last year the new VC told us that we had to "engage with the market place", and I took up the challenge.' His eyes had lit up. 'A chance to make some real money.'

Okay, Vince had thought, *so it's not just about the glory*. Surely Allan would've earned a fair pile over the years—must've blown it all on the gee gees and the dolce vitae.

'And now I have my new baby to think of,' he'd gone on excitedly. 'The conception was difficult, the gestation long, but now hopefully the birth is *imminent*. Abgrow will be the firstborn progeny of the newly established marketing arm of the University!'

Allan's enthusiasm was palpable and Vince was to learn all about abalone farming one autumn night after a typically Bacchanalian Findlay dinner party.

A band of local epicureans (plus Vince) had dined sumptuously on Allan's famous hand-made gnocchi ('Thanks, Suzie—really just peasant food after all'), *very* slowly braised lamb shanks with sweet potato mash, and finishing with tiramisu ('I *know*, Jamie, but it's worth it!'), all matched with wines from Allan's extensive cellar. Eventually the party broke up, leaving just Vince ('on the wagon, poor Vincenzo, our new best friend') and the hosts. But of course the show had to go on.

'Did you know that Australia supplies over forty percent of the world's wild abalone?' Allan asked, sipping on a luscious looking dessert wine.

'But the arse has dropped out of that caper, hasn't it?' asked Vince. 'Since the glory days.'

Allan snorted. 'Hardly, Vincenzo. True, the market value used to be fifty dollars per kilogram, but it's still close to thirty. Not bad for ugly looking marine snails!'

'What happened?'

'Market forces. Competition and overfishing due to overly generous quota allocation in the past.' Allan paused and refilled his glass. 'Since that nasty ganglioneuritis virus, the Western Zone quota has been reduced from twenty tonnes annually to three tonnes for each access licence.'

Vince nodded. 'Still the same number of guys diving?'

Allan shook his head. 'Used to be fourteen divers harvesting two hundred and eighty tonnes, but now the zone's total quota has been reduced to less than sixty tonnes, it's no longer viable for that many divers.'

'What are these ab licenses worth, mate?'

'Pre-virus, they used to be up to six million dollars. Each diver had an annual limit of twenty tonne, and at about fifty dollars a kilo, they could each pull up a good million dollars' worth a year. Sometimes in less than fifty days!'

'Shit, mate,' Vince said, doing some rough calculations in his head. 'That's about twenty thousand bucks for a day's work—the buggers were even better paid than cataract surgeons!'

Allan nodded. 'But now the quota's down and the price has dropped, you can get a license for less than a mill.'

He got up and changed the LP in his state-of-the-art Bang and Olufsen sound system. ('The vinyl sound is *so* much more authentic.') Cool notes from John Coltrane's saxophone permeated through the room.

'Wild abalone are already fished out in some reefs,' Allan added, after resuming his seat, 'and with the ocean warming due and progressive habitat damage, the future, Doctor, will be the farmed product.' He raised his glass in a toast. 'Almost all our catch is exported and the potential for abalone aquaculture in this country is *huge.*'

'Surely they must be farming it overseas too, Allan?' Rita asked as she cleared away the plates.

'Oh yes, love, they've been doing it in China for years and they've had trouble with water quality and typhoon damage.' He paused and waved his index finger. 'But they are getting their act together and producing hundreds of tonnes. So we need to pull out our fingers and establish a niche in the market.'

'If there's such a big quid in it, mate,' said Vince, 'surely there must be abalone nurseries in other parts of Oz?'

Allan nodded and pointed south-west with a dramatic sweep of his arm, knocking over a vase of flowers. 'Indeed, Vinzenzo. They started over fifteen years ago in South Australia and Tassie, but just shore-based efforts. Ours is going to be green and clean and the *full box and dice.*' He paused to refill his glass. 'We'll have a hatchery and nursery tanks in a sheltered bay over at Killarney and an ocean-based grow-out facility off shore. The conditions are ideal, with good quality water and very little pollution. And, we will do the processing, canning and vacuum packing out in the industrial estate.' His eyes lit up. 'We'll control it all, from the ocean to the table. No middle man!'

Vince cut himself a wedge of the Timboon Brie and a slice of quince paste—made by Allan of course—and topped up his mineral water—Italian naturally.

'And the *really* big deal,' Allan went on, red faced and excited, 'is that the exquisite Polly Cotter has developed a hybrid between the greenlip and the blacklip abalone, which is resistant to that herpes virus that almost wiped out the industry in Victoria.'

'Herpes!' interjected Vince. 'You've just got to get those randy abalone to wear condoms, mate!'

Allan ignored the gag—he was on a roll. 'And, this new hybrid will grow much faster and that's the key to quick return on investment.' She's a brilliant scientist, Vincenzo, and a lovely girl.'

Rita raised her eyebrows and started carting the dinner party debris out to the kitchen—Allan obviously saw himself purely as a culinary artist, unsuited to the more banal scullery duties, but Vince gave her a hand. Allan came out to make the coffee, ('Fairtrade from East Timor—it's the *least* we can do.') Another of his self-proclaimed areas of expertise.

With a theatrical 'voila!' Allan placed three espressos boasting perfect cremas on the large mahogany dining table and passed around some panforte, before reaching his peroration, voice rising and eyes blazing. 'But here's the thing—wild abalone fishing is limited by the minimum harvest size of one hundred and twenty millimetres, whereas there is no limit for the farmed product.'

He raised his coffee cup in a toast. 'So when the wild variety is eventually decimated by the virus or fished out completely, Abgrow will *clean up!*'

* * *

Today, as Vince glanced at Allan across the panel, he could see none of that night's verve and enthusiasm. The Professor looked tired and disinterested as they sat waiting for the Easybeats to finish. Vince followed straight on with a long Van Morrison track to give Allan time to find his feet.

'How are things, mate?' he asked, after checking the mikes were off. 'I hear you won a gold medal or something.'

Allan preened like a peacock for an instant. 'The 2016 Aquaculture Australia Award for Entrepreneurship, *if* you don't mind, Vince.'

'Enjoy yourself?'

'Oh yes. Went down the night before and stayed at a pad in South-bank—very posh, views of the bay and dinner at Vue de Monde, eighteen holes at Royal Melbourne the next day, then off to the Crown ballroom for the presentation—black tie and all the trimmings.'

Couldn't imagine anything worse. 'Wacko, mate, sounds a bit flash.'

Allan collapsed again like a deflated balloon. 'Feels a bit hollow really, with Polly … you know …'

'I'm guessing you're upset about her.'

'I just can't believe it, Vincenzo,' he answered. 'It's such a bloody shock.'

'Big loss to the department?'

'Oh yes, a big loss. Polly had started breeding our new hybrid abalone from elite brood stock she'd gathered in the wild, completely uncontaminated by the virus. She was this close to finalising the ecosystem for the next phase.' Allan held up is thumb and forefinger, almost touching.

'It will halve the time to grow-out, and so we'll be able to harvest our first abalone within eighteen months and we are almost set to start selling our larvae and juveniles.'

He fell quiet for a minute or so and then shook his head. 'But it's not only that, it's … it's like … the end of a dream.'

Seemed to Vince the dream was almost a reality. 'But you're telling me Polly had virtually completed her work for you. Surely Abgrow's up and running now?'

Allan sat silently, seemingly lost in thought. Eventually he responded. 'That's right, Vincenzo—up and running. But, she still …' He paused again, sighed and glanced across at Vince. 'So what happened to her, Doctor?'

What is it with these people? The concept of medical confidentiality seems to be unknown in this town! And why was Allan taking Polly's death so personally? *For Christ's sake, if anyone, apart from the family, should be affected by it, it's bloody well me. It's my neck and professional career on the chopping block, not Allan's. And I don't bloody know what happened anyway!*

He returned Allan's enquiring gaze. The Professor was on the wrong side of fifty but was a notoriously vain, almost narcissistic man. What looked like casual elegance was the result of much time spent at the hairdresser, gym and trendy clothes shops.

Allan enjoyed the good life, but Vince knew he looked after himself too, balancing his excesses with exercise and a healthy diet. The only exception was his smoking, which for an intelligent man with chronic asthma, defied logic. Vince had long since given up trying to change patients' self-destructive behaviour, although he himself knew it was possible.

Today, however, Allan's hair was unkempt, he was dressed in an old tracksuit and looked badly in need of a sleep. For a change, Vince felt well groomed by comparison.

'You know I can't discuss Polly's case with you, Allan,' he responded pompously. As Van the Man warbled his last notes, Vince faded him out, played a promo for the afternoon's shows and turned on the mikes.

'Welcome to Friday on My Mind on Breakers FM. It's Vince in the saddle and Allan riding shotgun.'

He glanced across the panel with an expectant look, but Allan was giving him nothing. He tried again. 'So, what's happening in the world, Allan?'

Allan reluctantly glanced at the newspaper in front of him. He kicked off but without his customary enthusiasm. 'Well, Vince, I see that our esteemed PM is talking up his new Border Protection Strategy. Sounds just like the last guy, just rebadged. Looks like Fortress Australia is still the plan.'

'Shouldn't be too hard,' Vince responded. 'What about a twenty-foot high stone wall right across the top of the country? Bit of barbed wire on top—that should do the job.'

Vince had no time for either side of politics; he reckoned they were all bastards, but he didn't mind a bit of political satire. He knew Allan was a dedicated greenie—a founding member of GreenCoast, a local environmental lobby group committed to maintaining the biodiversity of the coastal environment. Vince had enough problems of his own without worrying about the rest of the bloody planet.

The ball was in Allan's court, but he just wasn't on his normal game, so Vince was forced to keep it in play himself.

'Those boat people—if we don't watch out they'll take over the whole country soon.'

He paused for a rejoinder, but Allan was mute. Bloody hell!

'It's just coming around to twenty-three past nine, time for a bit more music. First we will have Ry Cooder with 'Little Sister', then a bit of cool horn from the lips of Miles Davis. You are listening to Breakers FM 109.3.'

'The thing that really worries me, Vince,' said Allan, suddenly waking from his trance, 'is the baby. Who's going to look after her?'

Vince just managed to turn the mikes off in time. 'Shit, Allan! Just watch the *on-air* light, mate,' he said crossly. 'And help me out here. I don't feel like doing this either, but we've got a bloody program to run!'

'I mean, a junkie is not an appropriate person to be responsible for the welfare of a baby, Vincenzo.' Allan seemed oblivious to Vince's entreaties. 'I wouldn't trust him with a kitten. All Emu is interested in is what he can squirt up his arm.'

There was no mistaking the contempt in Allan's voice.

'But he is Indigo's father, mate, and it's really none of your business. He's got good support, so let's just see what happens, okay?'

'Really, Doctor?' said Allan, with the most animation he'd displayed all morning, then added darkly, 'We'll see what happens all right.'

Vince was surprised at the vehemence in Allan's voice. He knew Emu had a big heroin habit in the past, but Polly had made him go to the local Alcohol and Drug Centre, where he'd detoxed and gone on a methadone program. Then he'd resumed his art studies at Deakin and been clean ever since. Hadn't he? Maybe Allan knew better.

'How do you even know Emu?' asked Vince, as he faded out Miles Davis and put on a promo tape about a meeting of the local Amnesty International Branch.

'Just through Polly. He's just not a fit person to look after a baby. Not that I'm any expert on fatherhood.'

Allan was struggling to stay on top of his emotions. Vince knew he and Rita had been unable to have children and it sounded like he was still very vulnerable about the issue.

The promo finished and Vince hurriedly put the mikes on. 'It's now twenty minutes away from ten and you are listening to Friday on my Mind here on Breakers FM, and it's time to have a look at the weather.'

Usually the person not operating the panel would do most of the chatting, allowing the guy in the hot seat to cue up tracks and focus on the controls, but Allan was still slumped in his chair looking at the floor, so Vince had to juggle both jobs.

'I have the Bureau of Meteorology forecast for today. We are expecting a cloudy day with a maximum of fifteen degrees. Let's have some more music with a Jackson Browne classic.'

He turned off the mikes as soon as 'Late for the Sky' started and followed it with the Community Calendar tape.

'The Jamieson Street Primary School Fete will be held on Sunday starting at eleven am. There will be an information night at eight o'clock on Monday at the Wilson lecture theatre at Deakin University, regarding the JIR drilling off the eastern end of Lady Bay. Mr Jonathan Harkin will answer questions about the environmental impact. The monthly Gem Collectors meeting will be held at the Temperance Hall on Thursday the Second at the usual time.'

He followed on with a Waifs track and glanced across the panel at Allan. 'Suppose you GreenCoast warriors will be out in force on Monday night, heckling the bullshit artist from JIR.'

'I will be there,' answered Allan, sparking up a bit. 'I've been playing a bit of golf with Jonathan Harkin and he's not such a bad guy. We've become quite good friends and it's his apartment I stayed in last night in Melbourne. He's a generous host.'

'Surprise, surprise,' said Vince caustically. 'What's that they say about a free lunch?'

'You are such a cynic,' Allan snapped. 'Jamiesons are sensitive to the cultural significance of the Aboriginal middens and the whale nursery concerns. Last year we suspended our objection to the project, pending their environmental impact study. It was all in the *Observer*. However, we'll still be holding them to account.'

This was news to Vince, although he only tended to read the local rag for the hatches and dispatches and footy scores. He vaguely remembered hearing that GreenCoast had initially opposed the drilling.

'Sounds like a backflip to me, but if the guy plays golf, he must be okay.'

'Come on, Vince,' Allan responded, raising his voice. 'To promote sustainable development, we have to work with industry! We'll just wait for their EIS before taking a final position.'

'Settle down, mate,' Vince said. 'I don't give a shit either way. I've got enough on my mind keeping human beings alive, let alone worrying about middens and bloody whales.'

The Waifs faded into the ether, so he turned on the mikes.

'That was London Still. It's now five to ten on Breakers FM and that's just about enough from Friday on My Mind. Stay tuned for Midday Metal. We'll go out with the Oils and 'Beds are Burning'—this one's especially for Allan.'

Vince turned off the mikes, gathered up his stuff, quickly vacated the seat and looked at Allan as he headed for the door.

'Next week, sunshine, pull your bloody finger out! The way I'm heading, you might be on your Pat Malone on Friday mornings soon enough.'

11

'Not hungry, Doc?'

Vince sat back in his chair, cradling a glass of the very best Warrnambool tap water, lost in thought. His entrée sat untouched in front of him. The table he was sharing with Elena Genovisi was at the rear of Fannies restaurant, well away from the hoi polloi and inevitable 'tableside' consultations—'Enjoying your tea, Dr Vince? Jackie's still got that gastro, it's fair squirtin' out.'

He'd met the senior constable at the end of his first month in Warrnambool. They'd both been part of a workshop—'Boyz Stuff'—for Year Ten lads from the local high school. Vince's topic had been the usual medical combo of STIs, contraception and sexual health—and Elena's session had been about the importance of keeping on the right side of the law. They'd chatted over tea and bikkies after the workshop, then dodged the mandatory sausage sizzle and gone to Fannies cafe for a feed instead. It turned out to be the first Friday night of many.

As far as Vince was concerned, that's all there was to it. Even the much-abused word 'platonic' overstated their friendship. Obviously a spunky young chick like Elena wouldn't regard a forty-something has-been like him as anything more than a buddy, and anyway, he was still a married man, wasn't he? Like he'd explained to his old man last year, 'I've been red carded by Lydia, Dad, but if I keep my bum clean, hopefully I'll be back in the team again next season.'

'You just got too big for your boots, son,' his father had responded sagely. 'You shoulda seen it coming.' Old Mick had been on the money. As usual.

Celibacy certainly had its drawbacks, but Vince had no intention of hooking up with any women in Warrnambool. This regular rendezvous with the senior constable was just another Friday night feed with a mate. Could've just as easily been with a bloke.

Vince figured Elena for early thirties, not that he knew when her birthday was, and over time he'd learnt something of her background. The Genovisis were dairy farmers, nearly fifty kilometres away near Simpson, and she had three brothers who were still there milking cows.

'I had no great love for gumboots, udders and mud, Doc, so I headed off to uni and did a degree in IT then enrolled in the Police Training College.' After some city postings she'd ended up back in Warrnambool and was keen to progress up the ranks and become a detective.

Elena had the olive skin and black hair of her ancestors, an angular face, finely-chiselled classical Roman nose and a permanent half smile. Her eyes were large, dark and liquid, reminding Vince of Dylan's 'Sad Eyed Lady of the Lowlands'. Her body was wiry but strong, with a physicality that he found vaguely sexy.

'Earth to Doc, come in please, Doc.'

Vince looked across the table at a vague shape that gradually sharpened into Elena.

'Sarge,' he said slowly and deliberately. 'Do you know what the state maternal mortality rate was in the last twelve months? Give up? Five out of sixty thousand births. And here's the kicker: how many have I lost in a twenty-year career? Answer—only one other. So you can understand why I might be a little preoccupied.'

Elena nodded. 'I saw the report in *The Observer*.'

Vince had also read the piece about Polly's death in the town's newspaper—not the best publicity for a local doctor. It was wedged between articles about the battle for Mosel and the relocation of the Warrnambool sale yards.

'Bad news travels fast round here,' he said. 'I've already had some of your guys grilling me.'

Two local detectives had interviewed Vince at the surgery last evening. Routine stuff for a reportable death but still unsettling.

'So Mr Eldrige is conducting the investigation?'

Vince had learnt that coronial duties in the bush were usually part of the local magistrate's job. 'No, Sarge, old Bernie's crook, apparently. The State Coroner's got the gig.' He paused, with a wry smile. 'An old sparring partner of mine.' *One I thought I'd seen the bloody back of.*

He lapsed into a sullen silence again.

After a few minutes Elena leant forward and briefly put her hand on his. 'Doc, these things happen. I'm sure no one's blaming you.'

'You just don't get it, Sarge,' Vince snorted, pulling his hand away. 'It's my name on the bed card, so it's my arse on the line.'

'Okay,' she said after a long silence. 'I know you can't discuss the medical details of this case, but, hypothetically, why would a healthy young woman die after childbirth?'

Vince rapidly went through the same list of possibilities he had discussed with Sarah Bell.

'Do you want to just run those past me again, Doc?' said Elena, pushing a strand of black hair behind her ear. 'But this time in English?'

He proceeded with an air of resignation. 'Okay, but you asked for it, Sarge. A big haemorrhage is the most common cause—obvious unless it's internal. Sometimes a bubble of the baby fluid can leak into the mother's circulation then go into the brain and cause a stroke—never seen it. Maybe a blood clot in a leg vein might escape and knock off a lung artery—happens occasionally. Her blood pressure might skyrocket and cause a haemorrhage in the brain—never seen it. Or, uncontrolled toxaemia causing a fatal convulsion—rare. Or there could always be some pre-existing medical thing like a heart problem. Thus ends the lesson in postpartum collapse.'

He had a big draught of water, laughed, then leant forward and dropped his voice. 'And guess what, Sarge? Just between you and me—this time, none of those things happened.'

A young waitress, sporting a long blond plait and belly button ring, collected their plates and carried them off to the kitchen.

Vince resumed his broody pondering. Sarah Bell had rung at lunchtime with Polly's chemistry and toxicology results. 'It was hypoglycaemia, Vince. Her serum glucose was barely recordable. Did she have diabetes or ketonuria?'

'That's just bullshit, Sarah,' he'd answered. 'Labouring women can drop their blood sugars because we don't let 'em eat in case they need a general anaesthetic later, but it doesn't kill them. Anyway, Polly had an IV and we'd run in some dextrose cos I thought she might need an epidural—that would have given her enough calories to go on with. And she had no ketones in her urine, and she didn't have bloody diabetes!'

Sarah had paused. 'Well, Vince, I can only tell you Polly Cotter died from hypoglycaemic coma, but I can't tell you why.'

'Thanks for nothing, Dr Bell,' he'd responded, then hung up and sworn.

As he sat there at Fannies five hours later, that word was still going around and around in his head. *Hypoglycaemia!* What was that about? It wasn't an answer, it was just more fucking questions!

He beckoned Elena forward and informed her about the lab finding, with a threat of terrible retribution if she told anyone. She frowned and spoke quietly. 'Isn't hypoglycaemia what you get if you skip meals and have too much starch? I thought it was just something you read about in women's magazines. I didn't realise you could die from it.'

Vince replied impatiently. 'We're not talking just a small dip in the blood sugar here, Sarge. As far as I know, only a big bloody dose of insulin could cause a fatal drop in blood sugar.'

Elena considered this in her usual analytical fashion. 'So did someone make a mistake about her insulin dose then, Doc? I didn't realise that Pol … I mean, patient X, even had diabetes.'

'She didn't.'

'Then why the insulin?'

'Exactly.' Vince knew he was being a smartarse, but tonight he was past caring.

'Could it have been given by mistake, Doc?'

Vince was rapidly tiring of this question and answer session. He shrugged. 'Who knows, Sarge? Beats the shit out of me.'

Elena, clearly pissed off, snapped her mouth shut, her lips a thin, angry line.

Vince sat forward. 'I'm sorry, Elena,' he whispered. 'But you just don't expect women to die in labour, and there are some really important people who will take a dim view of this. And, I already have form.'

Elena frowned. 'What do you mean, Doc?'

Vince paused then shook his head. 'I'll tell you one day. When you've got a few hours and a box of tissues to spare.'

12

Vince ran into Danny Nguyen on Monday morning in front of the X-ray department.

Vince had been on call for the weekend, and two days and three nights of being tied to the mobile phone had just come to an end. It wasn't just the mums of sick kids, and old blokes with chest pains who hassled him, but the families in domestic crises and the crazies who decided at three o'clock Sunday morning that they can't cope anymore.

'How are things, Ox?'

Just tickety boo, Dan, thought Vince. *About to be flushed down the professional dunny, that's all.* 'Happy to have another on-call weekend behind me, mate.'

Danny laughed. 'I know how you feel. Any news on that girl of yours who went to heaven last week?'

Vince's post on-call euphoria immediately evaporated. He gave Danny a brief outline of the state of play and posed the question that had been eating away at him all weekend. 'Mate, what would cause fatal hypoglycaemia in a non-diabetic?'

Danny thought for a minute then shook his head. 'Nothing, Ox. Perhaps some weird endocrine thing or poisoning maybe, but that would show up in the forensic lab results.' He paused. 'Unless one of the nurses *thought* she had diabetes, found her blood sugar was elevated, then gave her too much insulin to bring it down.'

Vince nodded. In-bloody-soluble! He'd scrutinised all Polly's notes at both the hospital and the clinic—no mention of diabetes. She'd had the usual Glucose Challenge Test at twenty-four weeks and passed with flying colours. 'Polly definitely didn't have diabetes. And, according to her labour ward records, no one tested her blood sugar. No reason to.' He shrugged his shoulders. 'Anyway, no midwife would administer insulin without a doctor's order.'

After leaving Danny as puzzled as he was himself, Vince had only baby Indigo still to see. She was now five days old and ready for home. Before she was discharged, Vince needed to do the routine baby check, so he palpated the soft fontanelles on her skull, peered in her ears and mouth, listened to her heart and lungs, looked at her spine, felt her tummy and checked her hips.

'How's she doing?' he asked Barbara Craig, after he documented his exam findings in the Maternal and Child Health Book.

'She's feeding well and having no problems at all. She's had her routine blood tests and her Hep B vaccination and she's ready to go.'

They were both painfully aware that something was missing from today's discharge ritual. Normally it would occur in the new mother's room and Vince would be examining her too, but there was another expectant woman in Polly's room and her shadow loomed large over the cot in the nursery. Sometimes the baby would be the ghostly presence. After a stillbirth there'd be a devastated woman to check, but no cot and no baby. Those poor girls couldn't get out of the place quickly enough, because the postnatal ward with its lactating women and crying babies was like a dagger to their hearts.

'How is Emu coping with the parenting job, Barbara?'

'Aaron's not too bad, Doctor,' she answered, expertly dressing Indy in clothes Emu's sister had dropped in. 'He's changed the babe a few times and done a couple of baths, and seems to have a fair understanding of feeding issues. I think he'll manage. With plenty of help.'

* * *

Vince left the hospital, raced down to the clinic and made a couple of quick phone calls, tying up some loose ends from the weekend. One was to Petra Smits.

'Listen, Princess, you know that old bloke with the crook shoulder that you sent to the physio on Friday? Jocka came back yesterday and he's got classic shingles. He told me you didn't even examine him and now it's too bloody late for the anti-virals!'

No response.

'And another thing. You didn't ask the nurses to give Polly Cotter any insulin the other night, did you?'

'Why would I do that?' came the indignant reply. 'That little hippie didn't even have diabetes.' Suddenly the volume went up. 'And why are you trying to blame me anyway? She was your patient, Dr Hanrahan!'

'I'll take that as a no,' replied Vince, then hung up. Talk about hysterical! He shook his head and looked at the morning schedule. First up was a meeting with Jamieson International Resources. What the hell?

He angrily picked up his phone again. 'Shirley, why are we having an appointment with a bloody mining company?'

'They want us to do medical services for their new drilling operation, Rooned.'

Vince groaned. 'You don't need me for that, Shirl. Industrial medicine's not my bag, and I've got a bit on my mind right now.'

'Get your bum in here, champ, we gotta all fly the flagpole. This stuff's like jam for old ropes.'

Even Vince was aware that hydrocarbon exploration had been developing apace along the local coastline. There were rich deposits of natural gas and oil in the Otway basin area, and a ready market. JIR had been drilling at various sites for a couple of years and apparently Woodside and Santos were trying to get in on the act too.

He went in to find the meeting just starting. 'So, blokes, what's happening?' Shirley was asking. 'You found a shitsload of oil out in the sea and you need a heap of workers to dig it up?'

'Something like that, Dr Tiang,' answered the JIR Health and Safety Manager, a likeable middle-aged man with a ruddy face and a shock of sandy hair. 'We have a lease for a large part of the ocean off the local coast and our seismic testing has indicated there is a large deposit of gas about fifteen kilometres off the western end of your beach, so we're going to set up a drilling rig there and a gas processing plant near Port

Campbell. We'll be employing about fifty locals and we need a reliable clinic to provide medical services.'

'We've heard this all before,' said the Prez. 'You've been poking about down there for a couple of years and the jobs for the locals seem to stop and start all the time.'

'This is different, Dr Menzies,' responded the other bloke, who Vince now recognised as the slick Jamiesons PR guy who'd come in last week for his travel vaccinations. 'They were on-shore projects, some seismic based, others wildcat, and a few that turned out to be dry. We're still operating down at Peterborough but our lease extends beyond there, and this Jupiter One well is the first one this close to your lovely city. It should have about twenty years' worth of gas, which we have already presold to a company in South Australia. So, Doctor,' he said as he sat back, flashing a dazzling smile, 'this time we are here to stay.'

'So where will the gas go, once you've found it?' asked Shirley.

'Oceangas are building a pipeline all the way across to Adelaide,' answered the sandy-haired man, 'and there will be lots more jobs on that project, too.'

'Who decides where these leases are?' Vince asked, feigning interest. 'I've never noticed any bloody boundary fences out there in the briny.'

'Well, Doctor,' answered Harkin, unruffled by Vince's sarcasm. 'The state government declares certain areas open for hydrocarbon exploration, then they call for bids from companies—who have to do environmental studies—and if you are successful you can start digging holes. Our current lease is over two hundred square kilometres.'

'How often do you hit pay dirt?' asked the Prez.

'We generally have a one in four strike rate, Dr Menzies, but with Jupiter One, we are very confident we're onto a big deposit.'

'So there'll be a bloody great drilling platform sitting off our beach for years and years,' exclaimed Shirley, earrings dancing.

'Not so, Dr Tiang,' responded the silky Mr Harkin. 'We will have pipes on the sea bed that will run from the well head into the cliff and up under the highway via a directional drill, ending up five hundred metres from the processing plant. Then we'll remove the drill rig and sink a manifold into the seabed with a valve to the pipe. So your horizon will stay picture perfect.'

Eventually Shirley and Lynne gave them a quote for the medicals, about twice their usual fee, and an agreement was reached.

'Doctors, just before you go,' said Lynne after showing the visitors out. 'Kate tells me there are missing morphine ampoules from the safe in the treatment room.'

'But they must have been signed out by one of the doctors, Lynne,' said Shirley.

'And counter-signed by one of the nurses,' added the Prez.

Lynne shook her head. 'Apparently not.'

'Shit a bricks,' snapped Shirley. 'Who's the slack bum here? You got to account for those bloody S8s guys! All I know, you could be giving them to your bloody selfs!'

13

Vince sat down at his desk, impatient to distract his troubled mind. If you didn't think about it, it wasn't happening, right?

He brought up his morning list to find that his first punter was Rita Findlay. He'd found that his messy overlap between friends and patients was endemic in country practice—the longer you stayed, the more of your friends became patients and vice versa. Not that Vince was looking to make friends, but the blurring of those boundaries could be tricky.

The clinic policy was that staff should attend other practices, but long-standing patients like Rita remained on a 'grandfather' clause. Not that she was a grandmother, in fact she wasn't even a mother. Vince knew she had endometriosis, a puzzling but common gynaecological malady that can cause infertility and was almost post-menopausal.

He scanned her file; Rita had last consulted him six months ago with wonky periods, chronic insomnia, and disabling hot flushes.

'I know what's happening, Vince,' she'd said on that occasion. 'But when's it going to be finished?'

'How long's a piece of string, Rita? It's not over till it's over.'

'Well, it hasn't done much for my libido, that's for sure.'

Vince had laughed. 'That's part of the deal, Rit. Al will just have to find another hobby.'

'Well, he always seems to find no shortage of those,' Rita had muttered. 'These days all his testosterone seems to be going into Abgrow. Talk about boys with their toys.'

Suddenly she'd sat forward and her voice had become tremulous. 'Trouble is Vince, I don't have any toys. I should have grown up children and should be looking forward to grandkids by now. Some days I just feel so jealous of those new mothers up on the ward, and when I get to the end of the piece of string, that door will be shut forever.'

Vince quickly called her in and looked up expectantly. He was used to seeing Rita in her nurse's uniform, but today she had on an elegant blue woollen dress and black leather boots. Judging from the wedding photos Vince had seen at the house, the young Rita had been a stunner, and despite the passage of thirty-odd years she was still a beautiful woman. Unlike her partner, Rita seemed content to age gracefully.

'So, Vincenzo,' she said in response to his quizzical glance, 'I've come for the big menopausal grease and oil change.'

Shit, thought Vince, there goes the morning. He unobtrusively hammered an angry email to Lynne: 'BOOK LONG APPOINTMENTS FOR WOMEN'S BLOODY HEALTH CHECKS!' He knew that by the time he did the pap smear, pelvic and breast examinations, discussed Hormone Replacement Therapy and random issues that he used to slough off to GPs, his schedule would be buggered.

Vince had also found that educated women like Rita no longer accepted medical advice on face value. Part of him yearned for the days when doctors were still on the pedestal casting pearls of wisdom in front of trusting patients. 'The punters used to do what we told 'em bud,' as Shirley put it, 'but now with Dr Google, they know more than us!'

Just when he thought the consultation was over, Rita paused as she reached the door and Vince's heart sank as he recognised the 'hand—on-the-doorknob' phenomenon, feared by all Geeps.

'Well, Vince,' Rita said, retaking her seat. 'I'm worried about Allan. He's behaving really oddly and I don't understand it.'

'What do you mean?'

'It's hard to explain … maybe it's a mid-life crisis or something.'

Never mind Allan, thought Vince, *I'm constantly in a mid-life crisis.*

'Rita, I'm not really allowed to discuss Allan's medical issues with you.' He mentally swapped his 'doctor' hat for his 'friend' hat. 'I know he's upset about Polly—she was obviously a very important member of his team.'

'Obviously,' agreed Rita with wry smile. 'Although I can't quite see why he's so distraught about it. It's not as if he was there.'

I know what you mean, thought Vince.

'But it's not about Polly Cotter. Since Abgrow started, his whole system of values has changed. GreenCoast used to be so important to him, but now he cares more about money.'

'He's probably just a victim of the natural tendency to lurch to the right with age,' Vince responded. 'I used to be a bit of a leftist myself in the old days—now I'm to the right of Attila the Hun.'

Rita looked unconvinced. 'But he used to be so committed to the environment, Vince. Remember when the council said we should be grateful to JIR for stimulating the local economy? Allan was ropeable.'

'Yeah, the famous "Moron Incident",' said Vince with a chuckle, recalling the series of headlines in the paper following the Mayor's effusive endorsement of JIR's alleged altruism last year.

Mayor Baxter backs generous JIR—'They're here to help us.'

'"Generous mining company"—what an oxymoron!' responds Professor.

'The only moron is the greenie in the ivory tower,' replies Mayor.

? Defamation action pending.

'That's the funniest thing I've ever seen in the *Observer*, Rita,' said Vince. 'Like I told Allan at the time, "you're not just a stirrer mate, but a bloody smartarse!"'

Rita was obviously not in the mood for humorous anecdotes. 'But then he changed his mind and decided the drilling was okay after all. I felt completely betrayed.'

Hardly a hanging offence, thought Vince. 'It's probably just part of the new Allan,' he commented with a wink. 'You know, the aquaculture entrepreneur. Remember he's a business man now.'

She sat back and shook her head. 'Perhaps that's all it is, Vince, but he's become so materialistic. He says the joint venture is taking off now and soon we'll have some serious money for a change.'

'Look, Rita, Allan's finances are none of my business. It's probably just a bit of a mid-life crisis.'

Vince was trying to wrap things up, but Rita was resisting. 'And we're off to the city every second weekend, going to the opera and expensive restaurants and staying at this swanky Southbank apartment that one of his golf mates owns. "We can have it any time we like", he told me last week, "instead of vicariously living the metro epicurean life, Rit, we can actually do it!"'

I should be so lucky, thought Vince. What's not to like? Sounded like Jonathan Harkin was a very generous host. 'Anyway, Rita,' he said, attempting to sum up. 'We both know Allan's always enjoyed the dolce vitae. He's probably just putting it all on plastic for now, expecting that soon he'll be able to live the dream.'

'But he's changed. You know, I don't trust that Fletcher Smit and I wish Abgrow had never happened.'

Rita glanced at her watch and suddenly jumped to her feet. 'Oh Vince, I've kept you so late. I'm really sorry. I know you've got a lot on your plate, too.'

Vince rose. 'Anytime, Rita. I'm afraid I haven't been much help.'

She kissed him on the cheek. 'Thanks so much, Vincenzo. I'm probably jumping at shadows. You've helped a lot by just listening. Please don't tell Allan I spoke to you.'

Vince put his head down and motored on through his list. It was his turn to tackle the daily mountain of repeat scripts—a job he loathed—but went in search of the list at lunchtime to find Petra had already done them.

'Dr Smit saw eighteen patients this morning,' said one of the receptionists, 'then asked if there was anything she could do to help out, so I gave her the repeats and she did 'em in a flash.'

'Bloody hell, Shaz,' exclaimed Vince. 'Will wonders never cease.'

He was halfway through his lunch—pie and sauce from the corner shop—when he got a call from Professor Lachlan McDonald.

'Good afternoon, Vincent. Thought I should inform you of the Board's initial decision regarding your recent maternal death.'

'Fire away, mate.' Heart in his mouth.

'You will receive formal notification, but the bottom line is that you are barred from obstetric cases until the Coroner completes his report.'

Not the end of the world, thought Vince.

'Off the record, however,' he added, 'unless that report identifies a cause of death exonerating you, then your current provisional registration to practice medicine will be revoked. Stat.'

Fuck! That is!

'I'm guessing hypoglycaemic coma won't cut it, Lachlan?'

The Professor laughed. "Fraid not, Vincent. It's a mode of death, not a cause.'

Vince hung up immediately and swore at the walls. He went straight to Shirley's room and told her the verdict.

She looked shocked, obviously shaken by the implications. 'McDonald doesn't beat around the bushes, does he?'

'I'm gunna strangle the vindictive little bastard.'

'Better not, Rooned. He's got you by the shorts and curly.'

'Shirl, I'm treading water and slowly sinking. Taking out little Lachie would at least give me some satisfaction.'

* * *

It was close to seven-thirty when Vince left the clinic. By the time he put on a plaster at the hospital and did a house call on the way home, it was almost nine when he pulled into his drive at the Snapper house. Deefer scampered about, wagging her tail in welcome as Vince changed into his old jeans and windcheater, put on his favourite Dylan LP—*Blood on the Tracks*—and looked in his tiny fridge for some tucker. Inside was a casserole dish with a note stuck to the top: 'Just some tea for you, Doctor Vince.'

Vince had lived on takeaways for most of his time in Warrnambool, supplemented by some home cooking from Mrs H and dinner at the Findlays' every month or so—a classic 'divorce diet'. *Even though I'm still bloody married.* After fifteen years of lavish entertaining in the eastern suburbs, private school, 'You really must try these divine quinoa stuffed chargrilled spatchcocks, darling' set, he'd lost interest in cooking altogether. Food was now just fuel.

Vince bombed the casserole in his decrepit microwave and wolfed down the delicious beef and vegetable stew. He then took Deef for a quick wander around the block before hitting the sack. After a weekend on call, he usually slept well, but as his body became more tired, his mind became sharper and filled with two images of dead mothers juxtaposed with a churchyard in the background.

Something told him sleep would not come easily tonight.

14

The next day passed with Vince on autopilot and enforced emotional bypass. Over the last year he'd perfected this technique, which allowed him to keep his head in check and do his job. While he still had a job.

His last punter was a woman with a thyroid problem, and as he showed her out, he suddenly had a light-bulb moment—an Endocrinologist might know the answer! He grabbed his mobile and rang Edward Curcovich, the consultant he used for pregnant diabetics back in the day.

'Hi Ed, how's the wild world of hormones?'

A laugh bubbled through the phone. 'Going well thanks, Vince. Haven't heard from you for a while.'

'Long story, mate. Tell me, Ed, why would a girl die of hypoglycaemia just after pushing a baby out?'

'From a glycaemic viewpoint, Vince, obviously diabetic ketoacidosis and hyperosmolar shock might cause intra or post-partum death—'

'Yeah, Ed,' Vince interrupted. 'But she wasn't a diabetic.'

'—but,' continued the unflappable diabetologist, 'while some decrease in blood glucose during labour is almost inevitable, it wouldn't be fatal—'

'—and she had an IV running with some dextrose, and no ketones in her urine—'

'—indeed,' responded Dr Curcovich patiently. 'So unless she had a pancreatic insulinoma, an inborn error of metabolism, a renal or adrenal abnormality or acute alcohol poisoning—'

'Just hang on, Ed.' Feeling like a student again, Vince scribbled down the list.

'—then a large dose of insulin would seem the likely differential diagnosis in this case.'

Great, thought Vince, leaving the small questions of *who, how* and especially *why?*

'Thanks, mate,' he replied. 'I owe you one.'

* * *

That evening Allan Findlay called at the Snapper house to collect Vince for the quarterly Abgrow Board meeting.

In a weak moment a few months ago he had agreed to join the Board as a non-voting community representative.

'Thanks, Vincenzo,' Allan had commented at the time. 'Marram's right into this corporative governance stuff and he says we need a dis-interested rep from the public. Next meeting's not till August.'

'I'm not *dis*interested, mate. I'm *un*interested.'

After vaguely agreeing to the gig, Vince promptly forgot all about it until Allan's reminder email that morning. It was the last thing he really felt like doing—he had some important couch sitting and sense-less naval gazing planned.

'So what do I have to do exactly, Allan?' he asked, getting into the car. 'I've got a fair bit on at the moment.'

'Not much at all, Vincenzo. It's just a compliance thing. You can have a snooze if you like.'

Well, one thing I do need is a good bloody sleep, thought Vince as they headed out along the highway.

On the way, Allan filled him in about the makeup of the Board. 'There's five members. As well as Marram and me, there will be John Palmer—Marram's financial advisor; Tony Katsaros—his right hand man at Nautilus Seafoods; and Dr Leanne Fischer, the Pro Vice-Chan-cellor of Deakin. The office manager from the Faculty of Marine Sci-ence attends as minutes secretary.'

Allan turned off the highway down the road into the university. 'I used to co-opt Polly to provide input from the breeding perspective. Give those number crunchers some biology to get their heads around.'

'Tell me something, mate,' said Vince, thinking he'd better pretend he was interested in abalone. 'What do the local ab divers think of Abgrow?'

'Well, naturally they were initially hostile to the scheme. They guard their patches most jealously and didn't want their monopoly to be undermined. But that's when I played my masterstroke, Vincenzo. A couple of years ago, a group of them had formed their own seafood marketing cooperative, mostly the brainchild of Marram Smit.'

'Why Marram, Allan?'

Allan chuckled, the first laugh Vince had heard from him recently. 'Marram grass was imported to the district from South Africa and now it's everywhere. Just like Fletcher.'

'Why did he leave South Africa?' asked Vince.

'He got into some sort of trouble, apparently.'

'Lot of strife over there around that time, mate.'

Allan nodded as he turned off the highway into the entrance to the university. 'I don't think it was about politics, Vincenzo. Anyway he came over here during the eighties, purchased an ab license and spent fifteen very lucrative years bringing those valuable creatures up off the sea floor.' Allan shifted in his seat. 'He was smart enough to get out just before the herpes virus arrived, then sold his license and turned businessman. Now he's got his fingers in just about every pie around the place. "You've taken root," I told him. "You're spreading over the whole district like that bloody grass!"'

Vince smiled; the Marram handle was right on the money. Fletcher certainly was ubiquitous. 'Someone told me that he played first grade rugby for Natal and if it hadn't been for the boycott during Apartheid he might have been a Springbok.'

'That's right, Vincenzo,' said Allan, 'although these days he would have been a Protea.'

Political correctness gone crazy, thought Vince. *There's nothing floral about Fletcher Smit.*

'But mate, wouldn't he have made a great ruckman for the Cats?'

Allan nodded. 'Better than our current bloke anyway.'

'Anyway,' he went on, 'back to Abgrow. We had the science but not the infrastructure and commercial expertise. So I pitched the concept of a joint venture to Marram, and Nautilus Seafoods came on board as a partner. To paraphrase Franklin Delano Roosevelt, Vincenzo: better to have the bastards on the inside pissing out than on the outside pissing in.'

'Makes sense,' said Vince.

'So we built an on-shore nursery tank facility over at Killarney, with pristine ocean water pumping through it.' Allan followed the winding drive through the floodlight Deakin grounds. 'And we're putting grow out cages about ten kilometres out to sea.'

Allan pulled up in his designated car park outside the university boardroom but made no move to get out. 'The set up costs were massive, Vincenzo, and, in strictest confidence, Marram overreached and Abgrow was almost scuttled.' He took the key out of the ignition. 'In the meantime, he's found a white knight and it looks like full steam ahead. I would've preferred to avoid private equity but this project is so important to me that I'll probably have to compromise.'

They got out of the car and walked into the nearby boardroom. Fletcher Smit greeted Vince with his ready smile, crushing handshake, and a big bear hug.

'Welcome aboard, bru. Howzit, Vincey?'

Jesus, we're hardly besties, mate! Vince had encountered that alpha male handshake before—I'm the leader of the pack, so look out!

Fletcher was a commanding presence at the head of the boardroom table, and seemed to be brimming with ideas, which he articulated in machine-gun bursts. He was a huge, muscular man, with tousled blond hair, a thick bull neck, and an animal-like physicality, accentuated by his cauliflower ears and crooked nose. After introducing Vince, he gave a brief rundown of the agenda, mentioned the passing of Polly Cotter, then looked around the table for general comments. There were some responses, but Allan seemed to be lost in thought.

'Come on, Professor,' Fletcher added in a jocular tone. 'I know you academics are deep thinkers but we need to have some blooming focus here, okay?'

He then invited a motion regarding Polly's death and Leanne

Fischer responded. 'Thank you, Mr Chairman. We at the university very much mourn the passing of Polly Cotter—a Deakin_alumnus and brilliant young scientist. I move that Abgrow send a condolence card and flowers to Aaron Quick.' The motion was seconded and passed. Allan simply nodded.

'Allan, we're all sorry about the tragic loss of Polly,' said Fletcher. 'Her contribution to Abgrow was outstanding. But the show must go on. That's what she would have wanted.'

'You know what she would have wanted, do you Marram?' said Allan, staring at the unopened financial reports in front of him.

Fletcher seemed used to Allan's churlishness and distracted manner. Vince figured he'd probably realised long ago that Allan was an ideas man and rarely scrutinised the fine print.

Fletcher guided the Board through the agenda and then Tony Katasaros and John Palmer gave their reports, followed by some concerned questions from around the table. Vince didn't have a copy of the full financials and wasn't expected to join that discussion; however, it was apparent even to him that Abgrow was haemorrhaging money.

The next agenda item was 'Funding Options—Fletcher Smit'.

Fletcher stood and took the floor, casting a large shadow under the standard-issue compact fluorescent light bulbs.

'Friends, we have a real problem just now. If we can't attract some funds, Abgrow will be finished.' He looked at Allan and Leanne. 'Ja, we have the science but the infrastructure is blimmin' expensive, so I have a proposal.' He scanned those around him in a challenging, almost belligerent fashion. 'You will know that Jamiesons International Resources are doing exploratory drilling off the coast. They are willing to underwrite Abgrow's ongoing expenses as a good will gesture.' There was an indignant exclamation of dissent from Leanne Fischer but he stared her down and continued. 'This will get us out of the shit and there are no strings attached. JIR will not have a seat on this Board and they won't expect anything from us.'

'But it's such a bad look,' said Professor Fischer. 'The university can't accept finance from an international resource company, and surely they will expect us to support their drilling.'

'Hey Prof, like I said, this good will stuff is just part of their PR.'

Leanne Fischer shook her head and everyone looked to Allan, who eventually spoke, his voice uncharacteristically quiet.

'I think Marram's right, Leanne. We don't have much choice. Abgrow needs that money or it will go under—we mustn't, *mustn't* let that happen,' he added with real passion.

Shit, thought Vince, *I didn't realise this thing was so important to Allan.*

Professor Fischer gave a resigned nod. 'The VC is also determined that the project succeed.'

Fletcher's aggressive posture was immediately replaced by a relaxed and cheerful demeanour. 'John and I will meet with Mr Harkin soon-soon and thrash out the details. Then we can move forward with our strategic plan.'

Doesn't he look like the cat that swallowed the cream.

'That brings me to the last item of general business. I propose we set up an education fund for Polly Cotter's baby—the Abgrow Indigo Quick Bursary.'

There was a murmur of assent and a motion was put and passed.

Fletcher then glanced around the table and smiled. 'On a happier note, I would like to congratulate Professor Findlay on his achievement—"The National Aquaculture Award for Entrepreneurship". Well deserved.'

There was a generous round of clapping, and Allan brightened up immediately. 'Thanks for your kind words, Mr Chairman,' he responded, 'but the award was really for the whole team.'

Fletcher Smit spread his big arms wide. 'But you had the idea, Allan.'

'So,' Fletcher went on, 'thanks for your attendance. A special thanks to the good doctor for his maiden innings. Any more general business? No? We'll have the full financials available before the AGM next month. Let's all redouble our efforts to move the thing a bit more quickly.' He paused, his gaze roaming those around the table. 'Good decision tonight, guys.'

Allan and Vince left as soon as the meeting ended and headed off towards the car, but turned when they heard running footsteps behind them.

Fletcher appeared out of the dark. 'Allan,' he called out. 'Wait up.

I had a call from a lad from the *Australian Financial Review*. They're doing a piece on entrepreneurship and joint projects between industry and universities and they'd heard about the award. I told them you were the creative force behind the whole thing and to contact you for an interview. Should be front page.'

What is Smit up to? Vince wondered. *Sounds like a snow job to me.*

'There's also talk of a piece on that Sunday morning business show on ABC TV.'

Allan paused and attempted a modest smile. 'Thanks, Marram, that was very kind of you. It is important for projects like ours to receive appropriate recognition and perhaps I can help other similar joint ventures to get off the ground. Naturally, I will acknowledge the crucial roles played by Nautilus Seafood and the rest of the team.'

Get your hand off it, mate. Fletcher is playing the oldest trick in the book here.

The South African beamed broadly and gave them a big joint hug, as if they'd both kicked the winning goal in a Grand Final.

They got into the car and headed off. As Allan turned on to the highway, Vince looked across at him—the naïve, vain bugger looked happier already. Smit obviously realised Allan's ego was even bigger than his libido, and he certainly knew how to stroke it.

15

After Allan dropped him home, Vince sent out for a pizza, flopped on the couch, and reflected on the meeting. One thing stood out—Fletcher Smit was a bully and a manipulator, and hopefully he wasn't in Abgrow purely to feather his own nest. Vince wondered what sort of trouble he'd run away from in South Africa. He shot off a text to Elena to see if she could find out. Not that it was any skin off Vince's nose if Fletcher was a crook, but he thought Allan should know.

He pulled out the list of conditions Ed Cercovich had given him and grimaced—it might as well have been in Swahili. He googled insulinoma: 'an insulin-secreting tumour of the pancreas gland causing hypoglycaemia'. That could explain it. He picked up his mobile and punched in Sarah's number.

'What about an insulinoma? It's an insulin—'

'—secreting pancreatic tumour. Good evening to you too, Vince,' she responded crossly. 'It's almost eleven. Ring me tomorrow.'

'Could you see if Polly had one?'

Sarah fired up. 'I sectioned her pancreas and no, there was no insulinoma. I do know my job, Vince!'

'What about renal or hepatic problems that might cause hypos?'

'NAD.'

'Inborn errors of metabolism?'

'No!'

'Did you check for alcohol poisoning?'

'What do you think? Of course—it's routine. Blood alcohol zero. Goodnight!

Vince tossed his phone on the coach; another bloody dead end! He never did like endocrinology. So what then? Someone in that labour ward gave Polly a big shot of insulin for reasons unknown? Crazy stuff!

The pizza-delivery boy duly arrived and Vince turned on the idiot box. It was day three of the second test at Mumbai and the Indians were batting. He sat in a trance munching his pizza, watching the overs come and go and the total steadily increase until the umpires removed the bails and he realised it was stumps. Vince looked at his watch: two forty-five!

'What the hell do you think you're doing, you dickhead?'

* * *

Next morning he woke early to find the air was warmer, the birds were singing, and quite unexpectedly flowers were appearing in his completely neglected front garden—a miracle of nature! He must've encountered numerous springtimes before but he'd been too busy to notice the natural world at all.

The change of season failed to improve Vince's mood. There was an eerie official inertia surrounding Polly's death, but he knew it wouldn't last. The VMIA couldn't see any grounds for a claim against him, but that was the least of his worries. The Coroner was still considering the matter and, as Vince knew, those legal wheels started very slowly but could suddenly accelerate down his blind side and crucify him on the home stretch. And Little Lachie would be waiting there to hammer the nails in.

Vince decided to ignore the advent of spring and turned over to resume his repose. However, his mind was already switched on and the bright sunshine was streaming in through his tattered curtains. Deefer, obviously convinced the day had started, was moaning and scratching at the door.

'All right,' he muttered to the world as he rolled out of bed. 'Have it your own bloody way.'

Vince looked at the mess on the couch—dirty clothes and empty pizza boxes, and the broader domestic chaos around it.

Minutes later he and Deefer clambered up the mound behind the Flume car park to check out the surf. As he gazed at the rolling waves below, two young guys came up the track on the same mission.

'Looken good, Doc,' said one, taking off his beanie and shaking out a blond mop. 'A one-metre swell and an off-shore wind. Let's get out there, Jacko.'

Vince had discovered the local surfing conditions were notoriously quixotic. The typical south-wester coming from beyond the breakwater produced an on-shore breeze and chopped up waves, resulting in widespread misery and increased dope consumption in the surfing fraternity. Then the wind could suddenly turn around, producing perfect sets of sculptured waves and a fast rip back out along a channel over the sandbar to ferry the surfers out the back again. Word would spread in seconds and the Flume car park would rapidly fill with utes, station wagons and bikes, and the ocean with wet-suited figures paddling out through the breakers.

'What's a middle-aged baldy like you doing out with the grommets, Doc?' called one of the hospital nurses who was walking down the track with her dog.

'Dunno, Ivy,' answered Vince, pulling on his wetsuit. 'Must be mad I reckon!'

Good question, he thought, *probably just a fruitless attempt to stem the passing of the years.* However, he wasn't the only one. There were lots of other older guys out there, mostly on mini Malibu boards, surf skis and stand-up paddleboards. Shirley's husband Gareth was a mature-age surfer as well.

Vince was purely out there for the therapy. He knew withdrawing into himself might send him down that slippery slope again, and as the shrink had put it: 'Lack of motivation and anhedonia are important early warning signs, Vincent.'

So he grabbed his board and trotted down the track, Deefer chasing the leg rope as it trailed in the sand.

16

When he got to work, Vince found Shirley sitting in the tearoom talking to Serena Jorgenson, a masseur and yoga teacher who operated from the Timor Street clinic three days a week. Serena was a thirty-two-year-old New Ager, who wore brightly-coloured cheese cloth shirts, floral happy pants, beaded dreadlocks and copious bangles that jingled and jangled and announced her imminent arrival in a room.

Serena leapt up and enfolded Vince in a warm embrace. 'Man, you look tense,' she exclaimed as he disentangled himself. 'What about a massage?'

'Yeah, Rooned, you stressed bloke,' said Shirley with a grin. 'Maybe you need some colon irrigation? Clean out the bloody toxins, mate.'

Vince knew Shirley had no more time for alternative therapies than he did. Sounded suspiciously like she'd told Serena he needed some chilling out. *What bullshit!*

'Think I'll give it a miss, Serena,' said Vince, taking a backward step. He admonished Shirley with a wave of his index finger and headed off to his room.

As he sat at his desk his mobile beeped with a message from the girls. Texting had become the *lingua franca* for Vince and the twins. However, their mother disapproved of this constant repartee. 'They need to concentrate on their homework, Vincent, not message you endlessly about old movies, football and juvenile TV shows.'

Vince knew it was really because these precious interactions with the girls were full of father-daughter in-jokes Lydia wasn't part of. Unlike Lydia, the girls also allowed him to be a Facebook friend and more recently an Instagram follower, although that scared him as much as it kept him in touch with their lives.

The message was from Georgie, the twin with attitude. *'What up Bins? We are good but suspended 4 a week 4 smoking can we come down? G x'*

Vince was happy for the girls to visit anytime, but, fearing the consequences of not discussing this plan with Lydia, decided to defer a decision until he knew more. Lydia blamed Vince for Georgie's smoking anyway—he'd been a smoker when they'd first met. ('Lids, that was twenty years ago, and smoking is not bloody genetic!')

The twins usually called him 'Bins', which was the closest Tessa, at two years old, could get to Vince's name. Lydia, on the other hand, had always insisted on 'Vincent', maintaining the diminutive was too casual for a city specialist. In those days, his pet name for her was 'Lids', and his brother—in-law Paddy used to refer to them collectively as 'The BinLids'.

He texted back a suitably disapproving reply, saying he would get back to them ASAP, fired up his computer and glanced at his morning's appointments. 'Oh no,' he groaned, 'not baby vaccinations again. I did them last week!'

This was Vince's job every second Monday morning and he had designed a system whereby he would see the infants first, make sure they were well, then flick-pass them through to the nurse who would explain the vaccines and do the jabbing. That way he would avoid the inevitable screaming and tears.

The only good thing about babies was that they never asked questions, but the parents certainly did—especially those first-time Serious Young Mothers, SYMs as Shirley dubbed them.

Just as Vince was about to kick off, his phone rang. 'What?' he snapped.

'It's Lynne. The nurses are attending a wound healing in-service this morning. You'll have to vaccinate the bubs yourself.'

'That's all I bloody need!'

He called in the first infant and immediately encountered a SYF with a seven-weeker for his first vaccine. The bloke wanted to know every last thing about all eight components and just as Vince was about to start, he asked: 'Doctor, can you guarantee this will not give Henry Asperger's Syndrome?'

'Probably not,' answered Vince, 'but I'm about to get Pissed-Off Doctor Syndrome and believe me, mate, it's not pretty!'

By the time he'd given the shots, completed the paperwork and herded the SYF and babe (both weeping) back out to the waiting room, he was already way behind.

He called in the next baby punter and realised with a jolt that it was Aaron Quick and Indigo. Aaron was universally called 'Emu', although with his black hair and narrow face, Vince reckoned he looked more like a crow.

'Why *Emu*, mate?' he'd asked Aaron out in the surf one morning.

'I inherited the name off me old man, Doc,' he'd responded with his slow grin. 'He had long skinny legs and a big bum and hair that stuck straight up like Homer Simpson and they reckon he used to run like a bloody emu when he was playen footy. Pop was called Emu, too.'

Emu carefully put the capsule bearing its precious cargo on the floor and slumped back in the chair.

Looked to Vince like he'd been doing it hard. 'So, mate, it's a tough gig looking after a little baby, eh?'

Emu looked at the floor. 'We're doin' all right, Doc. Just get on with it.'

Vince had called Emu with Polly's post-mortem results but had not seen him since that morning in front of the hospital. 'Trouble with these new bubs, they don't come with an instruction manual.'

He generally got a smile of agreement with that one, but Emu just shrugged his thin shoulders and sat forward. 'Let's just cut the bullshit and do the business.' He seemed more angry than sad.

'I know you must be feeling very pissed off, mate, just thought you might need some help.'

Emu snorted derisively and handed over the Maternal and Child Health Book containing Indy's life story so far: her birth details, dimensions recorded on percentile charts, and developmental assessments—already opened at the vaccination page. In this case, Vince realised, the Maternal section of the book was sadly superfluous.

Vince saw from Indy's clinic record that she'd been in the previous week. 'Mate, I see here Dr Smit diagnosed Indy with reflux. How did she go with the omeprazole?'

'I didn't give it her, Doc. I don't reckon that chick knew what she was talkin' about. I just told her Indy wasn't sleeping so good, and she didn't ask no questions or nothin'. Just gave me the script.'

Fantastic, thought Vince, *now the Princess is medicating healthy babies!*

'We seen her dancin' with some guys down the Cally one night, Doc, pissed as a maggot. She had a real big night and Pol and me drove her home, but now she reckons she's never seen me before. Probably too wasted to remember.'

We've all been there, Vince reflected as he drew up the vaccines. *Although not ideal behaviour for a doctor in a small community.* He watched Emu expertly undress the sleeping Indy. Her baby gear was in a large pink plastic bag, patterned with blue flowers and red teddies, bulging with nappies, pins, bottles and bibs, which all looked a little incongruous alongside Emu, with his black dreadlocks, assorted facial piercings and torn, black sleeveless shirt with 'WICKED' emblazoned across the front.

Vince went with his usual quick jab-jab, element-of-surprise approach. He'd learnt it was impossible to charm a new baby into accepting sharp pricks voluntarily. Indigo swallowed the oral rotavirus dose happily enough, then after the first injection she opened her eyes wide and looked puzzled, then after the second jab she took a big breath and let out one mighty howl, then immediately reverted to peaceful somnolence.

'She's a cracker, Emu,' Vince said as he disposed of the needles in the sharps container.

'Yeah, Doc Hanrahan,' he responded as he changed her nappy and dressed her again. 'Pretty cruisy like her mum.' For an instant, Emu's features softened and a half-smile played on his gaunt features. 'We do all right, me and Indy,' he said, looking Vince face-on for the first time. 'But some people need to stop stuffin' us around.'

Vince was puzzled. 'Who do you mean, mate?'

'That old bastard Findlay. He keeps wantin' to play with her and give her dopey presents and shit.'

'Emu, he was Polly's supervisor. He's probably just trying to help.'

Emu gave a sardonic laugh. 'Bloody well helpin' himself, ya mean.'

Vince glanced at him quizzically. Emu avoided his gaze and starting packing up Indy's gear, then stopped, took a deep breath, and looked up again.

'He took Polly to stay in some flash joint at a conference in Melbourne last year and like the dirty old man he is, got her pissed and got into her pants. Then later, when Polly told him she was knocked up, he said he'd always wanted to be a father, yadda yadda, and that he wanted to move in with her and play happy bloody families.'

Vince reeled at this bombshell.

'Pol told him to piss off and he went ape-shit and tried to turn her against me. As if she'd wanna live with him, he's fucken older than my dad!'

It took Vince a minute or two to digest all this, let alone know if he believed it.

'So who is Indigo's father, Emu?'

Emu answered immediately. 'Shit, they only did it once, who d'ya reckon? An old bloke like that would hardly even be up to it.'

'But if paternity is an issue, mate, then surely—'

Emu shook his head as he rocked Indy back and forward. 'It's *not* a fucken issue, Doc. Indy's mine and that's all there is to it.' He gave a sudden grin as he played with Indigo's fingers. 'Anyway, Findlay knows what the deal is. I'm not lettin' the bastard off the hook. He's got a guilty conscience, just like the rest of youse,' he added darkly, zipping up Indy's bag.

Emu's pale face bore such a look of hostility that Vince flinched. 'Listen, Emu, I can understand the way you feel, but—'

'Save it, Dr Hanrahan,' interrupted Emu, picking up Indy and loping towards the door. 'I'm goin' home to look after my baby.'

Vince's head was spinning as they left—what the hell was that about? Surely Allan couldn't be the baby's father?

'Of course he could,' he said out loud. He'd just had one of those instant recalls like in the movies—a rapid movement of the shot back through time accompanied by a supersonic boom sound.

Allan Findlay had come to see Vince late last year at the medical clinic out at Deakin. Shirley operated a branch office on campus three days a week, staffed by the doctors on a roster. It must have been Melbourne Cup day because Vince remembered the Student Services staff inviting him to join their sweep. The clinic was really for students but one or two academics often rolled up as well. Allan had been Vince's only client that day—the students were probably all at the pub watching the races.

Allan had appeared distracted and had waved off Vince's light-hearted banter about the Melbourne Cup.

'Very open field this year, Vincenzo, and I never bet on the Cup—it's a race for the mugs. Look, I'll cut straight to the chase. I am actually inquiring on behalf of a student. What can you tell me about paternity testing?'

'Well, it can be straight forward,' Vince had replied, 'you just need the blood groups of the baby and potential fathers and some candidates can be excluded right off the bat.'

'But there must be a more definitive technique, Vincenzo.'

'Okay sunshine, I'm getting to it. We take scrapings for DNA testing from inside the cheeks and gums of the mother, baby, and putative fathers and send it to the Forensic Institute lab in Melbourne.'

'Then how long till you get the result?'

'About ten working days from memory, mate. Is it one of your marine science freshers? Must have taken one of your genetics pracs too seriously.'

'Something like that, Vince. But there must be some way of deciding paternity before the baby is born.'

'These days we can determine the baby's genetic make-up from a maternal blood test at around nine weeks or so, but it costs several hundred bucks—way beyond the budget of most students. You better send her in to see me.'

So, thought Vince as he called in his next small victim, *Allan's sudden interest in paternity testing last year may well have been about a student all right—one student in particular.*

17

'That was Missy Higgins from her new album. It's now twelve past nine on this beautiful Friday morning on Breakers FM and folks, Vince will join us soon. Here's a message about the upcoming Trivia Night at the Surf Club.'

Sounds like Allan's back on song, thought Vince as he parked next to the pub—late as usual. Since Monday he'd been head down and bum up, no time for speculation about Indy's bloodlines or her mother's death, and suddenly it was Friday morning. He raced into the tiny studio and Allan put on a long track to enable him to get in position.

'Sorry, mate,' said Vince, putting on his headphones. 'Got stuck in Palliative Care.' One of his elderly punters had just died of pneumonia after a long battle with cancer and Una, the new widow, had been up for a chat.

'I met Stan at a dance during the war, Doctor. He looked so handsome in his uniform. You know,' she'd added, smiling through her tears, 'in fifty-three years of marriage we never had a cross word.'

Bloody hell, Vince reflected, he and Lydia had packed their seventeen years with cross words—it was more like trench warfare than marriage. As he raced down the hospital stairs, he was shocked to find his own eyes brimming with tears.

Allan phased out the track and turned on the mikes. 'Welcome, Vince. Tell the listeners what's coming down in this planet, world, country, state or little town of ours?'

He's obviously regained his groove, thought Vince darkly. *Good for him.* He summoned up some mental energy and looked at the paper. 'Allan, the UN Security Council has been urgently convened to discuss the Saudi crisis and the Reserve Bank plans another hike in interest rates.'

Allan hunched his shoulders and spread his hands in mock horror, as if to say, 'Can't you do any better than that?'

'Well listeners, you heard it here first! We'll leave you with that thought and go to Ben Harper.'

He turned off the mikes. 'Went for a run this morning, Vincenzo,' he said, standing up from the panel and stretching his legs. 'First for a while. Thought I might take the surf ski out tomorrow morning. Are you up for it?'

'Maybe, Allan, but I've got a few things to sort out. Listen, mate,' he continued, 'Emu Quick told me the two of you had some issues about Polly's baby.'

'Did he indeed?' said Allan, as he shuffled through his CDs. 'Issues eh? Well, Vincenzo, I've now taken your advice and pulled my oar back out again. The baby is fine and it's absolutely none of my business anyway. So,' he added, as Ben Harper approached his last few chords, 'the path ahead is now very clear and soon I'll have no issues with Emu at all.'

What the hell was that about?

Allan smiled and turned the mikes back on and they proceeded with the rest of the show then headed their separate ways.

* * *

Vince dumped his medical bag in the corner of his room, sat down at his desk and got another text from Georgie. *'Yo Bins, coming on tonight's train, mum shitty ++ LOL. G x'*

Lydia had rung Vince during the week and told him she was sending the twins down for him to read them the riot act about their smoking and the resulting suspensions. 'They won't listen to me, Vincent, and this disgusting habit really has to stop. I saw that *7.30 Report* special—it starts with smoking and next thing they're stealing money for ice! Mum feels it is the thin end of the wedge and who knows what it might lead to?'

Vince had sighed, no point arguing—it was a no-win situation. 'I'll do my best to show them the error of their ways, Lids, and tell your mother I will work on that wedge angle.' *Who gives a shit what that old dragon thinks anyway?*

Tonight's train, he realised with a jolt. *Bugger!* He was going to have to clean the house and stock up the fridge. Hadn't even thrown out those pizza boxes yet. And were there any clean sheets? There was a sleeping bag somewhere.

Before he kicked off, Vince dialled the mid floor; something was eating at him.

'Barbara, I want to ask you something.'

'Good morning, Dr Hanrahan. I'm well thanks, what can I do for you?'

He got the sarcasm but was in no mood for social niceties. 'Is insulin normally kept in the labour ward, like on the trolley or the shelves?'

'No, Doctor, in the fridge in the room next door. You can only store insulin at room temperature if it's currently in use, and even then not in the labour ward. And of course you know we never use insulin in the Low Risk Birth Room.'

Vince grunted, 'Ta, bye,' and hung up. So a midwife couldn't give insulin to someone by grabbing the wrong ampoule by mistake—so much for the 'shit happens' theory. Fair enough, he concluded, that just left one possibility—someone actually murdered Polly Cotter. The Board's gunna love that!

He forced that shocking conclusion off his mental front screen and looked at his appointment list. 'Jesus H Christ,' he muttered; it was a shocker, double-booked and extras galore. Fridays were always busy, but this was ridiculous! He phoned Lynne. 'What's bloody well going on?'

'You know Pete's on a family holiday in Queensland, and Dr Smit is unwell—again.'

That'd be right, the Princess having another bloody sickie.

He grabbed his stethoscope and called in the first punter.

18

Elena had been sitting patiently by herself at Fannies for over half an hour when Vince suddenly appeared and flopped down in the chair opposite, completely knackered.

'Hard day at the office, Doc?'

'Up to my arse in alligators all day, Sarge.'

'Flat out like a lizard drinking, eh?'

Vince smiled. Elena could certainly hold her own when it came to Aussie bush vernacular. Bit different to the ladies back in Canterbury.

'You said it. And the twins are coming on the nine-forty train tonight. Don't let me forget to pick them up, Sarge.'

'Why are your Fridays always like this, Doc?'

'By the end of the week,' he answered slowly, munching on a fresh spring roll—his usual starter, 'spot fires erupt into a big blaze and the punters panic as the weekend approaches. And to make matters worse, today Petra Smit, our registrar, was allegedly crook, so I was flat chat.'

'Is that Fletcher's daughter?' asked Elena.

'Yeah, Petra's a bit of liability really. One minute she's all charm and buzzing like a bee and next thing her lights are out or she's AWOL. Maybe she's bipolar or something.'

'We all have our off days, Doc.'

He gestured in mock horror. 'What, Sarge, even me?'

'Not going there, Doc,' she said with a smile. 'Anyway, I did some research, as per your instructions, and I can tell you Fletcher Smit spent a year at the Westville Prison in Durban for manslaughter in nineteen ninety eight.'

'Good job, Sarge! How the hell did you discover that?'

'Via our very own Australian Federal Police, Doc. They're Interpol's National Central Bureau in Australia.'

'In other words, they know how to find out stuff.'

'Exactly. Smit was a businessman in Durban in the late nineties with a string of dive shops. One day his BMW was carjacked and he tracked down the perpetrator and beat him to death with a tyre lever.'

'Shit,' said Vince. 'Isn't that murder?'

'Well … the victim was a black man and Fletcher had a good lawyer and pleaded self-defence. Turned out he had huge debts and after his release he was bankrupted, then he and Suzie and the eleven-year-old Petra emigrated to Oz, leaving some angry creditors behind.'

Maybe I better pass that on to Allan. 'Thanks, Sarge, you should be in the CIB.'

'It's now called the CIU, the Criminal Investigation Unit,' she responded, 'and I have just been accepted into the Detective Training School.'

Vince raised his water glass. 'Congratulations, Sherlock.'

'The DTS has a very high failure rate, Doc, so don't pop the champagne yet. In the meantime, I have been seconded to the local CIU.'

'Are you the only uniform there?'

'Yeah, and the only female too.' Elena laughed. 'So far the boys seem underwhelmed.'

Vince took a drink and looked at Elena for the first time since his arrival. She was wearing a snugly fitting pink top with short sleeves and a pretty shell necklace, and she looked lovely.

'You're done up a bit flash, Sarge. What happened to the netball club windcheater?'

Elena blushed, obviously surprised by Vince's unexpected compliment. 'It's a warm spring evening, Doc, in case you hadn't noticed.'

'I've noticed,' he said, grabbing a menu.

'How's Aaron Quick going with the baby?' she asked, after they'd ordered their main courses. Every Friday night they had the same—the waiters scarcely needed to ask. They'd eaten through the menu several times over and had settled on their favourites. Fannies had started life as a humble fish and chip shop and was then rebadged as a groovy café with blackboard menus and funky wait staff. Fletcher Smit, the owner, had introduced some Thai and Malaysian dishes, served on oversized white plates with side salads. Vince figured it was as good as you could get in this culinary desert.

'Seems to be okay as far as I can tell, but he's not a happy camper.'

'Hardly surprising, Doc. Girlfriend dead and a new baby to look after.'

Vince nodded, cleaned up his spring rolls, and sat back ruminating. He was still puzzled about Allan. Why was he so upbeat all of a sudden? And how was it that Emu was now fine as a father after all?

'Allan Findlay seems to be in good form again, Sarge,' he commented after moment's pause, failing to come up with any answers. 'He took Polly's death really hard at the start, but he was back on track on the radio this morning.'

Elena shook her head. 'I just can't work the Prof out, Doc. He virtually started GreenCoast and gave us great cred with his environmental science background, and when JIR started test drilling he filed an objection with the EPA to block it.' She paused as their food arrived. 'Then last year he suddenly put up a motion that we suspend our objection pending the JIR Environmental Impact Study—which is taking forever—and rammed it through the meeting.' She nodded towards the beach. 'So now there they are, with that great big platform, endangering marine life for miles.'

'I'd forgotten you were a tree hugger, Sarge,' said Vince, vaguely aware that Elena was secretary of GreenCoast. He was continually amazed by the complexities behind Elena's deceptively simple outward persona.

'I just can't understand it, Doc,' she continued. 'Anyone would think the Prof was on the JIR payroll.' She shrugged and started on her pasta.

Allan wouldn't do that, would he? A bit of philandering's one thing, but selling out your principles? On the other hand, it would explain some of that stuff Rita was talking about the other day, and …

He suddenly sat forward, energised. 'I tell you what, Elena. You mightn't be too wide off the mark there.' He had a quick look around to make sure they weren't being overheard. 'Allan's become mates with Jonathan Harkin, that little PR weasel from JIR, and he seems to be living the life of Riley these days, so maybe he has sold his soul to the devil.'

'Hang on there, Doc,' she said, putting her fork down. 'It was just a throwaway line. He's probably just a middle-aged man who's getting more pragmatic in his old age.'

'Careful, Sarge, I'm not far off middle-aged myself.'

'And the Prof's an entrepreneur himself now, so he's just got more sympathy for the commercial point of view.'

Vince considered this rationalisation for a minute; it sounded like Elena was trying to convince herself. 'Sarge, were Polly and Emu part of GreenCoast?'

'Certainly, and quite actively, too. Aaron is still involved in our campaigns. He doesn't go to many meetings though, it's not really his scene.'

'Wrong demographic, eh Sarge? Too middle class for our Emu.'

Elena laughed; a pretty sound. 'Not true, Doc. GreenCoast is a broad church, ranging from the "conservative with a conscience" set—aka "the Doctors Wives", to the more radical student group—"the Profs Disciples"—and everything in between.'

They finished their meals in silence, Vince seriously considering the idea that Allan was being bribed. Not that he was about to lose any sleep over it; he was used to being let down by people he got close to—good reason to keep your bloody distance. His only concern was if Allan had made this Faustian pact, he'd compromised himself further. *Forget it mate,* he told himself, *you've got enough of your own shit to sort out!*

'So Doc, any sign of that Coroner's report?' Elena had an uncanny habit of knowing what was on his mind.

'Not yet, Sarge, it's a *bloody* long process. Specially if there's an inquest.'

Elena leant forward. 'But no one will be pointing the finger at you, Doc.'

'I'm not worried about criminal charges, Sarge,' Vince responded impatiently. 'But if the Coroner can't find a cause of death that satisfies the Medical Board, my professional registration will go down the dunny. I'm like one of your punters who've blown a heap of demerit points—one more and I lose my license. I'm already benched from obstetric cases until the whole thing is sorted out.'

'That's pretty tough, Doc. You really enjoy delivering babies, don't you?'

'I don't want to come over too warm and fuzzy here, Sarge, but after all these years I do still get a kick out if it.'

Considering his teetotal, not to mention celibate lifestyle, Obstetrics was about the only thing that had been providing him with any thrills. How sad was that?

'Anyway, now I'm not on a specialist's income, soon I won't be able to afford the medical malpractice insurance you need for Obstetrics.' He suddenly laughed wryly.

'I think I missed the joke,' said Elena.

'Well, Sarge, last year my accountant got me to sign my assets over to Lydia in case I got sued. But the divorce rate is about fifty times the litigation rate, so if we don't get back together, she'll keep the lot.'

It was now after eight-thirty and while Elena hailed a waitress to order their coffees, Vince was debating whether he should mention Emu's allegations about Allan and a crazy notion that had just appeared in his head.

He dropped his voice to a whisper again. 'Elena, I will have to kill you after I tell you this, but here goes. I'm pretty sure someone knocked Polly Cotter off with a big dose of insulin—on purpose.'

Elena's large eyes grew even larger.

'I know, I know, just hear me out.' Vince drummed his fingers on the table. 'Say Allan was being bribed by JIR to support the drilling and he and Polly were having an affair—I'm not saying it's true, Sarge,' he added as Elena's eyebrows headed north, 'and Polly got pregnant. Then she found out about the contra and threatened to blab about him being the baby's father unless he withdrew his support for JIR.' He paused, reluctant to articulate the unthinkable. 'Then Allan killed Polly.'

Vince sat back and sipped his coffee. Elena was still leaning forward across the table with an incredulous look on her face. 'But how could he, Doc? He wasn't even at the birth.'

'No Sarge, he wasn't,' Vince paused. 'But Rita was.'

Suddenly the distant sound of the Melbourne train whistling as it came down through the cutting alerted him to the time. 'Shit, the bloody twins! I've got to go, mate.'

He jumped up, leaving this outlandish theory hanging like a giant question mark; he gave Elena a brotherly peck on the cheek and hurried off to the station.

19

Vince immediately dismissed labour-ward murder conspiracy theories from his_mind, jumped into Benny, headed down Liebig Street then turned right into Merri, around the dirty angel, and arrived at the station just as the train pulled in. He rushed onto the platform and nonchalantly leant on the red brick wall, yawning as if he'd been waiting for hours. The girls were last off the first class carriage ('I don't want them mixing with the hoi polloi, Vincent'). He gave them both a big hug, which they endured rather than reciprocated, and ferried them to the Snapper house.

He then presented them with pizzas for dinner—one medium Marinara and one large Fannies Special—their respective favourites.

'Silly old Bins,' said Georgie. 'We sooo don't eat pizza anymore. What do you think we are—ten? Look how fat I am!' she exclaimed, displaying her waif-like frame. 'I'm just on carrot juice this weekend.'

Tessa had apparently become a vegan and so seafood, anchovies and salami were now all beyond the pale. Vince wrapped the pizzas in foil and put them in the fridge, then ordered acceptable alternatives from the Noodle Nook.

'Sorry to be a pain, Bins,' said Tessa, sitting on Vince's old couch, having cleared a space amongst the old books and DVDs.

'We told you we were pizza-free back at Easter,' added Georgie, giving him a tickle. 'You must be getting Alzheimers or something.'

'Got a bit on my mind, Georgie—work stuff. Never mind, I'll have 'em for breakfast.' *Wouldn't be the first time; standard fare when I was drinking.*

'Cold pizza for breakfast is disgusting,' Tessa declared. 'You've got to look after yourself better than that, Dad.'

'Totes,' added Georgie. 'Isn't health, like, supposed to be your thing? You are a doctor, right?'

Yeah, but for how much longer? thought Vince.

'Dad, you can't just throw those boxes in the rubbish. You know there is a thing called recycling? It's kind of a big deal. Do they even do it down here?' Seemed Tessa was now an environmentalist with a new choppy hairdo and an arm full of wristbands supporting worthy causes.

The girls had turned sixteen since their last visit and Vince noticed things were different. Mercifully, the days of Justin Bieber and One Direction on high rotation appeared to be over. Tessa had moved on to Vance Joy and Georgie liked pretty much anything she could dance to. They were both in full campaign mode for Falls Festival tickets for Christmas, but at sixteen it wasn't going to happen.

They were identical—almost Vince's height ('Oh my God, Bins, were you trying to breed basketball players?'), with their mother's killer smiles and auburn manes, but they were different in so many ways. Georgie, despite her claims to the contrary, really was a smoker and a party girl. Her hair colour seemed to vary from week to week and she loved the buzz of the big city and glamming up for a big night out.

After dinner, Vince and the girls devoured a block and half of chocolate—'Has to be the dark stuff now,' said Tessa, 'vegan friendly'—they chatted about school, life, movies and the planet, until all three were yawning and went off to bed.

'Well, at least we have a bed each now, Bins,' said Georgie after surveying the ancient double bunks Vince had borrowed from Mrs Harrington.

'Yeah,' added Tessa, 'just perfect … if we were eight-year-old boys!'

For his part, Vince turned in with a relatively happy heart—these weekends were pure gold. Thoughts of dead mothers and Lachie McDonald were temporarily banished.

* * *

The twins had a predictably slow start to Saturday morning, with a late breakfast followed by a detailed inspection of the contents of Vince's wardrobe.

'Bins, you have just the grossest clothes,' said Georgie, wrinkling her nose. 'You used to dress awesome when we were young. Even Ivan the Terrible dresses better than you.'

'Who's Ivan the Terrible? One of your new teachers? Gee, your school goes through a few.'

Georgie yelped as Tessa trod on her foot and the girls exchanged sheepish looks. A horrible truth suddenly dawned on Vince. 'Girls, tell me Mum hasn't got a boyfriend.'

'Yeah, well, sort of, Bins,' Georgie finally said. 'Hasn't Mum mentioned him? He's a plastic surgeon. Probably about your age. Awful sense of humour, but he does have a pretty cool beach house.'

Vince shook his head. So this was obviously 'the friend with a place in Portsea' where the twins had spent Christmas, hopefully not a 'friend with benefits'. So much for 'After all that unpleasantness, Vincent, and with you down in the country, I think we should just have a break.'

Vince had optimistically clung to the dream that if he could get his life back together, they could get back together, but his hopes of a reconciliation with the woman he loved had just taken a big hit. *I can't involve the girls in any of that stuff.*

'Listen guys, if this Ivan is a plastic surgeon, he has to dress up to convince Brighton ladies he's the right man to relieve them of a chin or three, but I'm not trying to impress the country bumpkins down in this neck of the woods. What they see is what they get.'

Georgie seem to sense it was time to change the subject. She held up a very old crumpled Quicksilver blue and white floral shirt. 'You certainly can't go dating Police Constable Elena in this old crap.'

'Guys, old married people like me don't go dating.' *Except Lydia obviously.* 'And even if I did, I don't think she and I would hit it off.'

'PC Elena is a cool chick, Bins.'

'Yeah, we would totally approve.'

He tried to drag the twins along to the local football in the afternoon but they had already organised to do the op shops. 'You go off with your little footy friends, Bins. We need some girl time.'

Vince called in at the supermarket after the game, and when Elena dropped the twins off, he greeted them with a passable defrosted vegetarian lasagne and a sad looking salad. They ate on their laps and knocked off four episodes of *Mad Men*, an old favourite, before rolling into bed.

As soon as Vince's head hit the pillow, the soporific effect of having the twins under his roof was interrupted by unsettling thoughts about Lydia and her new squeeze. *No point fretting about it,* he told himself, *probably inevitable.* That worry was immediately replaced by graphic images of a dead girl on a floor, which then morphed into a dream sequence of Rita Findlay drawing up a syringe full of insulin.

'Hey, Bins, are you okay?' Tessa's voice suddenly sliced into his consciousness. He opened his eyes to find her standing at the end of his bed.

'You were calling out in your sleep, Dad. Having a bad dream maybe?'

'Yeah, Tess, that's right, don't worry about it, sweetie. I'll be fine, you go back off to bed.'

* * *

The next morning they took Deefer for a long walk from the Breakwater all the way round to the Hopkin's river mouth. As they trudged through the soft sand, Vince's mind automatically began replaying his outlandish theory about Polly's death until Georgie's insistent voice suddenly intruded.

'Twins to Bins, twins to Bins! Are you copying, Bins?'

Vince jerked himself back to reality. 'Oh yeah … What were you saying, Georgie?'

'We were telling you about Ivan the Terrible's nerdy son Ger—*ard*. We call him Jerry, and Ivan really cuts sick.'

Vince nodded vaguely. 'Good job, girls.'

'You're not tuning in, Bins,' said Georgie. 'What's the deal?'

'Look, I really shouldn't be talking to you guys about this stuff, your mother would kill me, but I had a young woman die in labour last week and it's going to play out badly for me.'

The twins nodded, identical worry lines creasing their brows.

'Did you do something wrong, Dad?' asked Tessa quietly.

'No, Tess, I didn't, but the authorities in Melbourne mightn't see it that way.' He took a deep breath. 'Not looking good.'

Georgie linked her arm through Vince's. 'Dad, sure you're not just jumping to conclusions?'

Vince noticed the twins exchanging knowing glances. *They're thinking I'm losing my grip. Again.*

'Anyway girls,' he said, knowing he'd overstepped the line. He was the parent after all. 'Enough of that stuff. Last one to the top of the hill has to wash Deefer!'

He hurled the dog's ball up the dune, and she took off after it.

* * *

After quick showers, they all jumped into Benny and headed over to Port Fairy for their traditional Sunday morning brunch at Rebecca's café. Vince needed to return the focus to their lives.

'Girls,' he said, 'there's been nothing new on your Facebook pages for months. What's going on?'

'Bins,' answered Tess, rolling her eyes. 'No one really uses Facebook anymore.'

'Plus, weird that you would even check it,' added Georgie. 'We mostly just Insta stuff.'

Vince frowned.

'We stalk the PC's Instagram account. Get her to teach you, Bins.'

'She posts really cool pics,' said Tess. 'PC Elena is way smart.'

'And she looks at you as if she knows what you're thinking but she doesn't try to analyse the crap out of what you say,' said Georgie as they sped along the highway, the wild ocean on the left and the verdant hills on the right.

'Yeah,' added Tessa with a nod. 'Not like Mum—the uber-neurotic— and the teachers who are so paranoid about everything.'

'In case we're turning into junkies—'

'—or hookers—'

'—so we have to do some bad stuff—'

'—just to make 'em feel like—'

'—they're on the right track—'

'—so then they're—'

'—satisfied.'

'—justified.'

'You mean to say …' Vince glanced at his daughters. 'That you do the wrong thing on purpose just to bait them?'

'Yeah, it's awesome, Bins. We call it "Twins Behaving Terribly",' responded Georgie, as they both burst into peals of laughter. 'Mum reads all these psychology books but she still can't figure us out.'

'PC Elena would just know it was all crap anyway—'

'—we were only smoking in the gym to get suspended so we could come down here—'

'—not to see you, of course, Bins, cos Ivan said you're a bad influence—'

'—just so we could—'

'—have a double cone at the Port ice creamery—'

'—play with Deefer—'

'—check out some hot locals—'

'—*as if*—'

'—and have a surf at the Flume.'

Vince laughed then almost cried, realising what he was missing. He knew he wasn't performing the duties of "father" to the degree outlined in any job description, but what choice did he have? The bloody Medical Board of Australia had forced him into this position.

* * *

Too quickly Sunday evening came around and he found himself back at the railway station with the girls—complete with new belly button studs, which, against his better judgment, they'd talked him into funding.

'Your mother already thinks I'm leading you astray, girls. Do you think this umbilical hardware is going to help?'

'It's cool, Bins, she *so* won't see them until we go to Noosa next summer. She'll cut sick then, but that's not like till forever.'

While they were waiting for the train, Vince gave the twins a lecture about smoking and licentious behaviour in general. This was met with the usual mixture of laughter and eye rolling. He frowned, put on his stern voice and notched up the volume.

'Hey guys, seriously, just listen up. There's no point acting up just to annoy your mother, because it will backfire and you definitely don't want to get kicked out of school. So just cool it, okay?' Same result.

'Enough of the Father-Daughter Talk already,' said Georgie.

'Yeah,' added Tessa, 'it's time for the *Daughter*—Father Talk, so hear this: we are worried about you, Dad. You need to take care of yourself better. You have to get some proper furniture and some pots and pans and a cleaning lady.'

'And your diet's crap.' Georgie produced a box from the back seat. 'Meet your new juicer, Bins—op shop special. Dr Bins, your prescription is two glasses of juiced carrots, apples, ginger, mint and kale taken by mouth each morning. Got it? Enough with the breakfast pizza.'

'And, Dad, you can't just sit around watching old TV series all the time. It's sad. Get out more. Or at least get Netflix.'

'Seriously, if you have work trouble, make sure you talk to the other doctors about stuff.'

'And maybe you should go back to that counsellor.'

Georgie summed up. 'Bins, it's time you got your shit together.'

Vince was gobsmacked and struggled for a response. Suddenly the train whistle blew loudly as it slowed around the last bend and pulled up with a screech at the platform. He instantly felt that familiar sensation of loneliness and self-pity. He wouldn't see them again until the following month when he'd promised to come up to their Parent-Teacher interviews. Apparently Lydia had a prior engagement, so Vince said he would come and fly the fatherly flag.

As the train pulled out, Tessa was already downloading a podcast and Georgie was making faces at the window. Vince waved, watched until the train disappeared around the bend, then walked back to Benny, which now felt huge, cold and empty.

* * *

Vince woke the next morning with the despondency that always followed a visit from the twins. He glanced at the time—just after six.

The clock radio was the only item from the matrimonial bedroom that had come with him. He got the radio and she kept everything else— except the overdraft!

He closed his eyes and tried to go back to sleep but the emotional vacuum that always followed the girls' departure rapidly refilled with anxiety—the elephant was back in the room and his mind started whirring …

Okay, so Polly Cotter died of hypoglycaemia and the only possible explanation is that some bloody person purposefully killed her with a large dose of insulin, but that won't satisfy the Board, so I'm going to have to find out who. I just want my old life back. Friday night's theory about Allan's potential motive seems ludicrous now and anyway, he wasn't even there. Who is this Ivan? Did Allan sell out on GreenCoast, and could he be Indy's father? Might as well just bloody ask him. As for Rita killing Polly … surely that's just bullshit! I'm missing the girls already. Must tell Allan about Fletcher's background—he doesn't sound like the best bloke to be in business with …

Vince shook himself, pulled on his mental handbrake and dragged himself out of bed. He knew he needed to get physical or his head would explode. So he dutifully pulled on his shorts, donned a T-shirt advertising tinea cream and grabbed his ancient runners, which he used for everything from jogging and fishing to walking on the beach.

'Bins, they smell like there's stuff growing in them.' The girls had tried to coax him into a shopping expedition, but with their usual lack of success.

'Fewer clothes means a smaller carbon footprint, right Tess?'

He snatched open the back door and Deefer starting yelping in anticipation. 'Feeling lazy today, mate, let's drive to the beach.'

He raised Benny's tailgate, Deef bounded in and they headed off. The old Swedish rustbucket was about as tired as Vince's runners. Volvo station wagons had been *de rigueur* around the leafy green eastern suburbs in the late eighties; just the thing for ferrying the children to kindergarten. Two hundred thousand kilometres later Benny was full of sand, rust and dog odours, as well as miscellaneous flotsam and jetsam, like random fishing tackle, fossilised Medicare vouchers and a single flipper.

Vince parked and they ambled up the embankment to the narrow walkway that led down to the sand. He went through his stretching routine and Deef did her customary wee on the beach. As Vince worked on his increasingly stiff muscles, he gazed out at the sea and was glad he'd made the effort. The ocean filled all his senses—the fresh salty tang, the crashing surf and the white horses shimmering and glittering, lit up by the first rays of the sunrise. In happier days, an absolute epiphany—this morning, just a temporary distraction.

He and Deef set off on the track running east from the surf club, along the dunes and high up above the beach. Vince paused and took in the view of the other side of the river mouth and the even wilder sea beyond. He'd raised quite a sweat; his chest heaved and his heart belted away. The sun had risen completely to reveal a magnificent but chilly spring morning. With the native bushes in flower and the sea the brightest of blues, despite himself, Vince felt grateful—to *someone*—to be part of it all.

As they commenced the return run, Deef lagged behind, fossicking in the scrub. She refused to follow despite Vince's stern beckoning. 'Why can't you be like other bloody dogs and just come when you're called?'

Cursing, he ran back up the hill, expecting to find her sniffing around an abandoned half sandwich or a chips wrapper. But this time she was really agitated, barking and sniffing and pulling. Vince followed her down the river side of the hill and, with a sickening shudder, saw what she had found.

A body. Pale, cold, and very dead.

Professor Allan Findlay.

20

'What's this, Vince—play it again, Sam? Twice in a month. We must stop meeting like this.'

Sarah and Vince both knew that contrary to popular opinion, Humphrey Bogart never actually said 'Play it again, Sam' in *Casablanca*, but Vince grimly nodded his acknowledgement of the reference. He wasn't in the mood for banter about old movies.

After the shock of finding Allan's body yesterday, the futile resuscitation attempt, ringing the coppers and ambos, and then the trauma of telling Rita, let alone trying to cope with his own feelings, Vince had barely slept. He felt like Basil Fawlty when he realised the world had completely turned against him and, brandishing a fist at the heavens, screamed, '*Thank you, God! Thank you so bloody much!*'

Vince felt completely numb. He was used to death, but shit, you don't discover the body of one of your mates every day! Especially one who happened to be a patient as well. Sarah Bell's casual attitude also shocked him; bloody pathologists, goes with the territory.

He glanced around the post-mortem room and responded with justifiable anger. 'Believe me, Sarah, I'm not planning to make a habit of it. The less time I spend in this bloody joint the better.'

Christ, he thought, *autopsies on two patients on the trot, I really don't need this!*

Again, he hadn't been able to sign a death certificate, which meant he had another Coroner's case on his hands; and so here he was, back in the PM room with Dr Sarah Bell. At least this time the answer was obvious: old-fashioned heart attack.

As he waited for Sarah to finish, Vince's phone beeped. It was a message from Holtens, the funeral directors. They were on his back to sign the death certificate ASAP, so they could tidy up their paperwork and proceed with the burial, but they would have to wait. Again.

Shirley had educated Vince about the local undertaking scene. Old 'Boxer', the eighty-two-year-old patriarch, would sometimes be waiting at the surgery door when the girls opened in the morning, chasing a certificate after an overnight death—a terrible shock for them if the deceased happened to be a neighbour or an old favourite.

Sarah removed her gown and gloves, washed her hands, then started recording the results on the computer. Vince studied Allan's lifeless body lying on the slab—skin ivory-white with mottled bruising and scarred by the freshly sutured autopsy incisions. He was shocked to find he felt little emotion—very much a case of 'Death, where is thy sting?'

The last time Vince had seen Allan, he'd been laying in the low coastal scrub, clad in his Pier to Pub shirt, red Nike running shorts, and top-of-the-range runners. Allan had always had a penchant for expensive sporting apparel, with the very best Italian boots for bush-walking, the newest wetsuits for surfing, and the biggest collection of cashmere golf sweaters this side of St Andrews. For Allan, looking the part had been crucial, but now he was just wearing a shroud.

'Well, Vince,' said Sarah, shutting down the computer, 'Professor Findlay died of an acute asthma attack. A bit of atheroma in the coronary arteries and some generalised atherosclerosis, but no sign of an infarct.'

'You mean chronic obstructive lung disease?' Vince asked, incredulous that Allan's heart hadn't been the cause of death.

Sarah shook her head. 'He had some chronic pulmonary changes but that didn't kill him.' She pointed at her screen. 'Bronchoconstriction, oedema, mucous plugging, respiratory failure. I'll let you know when the chemistry and toxicology come through, but acute asthma was definitely the cause of death.'

Vince shook his head slowly. 'I just don't buy that, Sarah. Allan was like a time bomb for an infarct. He had all the risk factors—hypertension, smoking, cholesterol and family history, but his asthma was well controlled. He was on the preventative inhaler, did regular peak flow readings, had a good Asthma Action Plan, and he'd virtually stopped smoking.'

He just couldn't believe the answer in Sarah's envelope.

'Well, asthma management is not my area of expertise, Vince,' Sarah responded, 'but even well-controlled asthmatics can still have fatal attacks. Maybe he just got slack about his medication or perhaps there was some overwhelming allergic trigger.'

'He wasn't allergic to anything, Sarah. We tested for all that last year.'

She paused then stood and gave him that special look. 'Obviously then, Vince, his asthma wasn't as stable as you thought.'

Vince saw red; stress and exhaustion tipping him over the edge. 'Listen, Sarah, Allan lost his twin sister to asthma as a child. He was obsessive about his monitoring and treatment and he was bloody well managed, so maybe you should look again!'

'I know you're upset, Vince,' Sarah responded angrily, 'but I don't care to have my professional competence questioned. All I can do as a pathologist is provide information. If you're after a more convenient answer, too bad!'

Vince stormed out of the hospital, climbed aboard Benny and headed towards the clinic After yesterday's events, he certainly had some catching up to do. *Fuck it! Bugger the punters. In fact, bugger the clinic!* He stopped, pulled out his mobile and rang Rita instead; she deserved a face-to-face explanation.

'Hi Rita. Sarah has finished the post-mortem and it seems Allan died of an acute asthma attack. Yeah I'm sure you are.' He looked at his watch. 'I'll call around now to have a talk about it if you like.'

Vince knew he would end up woefully late for the morning's consulting. Too bad—Allan and Rita were his oldest Warrnambool friends. He did a U-turn in Timor Street and headed back past the hospital, then turned left and joined Merri Crescent with its row of stately homes at the top of the hill.

Been a bit of money spent around the place, Vince thought as he pulled up outside the elegant Victorian sandstone house. The fence had been freshly painted, the original wrought iron lace work on the veranda had been replaced and the second-storey extension, which had been years in the building, looked to be almost finished. He walked down the curving brick path, flanked by standard roses, up onto the tessellated veranda, and knocked on the imposing four-panel red timber door inset with magnificent stained glass.

Rita opened the door, eyes red and puffy and lips drawn, and although time had changed the colour of her luxuriant mane, today her face was as white as her hair. Vince gave her a stiff hug.

'I was just sitting in the front room looking at the roses,' said Rita, coming out onto the veranda. 'Remember when Allan went through that phase?'

The 'rose phase' was one of many transient projects Allan had embraced over the years. Vince knew these episodic crazes kept him stable, because, despite his reputation as a bon vivant, unless he had a new passion to focus on he would default to a form of chronic low-level depression.

These serial enthusiasms reminded Vince of Mr Toad from *The Wind in the Willows*. There was always a new exciting challenge around the corner, and although Rita was really the gardener of the pair, last year Allan had become obsessed about winning the competition for Best Rose at the St Andrew's Church garden show, and had thrown himself heart and soul into roses until he'd achieved his aim.

'Oh yes, I remember that, Rit. For months it was all he talked about,' said Vince as they both looked at the emerging blooms.

He followed Rita inside and they sat in the family room at the rear of the home. The house sat up high and had panoramic views across South Warrnambool to the sea—a single uninterrupted sweep from the Surf Club across Lady Bay. On a clear day you could see Port Fairy to the west. Vince used to joke with Allan and Rita that they could wave at the hoi polloi like him down in the badlands of the south, as they sipped their G and Ts on the deep veranda. 'Like two relics of the Raj having tiffin at Raffles, what!'

Rita sat back in her chair, took in a big breath, then burst into tears. Vince willed himself to comfort her and say those things he knew he should, but just couldn't. Oddly, he was able to pour out the normal platitudes with the punters he scarcely knew, but he couldn't do it for people he really cared for. Maybe Lydia was right about his emotional health. He handed Rita a tissue, patted her on the shoulder and waited for her to regain her composure.

'Look, Rita, do you mind if I have a look at Allan's meds?' Vince asked after he had explained the post-mortem results as best he could. 'In view of that asthma finding, I am just wondering about his compliance with his puffers, although we both know he was usually spot on.'

Rita took him through to Allan's bathroom and showed him the neatly laid out array of asthma puffers. It certainly appeared that he was very careful about using prescribed treatments. He'd also recorded all his Peak Flow Meter readings carefully in a book and Vince noticed that even on the day before he died, his was blowing four hundred and seventy-five litres per minute, which was excellent for Allan.

Rita also showed Vince his other pill packets for his cholesterol and blood pressure medications, which were all as expected. But there was one name that Vince didn't recognise at all: *Propranolol 40 mg, take 2, 4 times daily.*

Where the hell did this come from? He turned the container around. It had been dispensed on the September the seventeenth—two days before Allan's death, and there it was—his own name on the label as the prescribing doctor. He suddenly experienced a rising sense of panic, made his apologies to Rita, and quickly walked out to his car.

'Christ! Bloody Propranolol, I don't believe it!' Vince shouted at his windscreen as he sped down the hill along Timor Street. He could see the sea through the Norfolk pines to his right and there looked to be a big swell, but there was more turbulence inside Vince's head than in the entire Great Southern Ocean.

He pulled up at the clinic car park with a scream of brakes and headed straight past the packed waiting room into his office, then rang through to the reception desk.

'Corrine, tell Dr Tiang to come to my room ASAP. Yes, yes, I know … Tough titties—they'll just have to bloody well wait!'

As his computer went through its preliminaries, Vince tried to suppress the feeling of terror that gripped his heart.

There was a knock on the door and Shirley poked her head in.

'What's so urgent, Rooned? I thought you must have a patient with a cardiac arrest or something. I'm halfway through draining a thrombosed pile on a bloke and, get this bud, he's actually crying. So I told him to man up and grow a pair of balls and—'

'Just sit down and shut up for a minute, and if this bloody computer ever shifts its arse, I will tell you what's so bloody urgent.'

She closed her mouth and did exactly what he said.

'To cut a long story short, I've just been to Allan's post-mortem and then to see Rita. According to Sarah, acute asthma was the cause of death, and amongst his medications I found a bottle of Propranolol. Apparently prescribed by me.'

'*Propranolol!*' said Shirley incredulously. 'What were you doing giving beta-blockers to an asthmatic, Rooned? Those buggers can trigger off life threatening bronchospasm and—'

'For Christ's sake, Shirley, thanks for stating the bleeding obvious. I know that!'

'I just thought you fanny mechanics mightn't know that asthma stuff.'

'The Royal College of Fanny Mechanics has sent me off the ground and I am shit scared the Medical Board of Australia is going to do the same thing! I just want you to look at this with me, just to confirm that I haven't completely lost my marbles.'

At last the computer was ready. Vince flashed through the Windows screens as fast as the gutless machine would let him.

'Maybe we need that big bloody terminal server after all.'

'Hey, Rooned, I told you we needed more grunts when we bought this hardware. Move over and let your grandmother suck the eggs.'

When she finally opened Allan's file, they scanned the list of his current medications—there was no Inderal to be seen, just his usual array of asthma medication and blood pressure tablets. Next, she brought up the record of his past prescriptions, and with his heart in his mouth Vince stared nervously at the monitor as Shirley rapidly scrolled down the list.

The screen suddenly came to a halt. 'Bingos!' Shirley exclaimed. 'There it is!'

Vince struggled to suppress the feeling of dread in his gut as he attempted to focus on the text. *15/09/16 Propranolol, 40mg, 2 tds, 100, repeats x 2, Hanrahan.*

'Looks like you wrote the script all right, Vincey.' Shirley spoke quietly now, deadly serious.

Vince shook his head, completely bewildered. 'But I just can't understand it. I know that beta-blockers are contra-indicated in asthma. I'm not bloody stupid.'

Shirley paused for a while, then stood and put her hand on his shoulder. 'There must be some mistake, bud. In the mean times, you better contact your medical defence mob.' She gave him a reassuring smile. 'Just in case.'

'*Again,*' Vince responded bitterly.

'Now I better get back to my sooky man and his bleeding bum. Let's talk after work. You look like you could do with some Propranolol yourself, Rooned.'

'Thanks for your help, Shirl.'

After she left, Vince sat staring at the monitor, as if he could erase the entry with the intensity of his gaze. He printed off a copy of that fateful script and exited from the screen. His heart was pounding and he was bathed in a cold sweat, and he knew there was one call he would have to make before he started consulting.

Bridget Ryan's card from MDVA was still sitting next to his telephone and she answered straight away. *Christ, it's like she'd been just sitting there waiting for me to ring again.*

'Guess who, Bridget? It's Vincent Hanrahan again.' He quickly went through the facts of the case.

'Okay, Vince,' she said, her tone cautious but anxious. 'I'll raise a file and send you some paperwork, then we'll need to have a detailed discussion. Any news on the Coronial inquiry regarding the Cotter girl?'

'Oh shit, Bridg, give me a break. One bloody thing at a time! The answer is no, I'm still waiting on that one.' Allan's death had almost displaced Polly Cotter from his mind. Almost, but not quite.

'Vince,' she commented, 'you've certainly got a *lot* going on.'

<h1 style="text-align:center">21</h1>

Vince glanced at his watch as he parked in the churchyard; *ten minutes late.* Normally he avoided funerals at all costs. And churches. Polly Cotter's body was still 'in the care of the Coroner', but because Vince had been able to put down a cause of death on Allan's certificate, this funeral was proceeding. Even though he'd worked late into the evening Vince had been behind the eight ball all morning, distracted by a sickening sense of confusion and foreboding.

A few minutes later he surreptitiously edged into the rear of the church hoping to blend in with the other latecomers standing along the back wall. However, he ran straight into James Wishart, a warden of St Andrew's Anglican Church. Jim was a seventy-one-year-old bachelor who lived with his maiden sister and had devoted his retirement almost exclusively to the church. He'd once come in to see Vince, requesting a prescription for Viagra, but due to the likely drug interaction with his angina tablets, Vince had told him it might be dangerous. However, he'd taken a script, 'just in case'.

St Andrews was a lovely nineteenth-century bluestone building featuring a square tower that was copied from a thirteenth-century church tower from an Oxfordshire village—so Vince had read on a plaque at the entrance. He was surprised a church of any kind would be the venue for Allan's funeral, as Vince figured the man was severely lapsed, if not an actual atheist. He recalled that Allan had attended Melbourne Grammar School, a Church of England outfit if ever there was one, and presumed the decision was in deference to his aged mother.

Despite Vince's protestations, Jim led him up the aisle and into the choir stalls adjacent to the organ and in full view of the congregation. His embarrassment was augmented by the fact that not only was he the only person up there, but also he was wearing a rather gaudy blue and orange floral tie the twins had brought home from Bali last year. Vince never wore a tie at work, having left the uniform of the 'City Specialist' back in Melbourne along with his Beemer and Melbourne Club membership. His only other tie was a dickey bow covered with Santas, which he'd felt would have been even less appropriate.

Rita, being comforted by her sister, was in the front row down to Vince's left, with the casket to his right. Next to her was an elderly lady, who Vince took to be Allan's mother, with a younger version of Allan. Next were a couple of rows of strangers, presumably extended family and old friends. Vince was familiar with the rest of the congregation— Deakin academics, students, and an array of people from the golf club, GreenCoast, the theatre group, surf club, and food and wine society.

The requiem service reminded Vince of a BBC period drama. The interior of the church seemed straight out of a Jane Austen novel, and the vicar, the Reverend Cobbs, a very diffident, mumbling fellow with the foppish air of a latter-day Bertie Wooster.

Fletcher Smit, who'd apparently volunteered his services, delivered the eulogy. Rita had originally rung and asked Vince, but he'd declined. 'Sorry Rit, until everything is sorted out, I'm probably not the best person for the job.' She'd had not been at work since Allan's death and he didn't know how he was going to explain the Propranolol script to her. *Bloody hell, I don't understand it myself!*

Fletcher spoke well, describing Allan's love for his wife, his sporting activities, his reputation as a *bon vivant* and *raconteur*, his work for the environment and his academic career, culminating in his involvement in Abgrow.

'Allan was a visionary,' he concluded, 'a creative thinker and a groundbreaker in forging links between academe and business.' He took off his glasses and looked toward the coffin. 'And a man I was proud to call my bru.'

Shit Fletch, laying it on a bit thick.

At the end of the service, Vince joined the pallbearers who shouldered Allan's coffin and led the procession down the aisle and out into the churchyard, to the strains of 'The Toreador Song' from Carmen, which was also the melody of the Geelong Football Club theme song. Vince smiled; Allan had once told him he wanted to be carried out to that aria—'Where footy meets Opera, Vincenzo.'

Vince stood amongst the throng alongside the two funeral directors, Holtens father and son, both looking suitably sombre in dark-green suits and grave expressions.

'Doc Hanrahan, you looked like a shag on a rock up there,' muttered young 'Stiffie' out of the corner of his mouth. 'I thought you were gunna start singing any minute.'

'More like a bloody parrot in that tie,' murmured old 'Boxer'. They both had the ability to impart such inappropriate observations, scarcely moving their lips, while still maintaining a perfect picture of solemn propriety, a feat that never ceased to amaze Vince.

'Sad occasion, Dr Hanrahan,' commented a well-dressed man standing next to Vince. He extended his hand. 'Jonathan Harkin—JIR. I met you a few weeks back at your surgery. I played golf with Al. He tended to slice off the tee, but his short game was brilliant.' He flashed his trademark smile. 'The last of the true believers, don't you think?'

Harkins, of course! Vince recognised him now; that smarmy little bugger. Not a hair out of place as usual. Harkin left his rhetorical question hovering in the air like a nine iron and moved on, a few drops of rain splashing onto his exquisitely-tailored suit.

Most of the mourners were coming up to Rita and offering condolences. Vince noticed Fletcher Smit attempt to envelope her in a big hug and speak in her ear. Rita seemed to ignore him and almost push the big South African away as she turned quickly on her heel to face some other well-wishers, including Fletcher's wife.

Fletch backed off clumsily, almost knocking over old Mrs Findlay. He then barked an order to Suzie, who abruptly dropped Rita's hand and hopped into the sporty red Porsche. Fletcher slammed her door, then lowered himself onto the white leather, mobile to his ear as they sped away.

There is an unsettling sense of veiled violence about that man, Vince reflected, *and obviously that veil occasionally falls.*

'Hey Doc, are you going to stand here all day getting soaked and staring at the sky? And do you have space for one small policewoman in that barely roadworthy conveyance?'

Vince stood on the grass beside the path that led to the front gate of the church. It was raining steadily but he barely noticed. He was at another funeral; another wet churchyard with another person walking up to him. *'Hanrahan! What are you doing here, you bastard? Haven't you done enough to ruin our bloody lives already?'*

He immediately hit his mental 'delete' button, as the psychologist had trained him, and focused on the dark uniformed shape in front of him. *Elena.*

'Yeah, come and hop in, Sarge. Plenty of space. Benny is a family wagon, even though I seem to be currently lacking a family.'

22

The rain had really settled in by the time they got out to the cemetery and found their way down to the graveside. The Warrnambool cemetery was on a hill in the eastern part of town, overlooking the stately Hopkins River—prime real estate.

The Reverend Cobbs, shielded by a large black umbrella held by the ever-attentive Mrs Cobbs, conducted the short ceremony, with the mourners dispersing soon after. Elena and Vince spoke briefly to Rita then walked back up to the car.

'Not going to the wake, Doc?'

He shook his head. 'No, Sarge, I'm not in the mood for that all that grog-fuelled revisionism.'

They gratefully sought refuge in Benny's capacious interior, staring in silence through the lashing bursts of rain across the headstones.

In the distance, the Hopkins river wound stolidly around the white buildings of Deakin University. The river was usually dressed in shimmering bright reflections, but today it was clad in black and grey.

After five minutes of steamy stillness, Elena broke the silence. 'So it was an asthma attack, eh Doc?'

Her words cut into Vince's consciousness with the abruptness of the first scalpel slash at a Caesarian section.

'The copper grapevine, Sarge. Why am I not surprised?'

'I didn't think people still died from asthma, with all the modern medications and everything.'

Vince gave a tight little laugh. 'It was a medication that actually killed Allan.' He glanced at her and raised his eyebrows. 'How's that for irony?'

'You've lost me, Doc.'

Vince took in a big breath then let it out slowly. He did the same twice more—a strategy he'd learnt from his therapist.

'Well, Sarge, Allan had just started a drug that can cause a dangerous exacerbation of asthma, and according to Sarah, asthma was the cause of death.'

'So where did he get this stuff?' asked Elena. 'Was it one of those herbal things you can buy over the counter?'

Vince sat hunched over the steering wheel. Tight chested. Muscles tense. Again he did the breathing thing and again there was a pause. 'It's called Propranolol,' he said quietly, 'and it's prescription only, and guess what? The script was written a week before it was dispensed … by me.'

A heavy silence filled the car.

'Everyone makes mistakes, Doc. Hard to keep up-to-date with every new pill that comes along,' Elena said softly.

Vince's anger suddenly boiled over. 'No, no, *no*. You don't understand!' He seized the steering wheel again. 'Inderal's been around forever. Every medical student knows it's contra-indicated for asthmatics! Jesus, Elena, I haven't done a lot of general practice but even I know it's a bloody no-brainer!' He pried his hands from the steering wheel and slumped back in his seat like a deflating balloon.

Elena paused for a few minutes before speaking again. 'But there are lots of people around with asthma. If this stuff is so dangerous, how come doctors still prescribe it?'

'Propranolol isn't dangerous in and of itself, Sarge. It's useful for stuff like thyroid disease, heart arrhythmias and migraine prevention. Even anxiety. The trick is not to give it to people with pre-existing problems like asthma.'

'And Allan had asthma?'

'*Yes*,' Vince responded. 'And also some chronic bronchitis and emphysema. But his actual asthma hadn't been that bad recently.'

Elena's brow furrowed in confusion. 'So what's the difference between asthma and emphysema, Doc?'

There was an edge to Vince's laugh again. 'You sound like my old respiratory medicine tutor, Sarge. Asthma is narrowing of the air pipes, which is reversible with a Ventolin puffer, but emphysema destroys the actual lung tissue.'

'So Allan was unlucky to have both, Doc?'

'Luck had nothing to do with it,' he retorted. 'Okay, he couldn't help inheriting asthma, but to smoke when you've got asthma already is stupid and to keep smoking when you're developing emphysema is just bloody ridiculous!'

They sat quietly for a few minutes, staring out the rain-lashed window. Vince knew his anger was driven by grief and confusion, but he was finding it hard to control.

'Perhaps he didn't understand the risk,' Elena offered. 'I mean, he would have started smoking years ago.'

'He knew all right, Sarge! And it wasn't just his lungs, he had high blood pressure as well. It was his heart I thought would bring him undone. Every time we went surfing or running it was at the back of my mind.'

'But if his health was that bad, Doc, how could he run at all?'

Vince sighed. 'He just went very slowly, Sarge, and he would always have Ventolin first and he limited his surfing to a gentle paddle on his surf ski or stand-up board. His marathon running and short board surfing days were long gone.'

Outside the wind had tapered down, and the rain had eased to a gentle drizzle. Vince nestled into his seat, loosened his tie, and lapsed into sullen silence.

'So, maybe he got the prescription from someone else,' Elena eventually said. 'He might have been doctor shopping.'

'Doctor shopping for beta-blockers, Sarge? Give me a break. Look I've checked on the computer and with the pharmacy. It was my script with my signature on the bottom and Rosie Lindley dispensed the stuff and sent it around to Allan's house.'

Vince felt the panic rising again as he turned to face her. 'But Elena, how could I have done it?' He then fell back in the seat, spent.

Elena looked at her watch. 'Doc, it's almost seven. How about we go round to your surgery and you show me how the IT system works and we might be able to figure out how it could have happened.'

Vince was shocked at the time; they'd been sitting in the cemetery car park for over an hour.

'Sure, Sarge,' he said with an air of resignation. 'Whatever you say.'

23

They pulled up outside the Timor Street clinic and found business was over for the day. They went straight into Vince's room and he pulled the patient chair around to his side of the desk so Elena could see the computer screen.

She looked around the bare walls of his office. 'Gee Doc,' she said, 'this is about as homely as the South Warrnambool netball club change rooms. This room has no personality at all.'

'Suits me fine,' said Vince, waiting for his computer to go through its paces. As he brought up Allan's file, Elena suddenly exclaimed, 'Doc, we've got to de-identify this information.'

Vince shrugged. 'Bit late now, Sarge.'

'IT fraud is the subject of my thesis, Doc. It's about restricting access to privileged information, and this is a case in point.'

She peeled off a long piece of wide surgical tape from Vince's dressings trolley and stuck it across the top of the screen obscuring any personal details. 'It could be anyone right, just a hypothetical case. Let's look at the file of Mr X.'

Vince nodded. 'First we have this front screen with a list of current medications and then—'

'Just hang on, Doc. Let's start with the basics. What's the program?'

Vince was the resident clinic Luddite but even he knew the name. 'It's "Medical Manager", Sarge, purpose-designed for medical practices.'

'So just go back to the start and show me how you got to this point.'

Vince shut down the program and returned to the desktop. Then he double clicked on the MM icon, put in a password, got back into Medical Manager, double clicked on 'Patients' then selected Allan's file. 'You need a bit more oomph here, Doc. This is like watching grass grow.'

'Apparently we need a new terminus server or some bloody thing.'

Elena chuckled. 'Okay, here it is. So now let's look at Mr X.'

Vince went straight to the 'Past Prescriptions' window, scrolled up the list and stopped at the Inderal script again. They both stared at the fateful entry on the screen.

15/09/16 Propranolol, 40mg, 2 tds, 100, 2 repeats.

'Okay, Doc, so we know when the prescription was written, that's just under a week ago. Did you see Mr X last Thursday?'

Obvious question, why hadn't he thought of that himself?

'I can't even bloody remember who I saw yesterday.' He clicked 'Past Visits'. 'Last time I saw him was Tuesday the thirteenth of August.'

He brought up his appointment list for September sixteenth. 'That was last Thursday. I didn't see any punters that day. I came in early, did some paperwork, and then went up to Ballarat for a sports medicine seminar. I remember now, it rained the whole time.'

'Well, Doc, if you didn't see him last week, you couldn't have written the script. Simple as that.' She raised her eyebrows quizzically.

'Allan was prone to chest infections,' Vince responded, his voice flat and tired. 'So we had a standing arrangement that when he got crook, such as shitty sputum, he would ring and I would write a script for antibiotics. Same with some of his other meds, too. Otherwise he would've been here every second day.'

He brought up the progress notes for Allan's last visit in August. 'His blood pressure was up that day, so I'd asked him to keep a record of his readings for a few weeks and said I would send a script to the chemist for additional treatment if necessary. Allan had a BP machine at home, so I get him, well, used to get him, to email the read outs to me.'

'So how was his blood pressure, Doc?'

Vince shook his head. 'Well that's the thing, it wasn't too bad so he didn't need any extra treatment. Coincidentally, Propranolol can be used for high blood pressure and Allan always looked up any prescribed treatments on the net, so perhaps that's what he thought it was for.'

'Maybe you misread a telephone request, Doc,' Elena said, 'and typed in Inderal instead of one of his normal tablets.'

'For God's sake, I'm not bloody illiterate, Sarge,' Vince said. 'And anyway, the computer would have warned me.'

'Come on, Doc, it's only a machine. Do you mean it talks to you or something? Get a grip.'

He silently brought up another file at random, then added "asthma" to the list of current illnesses and typed 'Inderal' in as a new medication. A red message popped up immediately—'*Warning, Propranolol can precipitate asthma attacks.*'

'Touché,' she murmured, then sat back, lost in thought. 'Doc, do you keep a record of those prescription requests?'

Vince gave a slow exasperated sigh. 'No Sarge, we just chuck 'em away. Of *course* we do, we have a book where all phone scripts are written.' He slowly walked out to reception, found the book and wearily tossed it onto the desk.

Elena flicked through the pages until she found the fifteenth of September. 'Nothing for Mr X on that date or nearby days at all, so that's not it.' She nodded. 'Okay Doc, so you didn't do it. Who else had access to your computer?'

'You need a password to get into the prescribing part of the software. No one else knows my password.'

Vince turned off the computer and got up. The thing was bloody inexplicable. Too many problems, not enough solutions.

'So there it is, Sarge. I hope you enjoyed playing detectives. Now, if you'll excuse me, I'm off to bed. I'm worried and pissed off, but most of all, I am tired. It has been a very long day.'

* * *

After dropping Elena at her place, it was almost nine by the time Vince got home. As he pulled into his carport he expected to hear Deefer barking hungrily but all was quiet. There was a plastic container at the back door with a note attached. *Just a bit of leftover tea. Kieran fed Deefer and took her for a run down the river.*

'Mrs Harrington, you're a life saver,' Vince said out loud. He noticed her front room light on and went around and knocked on the door.

She appeared in her dressing gown and slippers, obviously surprised by such a late visit.

'Sorry, Mrs H,' Vince said. 'Just wanted to say thanks for the tucker, you've been spoiling me lately.'

'No worries, Dr Vince, but you keep such long hours and you don't look after yourself too good.' She peered at him under the dim overhead light. 'And you need to run an iron over your clothes and have a shave, make them lovely girls proud of their dad.'

'Yeah thanks,' he responded shortly. 'Believe me, Mrs H, a crumpled shirt's the least of my bloody worries. Er, sorry, Mrs H.' His tone was now softer and kinder. 'Lot going on.'

'No worries.' Mrs Harrington nodded, chins wobbling. 'Fancy Professor Findlay going like that, Dr Vince,' she commented, obviously seizing the opportunity for some goss. 'Them greenies aren't good for Warrnambool anyway. Like I told young Kieran, you can't stop progress, and—'

'I better get in and have that food, Mrs H. Say thanks to Kieran for me. Goodnight.'

He trudged back through his front door and into the kitchen, bunged the food into the microwave and sculled a Coke. Then he ate the tasty shepherd's pie standing at the sink, staggered into his bedroom, pulled off his gear and collapsed into bed.

He was lost in a deep if uneasy sleep, then in what seemed like seconds he was woken by the sound of his mobile. *'We are Geelong, the greatest team of—'*

'Hanrahan,' he muttered, expecting the voice of a nurse or punter on the other end. 'Oh, Elena, it's you. No, that's okay.' He glanced at the time—two forty-five.

'Look, Doc, I'm sorry to wake you, but I think I may have figured it out. So you go into Medical Manager in the morning, right, and then do you leave it open at your password level all day?'

Vince dragged himself into a sitting position. 'Just hang on for a sec,

Elena, let me wake up a bit before the interrogation starts. Um … yeah, it's open all day. Except if I'm going to be out of the rooms for any length of time. Then I close it down.'

'So what about over lunch? Or, if you have to go up to the hospital?'

He rubbed a hand down his face, trying to rid the vestiges of sleep. 'Well, same story. Even when I'm in the dunny, Sarge. In theory.'

'In practice, Doc?'

'Well, actually I get a little slack about it.'

'So a lot of the time, when you're not in the room, anyone could just sit at your computer, access any patient's screen and type in the name of any drug and print it out.'

'Well, yeah, I guess so. Yes,' Vince admitted, now completely awake, 'but they would have to be able to operate the program.'

Elena laughed down the phone. 'Believe me, Doc, it's not rocket science. The icons are self-explanatory and the patient coding is alphabetical. That bit would be simple. But the script would then have to be signed by the doctor.'

'Sarge,' he said, 'anyone in the office could forge my signature. There are documents autographed by me all over the place.'

'Well, I can believe that,' Elena admitted. 'I've seen it before, it's just a V and an H and a squiggly line.'

As the implications of all this filtered through, Vince's mind began to race. 'Elena, I think you might be onto something,' he said. 'Any of the staff could have done it.'

'What about a patient? Maybe when you popped out of the room for a minute to get an instrument or something?'

Vince thought on that. 'Yeah, but they'd have to know exactly what they were doing, and it would be a huge risk. No, I reckon someone on the inside must've done the script and put it in the pharmacy pick-up box, and then the medication would've been delivered to Allan's house. He would've assumed it was a new blood pressure tablet and taken it as per the instructions on the bottle, then -'

'Whoa Doc,' Elena interrupted. 'I don't think we're going to get the complete answer tonight. I just wanted to clarify the access issue. Let's sleep on it, yeah?'

24

'*We are Geelong, we're always on the ball. We-e play the game as it should be played—*'

The next morning Vince woke to the familiar sound of his mobile and realised it was after eight and he'd slept in big time. After Elena's early-morning call, his mind had buzzed for the rest of the night with theories and possible explanations that might solve the puzzle and get him off the hook. One hook anyway. And if he was going down the gurgler over Polly Cotter, he might as well take whoever wrote that bloody script with him.

He picked up his singing phone and swapped one din for another. It was Lydia and she got straight down to business.

'Vincent, don't forget the girls' Parent-Teacher interviews tomorrow night.'

He sat up and rubbed his head. 'Hi Lydia, how's life in the big city? Pleasure to speak to you, too. Interviews? First I've heard of it.'

Vince had in fact already cancelled his appointments for Friday. He needed to go down to town anyway to have a D and M with the goons at the Victorian Medical Defence Association and 'may as well kill two birds with one stone,' as he'd told Shirley. 'Poor words choice, Rooned,' she'd responded.

'The girls are not behaving well at all, and I am very worried about them,' Lydia went on, ignoring his sarcasm. 'Georgia has dropped French and Tessa was suspended for wearing a No Blood for Oil badge at choir. I don't want them turning into delinquents, Vincent.'

'Giving away a poncy European lingo is hardly indicative of an impending slide into a life of crime. And a little political passion is not a hanging offence either. I do recall you manning the barricades at those anti-nuke demos in the eighties, Lids, or had you forgotten?'

'Be that as it may,' she went on tersely, having obviously left her mildly pink days far behind. 'I want you to go to those school interviews, find out what's going on, and lay it on the line to the girls. I would go, but I'm accompanying a friend to *Tristan and Isolde*. Ivan adores his Wagner.'

'And Ivan is *who* exactly?' Might as well hear it from the horse's mouth.

'He's just someone I met at the tennis club,' responded Lydia in an embarrassed voice, 'and we've been to a few shows together. That's all.'

'Only wankers like Wagner,' responded Vince. 'That's a quote from Lydia Hanrahan circa ten years ago, remember?'

'I will hang up if you're going to be offensive.'

'I do plan to return to Melbourne next year, Lids,' added Vince in a more conciliatory tone. 'You know that. Then we can go the whole bloody Ring Cycle if you want.'

There was a long pause. 'This is not the time to discuss next year, Vincent.'

He glanced at his watch. *Thursday, shit—I'm supposed to be going to the opera to myself tonight!* He and Sarah had a joint subscription to the local Performing Arts Centre theatre season and a regional company was doing *La Bohème*. Vince had been tempted to bail, but instantly decided to go—out of spite.

'All right Lydia, all right,' he said. 'You guys knock yourselves out, I'll go wave the big stick.'

* * *

Vince arrived at the clinic to find he was on the road for the morning. He had a gang of oldies whom he visited monthly and today was the day. *At least I can do that on cruise control.* He called into his consulting room to pick up his gear and found a young woman with a baby on her lap sitting expectantly outside his door.

'Thanks for squeezing us in, Dr Vince,' she said, as he barged past her into his room.

That'd be right! He picked up the phone and gave the Practice Manager a serve. 'I can't be in two bloody places at once, Lynne. So no extras, understand?'

'It's Gabrielle, Emu's sister, with baby Indigo, Vince. Apparently you said you'd see her any time.'

Vince's anger morphed into anxiety and helplessness. He fought to slow down his pounding heart and summoned them in. 'So what's the story, Gab?'

Gabrielle took a breath. 'Well, Indy's got this cold, and her nose is blocked, and she's got a nasty cough down on her little chest.'

Vince carefully examined the well-looking Indigo then looked up. 'She's just got a virus, Gab. Your own kids would've have lots of these when they were little. Just use some baby saline nose drops, keep her fluids up, Panadol if she gets a fever and call me if she gets worse. Understood?' He handed her a card and indicated his personal mobile number. *Never done that before,* he told himself. *What's that about?*

He stood, smiled and nodded towards the door, but Gabrielle made no move to get up. *Oh shit, what now?*

'Dr Vince, I just wanted to talk to you about Aaron. I'm a bit worried about him.'

Vince took his seat again.

'He's hangin' around with some of those dope heads again. I know he won't go back on the drugs, not with Indy; but he's gone a bit funny. All quiet and jumpy. He hasn't rang Mum for weeks.'

'Well, he's had a fair bit to deal with, Gabby. These guys are probably just his surfing mates. Just cos they've got a few tatts doesn't mean they're crooks.'

Gabrielle still looked worried. 'But they seem to have some sort of hold over him, and I don't want them coming around and smoking bongs and that near Indy.'

Vince looked at his watch and stood. 'I wouldn't worry about it, Gabby. Emu's only a kid himself.'

I certainly hope that's all it is, he reflected. Maybe Emu had drifted back to his old ways. And, he was in the labour ward that night, so could he have given that fatal injection? Too right, but why? Jealousy? Some sort of drug connection?

Vince hustled Gabrielle and Indy out and quickly perused his nursing-home patient list. There were some names there he didn't recognise.

'*Sharon*,' he roared at the receptionist. 'Who are these other four buggers?'

'They're Dr Smit's patients, Dr Hanrahan,' she responded nervously. 'She's unwell this morning and asked if you could see them as you're going to Riverview anyway.'

'Bloody hell,' said Vince, 'she's always bloody unwell!' He shook his head and threw the four extra Medicare vouchers back on the reception desk. 'You know what, she can go out there tomorrow and see them herself! *If* her delicate health allows.' He clenched his teeth and walked resolutely towards the back door.

'Hey Rooned, just a quick word before you go,' called Shirley as he strode past, beckoning him into her room.

'Shirley, what is it?' he asked, trying to control his anger. 'I'm bloody well late already! And you've got to do something about that Princess Petra.'

'Sorry champ, but I saw your Mrs Dove yesterday. She just came in for a script for diuretics. I did her electrolytes and she's a bit low in potassium so I figure she needs to eat more bananas.'

Hardly life and death stuff. Shirley's obviously angling for a chat. Why don't people just leave me alone?

'So bud, thought you might like to discuss this stuff about Allan?'

Vince just shrugged; he was sick to death of even thinking about it, let alone talking about it.

'Must be some big mistake,' she went on. 'You didn't know much about general practice at the start, Rooned, but fair suck of the sausage, mate, you've been taught by a bloody expert.'

For a temporarily deregistered consultant like Vince to work as a GP, he had to be under the guidance of a Royal Australian College of General Practice approved mentor and study for the College fellowship exam. Shirley was that mentor and they'd had weekly tutorials about everything from infantile eczema to gout—stuff he hadn't thought about since medical school and the year or so he'd spent as a fledgling GP before jumping ship and specialising in O and G.

Shirley sat at her desk and took a deep breath. 'Vincey, you've been like a cat on a hot tin lately. And you were in your room early the day that script was written. Maybe you just flopped out and made a blue with the prescription. Just cos of the pressures, mate.'

Oh shit, if Shirley doesn't believe me, those bastards in Melbourne certainly won't!

'Listen Dr Tiang, get this—I've thought long and hard that I might have done it—stress, ignorance, whatever. But you know what, I bloody well didn't. So put that in your pipe and smoke it!'

Shirley put her hands up in mock surrender. 'Fair enough, cobber. Just had to ask the question.'

'Someone must have accessed my computer, printed out the script and forged my signature. We all have Medical Manager open all day long. Anyone here could have done it.'

Shirley tilted her head, frowned and looked bewildered. 'Shit bud, that's a big call. You mean me and the Prez? Or Petra?'

'Or the nurses, or any of the staff. Maybe even one of the punters.'

'But it would have to be someone medical, Rooned, to know about beta-blockers and asthma.'

'Yeah,' he said, picking up his bag. 'And someone who wanted Allan dead and me in the shit. So if you do manage to figure it out, Shirl, feel free to pass the answer on. The Board already have me on their Most Wanted list. Just wait till they hear about this!'

Vince left Shirley open-mouthed and headed out to Benny. *Time for some serious thinking.* As he turned up Timor Street his mind started racing with possible names. He could think of plenty of *who* and *when* but very little *why*, and decided to do a mental roll call of the clinic staff.

Okay, he thought as he pulled onto the highway, *let's start at the top. Shirley*, he said to himself as he drove towards Riverside nursing home. She had the means, opportunity and knowledge but absolutely no motive, and she certainly had no interest in Vince being in strife. *The Prez?* Same story.

He arrived at Riverside, parked and went through sliding doors into the main foyer. It was originally a stately home built on the banks of the Hopkins River over a hundred years ago and had been turned into a nursing home in the seventies. Now it boasted two high-dependency wards, a large hostel, and independent living units dotted throughout the grounds. Vince had a couple of customers in each section and it took him nearly an hour to see them all. As he drove away, he considered some other names.

Lynne? The Practice Manager had plenty of access and was often fiddling about with the doctors' computers, but had no knowledge of pharmacology—and again, why? *The receptionists?* Limited access and ditto. *I do yell at them a bit, but surely they don't take it personally and bear grudges … do they?*

His next destination was a private nursing home on the eastern edge of the city—modern but impersonal. Vince had two inmates to visit and both were pleasantly bewildered and chronically constipated. As always.

So that just left the practice nurses—access and knowledge, but no reason. Kate barely knew Allan, and Rita, well, she had no motive either. Or did she? Vince was shocked to find himself considering the possibility. She wouldn't be the first long-suffering wife to resent her husband's serial philandering, and there was also Allan's U-turn on the drilling. Would a fervent greenie kill her husband for that? Hardly. Still, Rita had to be on the list for the script. And she was also in the labour ward the night Polly died, so maybe the deaths were connected and she did both. *Easy mate,* he told himself, *that's unthinkable!*

Now there were just the house calls to do. First up was a sixty-six-year-old widow who had been ravaged by Rheumatoid Arthritis. Despite this, she maintained a prodigious output of crocheted dolls and soft toys and her unit was crammed to the rafters with the results of her labours. As always, Vince drove away, humble with admiration for this unfailingly cheerful lady when he suddenly realised he'd forgotten Petra Smit, the feisty GP Registrar.

She was a lazy smartarse who had the means and certainly knew Allan—he was an old family friend. Petra was also in the labour ward that night. But why the hell would she want Allan dead? Or Polly?

'And that,' Vince said out loud, as he turned up past the brickworks, 'is the end of the list. Big bloody help that was!'

His last call was to a seventy-three-year-old from up country, another widow. As he was taking her blood pressure, another name inserted itself onto his consciousness—*Jonathan Harkin*. He recalled seeing the name last night on his list of patients from the day the Inderal script was written and even remembered the visit. Harkin needed a Hepatitis A booster as a follow up from his earlier travel shots. But why him?

Mrs Jervies suddenly winced and Vince realised he'd left the BP cuff pumped up flat out on her arm for over a minute. He quickly let it down, finished his examination and made his goodbyes, pushing further speculation from his mind.

By the time he got back to the clinic, Vince's first patient had been waiting fifteen minutes, so he got straight down to work and mowed through his morning session. He then grabbed a coffee, sat back and opened his mail. There were two large envelopes, one buff coloured from the Coroner's office and a white one from the Medical Board. An icy hand gripped his guts. He tore open the end of the first one and hurriedly read the contents. There was the usual bureaucratic blah blah and the detailed post-mortem findings, then ... 'death due to hypoglycaemic coma of unknown aetiology ... a Coronial Inquest to be held in due course.'

Just what I bloody need, thought Vince. *Let's see what the Board has to say*. Impatiently he ripped open the other envelope.

'The Medical Practitioner's Board of Australia has investigated the matter of the postpartum death of Ms Polly Maree Cotter at Warrnambool Base Hospital on 15/7/2016 and finds no evidence of culpability on your part. However, given your past record and the open finding by the Coroner, your Supervised Obstetric Privileges have been suspended indefinitely and your Provisional Registration will be reviewed at the end of the year.'

'Reviewed!' muttered Vince. Unless he could find out who gave Polly that insulin, 'reviewed' would turn into 'terminated', and come December, Little Lachie would have his balls!

He immediately went to Shirley's room. She was on the phone, so he dropped the two letters on her desk.

'Well Monica, the swab shows that it's chlamydia all right. Yeah, stands out like dog's balls in a snowstorm. Could be, could be, it certainly wasn't a present from Santa. Yeah, that's right Mon, cut 'em off.'

Shirley read Vince's letters while she handled this delicate phone consultation with her usual mixture of clinical acumen and sledgehammer diplomacy.

'Shit,' she exclaimed, earrings jangling. 'Those buggers play hardballs—they still leaving you in the sins bin with the babies. At least they haven't pulled the pins completely, champ. Any news about Allan's case?'

'Give me a break,' Vince snapped. 'One fucking thing at a time!' He slumped into Shirley's patient chair.

'The toxicology results show there was Propranolol present in Allan's blood, and the Coroner's office tells me there will have to be an inquest and maybe even a bloody exhumation. So, despite this temporary stay of execution,' he pointed to the letters on her desk, 'I'm still in deep shit.'

Shirley simply nodded. Not much she could say.

'I'm starting to think these two deaths were linked. And I'm sure that script was an inside job.'

'But I just don't believe anyone here would do that.' She looked worried; Vince knew the reputation of the clinic was Shirley's main priority.

'Listen, yesterday I got some interesting mails too,' she said, passing him a letter. 'That's Petra's profile from the National Prescribing Service.'

'Aren't those NPS charts supposed to go to the individual doctors.'

'Yeah buddy, but I always have a peek on the way past. I'm the boss, remember? This one's about benzos, and have a captain look at Petra's result.'

The curve clearly showed that her rate of benzodiazepine prescribing was way above the average.

'What's that about?' said Vince. 'Do all her punters have panic disorder or muscle spasm?'

'More like she's a soft touch for benzo junkies. I spoke to her about it last night and she fire up big times. She reckon it's none of my business and we are always picking on her and she's trying her best, then she burst in bloody tears and rushed out!'

True to form. Erratic and paranoid.

'You'll have to report her to my good mates the Medical Board of Australia. Why don't I tell the bastards myself when I see them tomorrow?'

25

After work, Vince drove up Merri Crescent to Rita's house—they needed to talk. As he pulled up in the gathering dusk, he saw Suzie and Fletcher getting into the red Porsche, so he made his way over and gave Suzie a peck on the check. She was looking typically glamorous—maybe just a little too blond and too tanned. *Must be pushing fifty*, thought Vince, *but you wouldn't know it*. Fletch jumped out of the car and gripped Vince's hand with his usual bone-crushing strength.

'How is she?' asked Vince, nodding towards the house.

'You know, as expected—upset,' responded Fletcher, closing the passenger door behind Suzie. 'Still not in the mood for talking,' he said, heading around to the driver's side and lowering himself in. 'Sad business, that's for sure. We all feel for her,' he added, pulling on his seatbelt. 'Abgrow's taken a big hit too, Vincey, with the loss of both Polly Cotter *and* Allan. But the Deakin people are appointing another Scientific Director. Important that we all carry on and grow the business—for Allan,' he said, pulling on his leather driving gloves.

Vince looked up at the house and thought of Rita in there—alone. 'Not going to do him much good now, mate.' His words were lost as Fletcher gunned the powerful engine and the Porsche disappeared down the road, gravel flying and Suzie waving.

Vince turned and walked up the drive and onto the deep veranda. He noticed a gleaming silver sporty Lexus sitting in front of the garage.

Haven't seen that vehicle before. The large front door swung open and Rita appeared, still looking lost and shattered. Allan was one of those larger than life blokes who leave an even bigger hole when they've gone.

'Sorry to arrive when you've just had visitors, Rita, but I thought we should have a chat.'

She smiled and nodded out to the street. 'It's fine, Vince. I really didn't feel like talking to them, so I said I was tired and excused myself.'

'Fair enough, too.' Vince gave her a pat on the shoulder. 'What happened to Allan's Subaru?' he said, looking over at the new car. 'The Lexus looks pretty swish.'

'Oh that. It only arrived last week,' said Rita, not even glancing towards the car. 'Allan bought it for me as a birthday present.'

Bought it for himself as Rita's birthday present more likely, thought Vince, as they went inside. 'I never saw Allan as a sports car man. Did he have a good day on the punt or something?'

To his dismay she started sobbing.

'Look, Rit, I'm sorry, just ignore me. I'm an insensitive bastard, talking about cars just after your husband's death. Forgive me.'

'No, it's not that. It's just …' Her voice faltered. She paused then regained her composure. 'Well, he ordered that car months ago, but it took ages to come because he wanted *that* colour. Then when it arrived last week he laughed and told me we'd have to sell it anyway. "I've killed that particular goose," he told me. The weird thing is that he seemed almost happy about it.'

Vince thought hard. What the hell was that about? 'Rita, do you know what any of that meant?'

'No idea, Vincenzo,' she answered in a flat distant voice. 'No idea.'

Maybe Allan's cash cow had dried up; perhaps JIR didn't need him anymore—although it sounded like Allan had opted out himself. He was surprised Rita hadn't joined the dots between JIR and Allan's gravy train. *Probably still in shock.*

He took a deep breath. 'Rita, Allan's asthma attack was almost certainly due to those Propranolol tablets I found here the day after he died. Beta-blockers like that are contra-indicated for asthmatics.'

Rita nodded, frowning.

'That script was generated by my computer, and although I can't imagine how I would or could have done it, the responsibility is mine.'

Rita sat forward after a pause and spoke in a low voice. 'Oh well, these things happen, especially with those on lots of different medication. And Allan didn't look after himself with his diet and smoking, so I expected something like this was always on the cards.'

'He definitely had his problems,' responded Vince, concerned that she hadn't understood the implications of what he'd said, 'but the Propranolol killed him.'

Rita looked around at him. 'Vince, I know you wouldn't have made a mistake like that. It must have been some computer error.'

Jesus! Maybe she's just in denial. 'I've reported this to the Coroner, Rita, so the death certificate I wrote after Allan's autopsy has been revoked and there'll now be a Coroner's inquiry.'

Rita started sobbing again. 'Can't they just accept that his time had come? I don't know if I can cope with an inquiry. It won't bring him back, will it?'

Vince frowned; seemed she was more dismayed at the prospect of an inquiry than at the probability that Vince killed Allan. Was she just a fatalist who really loved her husband? Or was there something she was trying to hide, something that might turn out badly for Allan? Or her? During his fruitless speculation about Polly's murder, Vince's mind had always automatically defaulted to 'impossible' every time Rita's name arose, but now that he really had his back to the wall, maybe it was time to take the gloves—and blinkers—off.

'That script was only dispensed a few days before Allan died, Rita. Do you remember him starting those tablets?'

She thought for a minute, a slight crease in her brow. 'Well, Rosie delivered some meds last Saturday morning and Allan presumed you'd sent her the script because of his hypertension. He thought you'd done it on the basis of his BP levels.'

Vince sat forward in the deep leather armchair. *Now we're getting to the guts of it.* 'That was the arrangement, but when Allan emailed his recent readings, they weren't too bad, so I wasn't planning to start him on anything new at all.'

Rita shrugged her shoulders. 'Well Allan told me on Sunday night he was going to start some new BP meds before his run Monday morning. He had great faith in you, Vince, and if he knew you wanted him to start a new medication he wouldn't have questioned it.'

Misplaced bloody faith. 'Do you mind telling me what Allan was doing last Sunday night?'

She sat back and looked out the bay window to the distant ocean. 'Well after dinner he went up in his office to check his emails and read through the Abgrow financials. The AGM was coming up and he'd received a whole pile of reports. Allan didn't usually bother with all that accounting stuff but this time he decided to read them all and then later he told me they didn't seem to make sense.'

Vince thought back to last month's Abgrow meeting. Allan hadn't even looked at the financials.

'He was hardly CPA material, was he?' Vince responded. 'I know the feeling. It's the same with our practice accounts—they might just as well be in Greek to me.'

Rita smiled and nodded. 'Allan was certainly no numbers man. I took him up a cup of coffee and he told me Abgrow seemed to be making lots more money than he expected, but expenses seemed to have got out of hand and most of it seemed to be disappearing into a black hole.'

'Welcome to the world of private enterprise, mate,' Vince said with a rare grin. 'That's exactly what Shirley tells our Practice Manager. But surely Abgrow isn't making any profits yet. They haven't even started harvesting the abalone, have they?'

'No, but they have been producing a lot of baby ones in their hatchery at Port Fairy and are selling them to other ocean-based abalone farms around the country.'

Sounds like the entrepreneurial skills of Fletcher Smit, thought Vince.

'Then I heard him on the phone until really late,' Rita continued. 'I'd gone to bed, but I think he was talking to Fletcher about the financials.' She began to get agitated and sat forward. 'Maybe the whole thing was falling over, and you know how much it meant to him. He wanted to set up a new department of Marine Ecological Sustainability with lots of partnerships with business and write books and …' She started sobbing again. 'I wish to God there had been no Abgrow at all. Allan was fine until he got the idea for that crazy project and then that wretched Fletcher Smit got involved.' Rita dabbed her eyes and looked up. 'Allan told me Fletcher was mixed up in something shady back in South Africa. He never should've gone into business with him. Allan was so naïve.'

Nothing to be gained by telling her about Fletcher's past now.

Rita put her face in her hands and Vince waited her out. When she spoke again, her voice was softer, slower. 'I don't know what time he went to bed, but I don't think he slept much because I heard him tossing and turning all night and then he got up early for his run.'

She looked out the window again, this time at the roses. 'After I took Allan that coffee, Vincenzo, I never saw him again.'

* * *

By the time Vince said his goodbyes to Rita, slipped home to feed the beast, swallowed some instant noodles and did the shower, shave and shoeshine thing, he was late for his date.

Sarah, immaculate in an evening dress, was waiting patiently in the foyer of the Performing Arts Centre when Vince rushed in. The Opera had started and the doors into the theatre had been firmly shut. She'd obviously had her hair done and made a big effort but Vince barely noticed. He mumbled an apology and Sarah schmoozed the usher into letting them sneak in the back and they sat down just ten minutes into the first act.

It took him until interval before he began to relax, but then, as always, he succumbed to the magic and allowed the performance to suspend reality for a couple of precious hours. Despite the thinness of the narrative and the variability of the singing, he greatly enjoyed the performance. During the closing stages, in which Mimi dies and Rodolfo sings the '*O mimi, tu piu non torni*' aria, Sarah passed Vince a tissue and he suddenly realised he had tears streaming down his face. Maybe the portrayal of a young woman's death had unlocked his emotions.

'Touch of hay fever,' he whispered.

'Sure, Vince,' she responded with a smile as the curtain closed.

'Are you okay?' Sarah asked as they stood in front of the theatre watching the crowd disperse. 'Not like you to come over all emotional during a bit of Puccini corn.'

Vince shrugged and blew his nose, and told her about the letters from the Coroner and the Medical Board.

'Sounds a bit ominous, but at least they acknowledged it wasn't your fault.'

'Yeah, Sarah, I might have won that small battle but I'm losing the bloody war. Unless I can work out what happened, Lachie McDonald will have me struck off by Christmas and the issue of Allan's death is still pending. Who knows where that's going to end?'

'Vince,' she said, her tone serious and clinical. 'How did an asthmatic like Allan come to be on beta-blockers?'

He looked to the heavens, palms upward. 'I wish I knew.' He told her briefly about the Propranolol prescription.

She looked puzzled and put her arm around him. 'Hang in, Ricky,' she said, as they walked to the car park. 'If you ever need to talk, you know where to find me.'

26

'You in a hurry, Doc? The Grand Prix isn't till next March.'

It was just after six am, and Vince and Elena were a few kilometres out of town on the Princes Highway heading for Melbourne. Vince had a full day of appointments. Apart from the VMDA, he had to see the Medical Board, the VMIA and Professor Lachlan McKenzie, culminating in the Parent-Teacher interviews for the girls in the evening. The only bright spot was the slap-up feed he'd promised the twins after their sentences were passed.

Elena was catching a ride with him for an introductory day at Detective Training School. Vince was to drop her in the city and then she planned to catch the bus out to the Police Academy at Mt Waverley. He'd noticed she was sans uniform and wearing a lovely orange flower-print spring dress, her hair down, and designer silver earrings catching the light. In a better mood, he might have noticed more.

'I figured you would be insurance against getting a speeding ticket,' Vince answered, slowing down.

'Don't bet on it.'

Vince put Benny on cruise control and told her about his letter from the Coroner.

The familiar crease of concentration appeared on her brow. 'So the good news and the bad news, Doc.'

'Well, not too much bloody good news. Polly's inquest won't be until next year and the Board will have given me the arse by then anyway.'

As he crested a hill, Vince was temporarily blinded by the sun, so he immediately pulled down the car visors, donned his sunglasses and put his hand up in an attempt to see past the fire ball. 'You cop the sunrise in the morning and the sunset in the evening,' he recalled Shirley complaining, after a recent daytrip to Melbourne. 'Old Sol's got you buggered both ways.'

They drove in silence for another ten minutes.

'Doc, what happened back in Melbourne for the Medical Board to send you down here?'

Vince immediately sat forward, tense. 'None of your bloody bus ...' He sighed. 'Well, let's just say, once upon a time I lost another girl in labour. Combination of hubris and bad luck. I almost got struck off.' He squinted into the sun. 'But they transported me down here to Coventry instead.' His tone and body language said: *don't go there.*

Elena seemed to get the message. She paused a while and watched the fences and paddocks rush past and long columns of dairy cows plodding towards dairies in the distance.

'How is Rita going?' she asked eventually.

'Struggling, as you'd expect,' Vince answered, concentrating carefully as the road curved and the sun came and went as if being turned on and off by a giant switch. 'I went to see her last night and ran into Fletcher Smit. He and Suzie were just leaving. You'll be pleased to hear Fletcher reckons Abgrow will still prosper without Allan.'

'Long as the bottom line's okay, that's the main thing, I guess,' said Elena.

That's a first: sarcasm from the Senior Constable. 'Anyway,' he went on, 'I told Rita about the Propranolol script and where it came from.'

Elena spun her face to Vince. 'I was thinking, you don't think all this pressure with Polly's death and everything ... that you might have just written it by mistake? You know, like a brain fade?'

Jesus, thought Vince, *not you as well!* 'I don't really give a rat's arse what anyone thinks, Sarge, but I've been maxing out on stress for almost two years, and I still know what's right and what's wrong!' He was suddenly energised by anger and frustration. 'So, the answer is *no,* I didn't write that script and if you don't believe me I'll pull over and you can get out and bloody well walk to Melbourne!'

Elena stiffened visibly and opened her mouth, then closed it again.

Vince squeezed the steering wheel hard and shook his head. *You bastard, Hanrahan. It was a fair enough question.*

'Sorry about that, Sarge,' he said, voice softer. 'Bit jumpy just now.'

'No prob, Doc.'

Vince slowed down as the speed limit dropped outside the next town.

'Any news from the Coroner about Professor Findlay's death yet?' asked Elena after a pause.

'No, but he'll probably bring down a finding of death due to acute asthma, precipitated by Propranolol, prescribed by yours truly,' responded Vince. 'Then the shit will really hit the fan.'

They had come to Terang, a town of a few thousand straddling the highway. The sign on the way in proclaimed it to be the 'Home of Gammalite—Dual Winner of the Inter Dominion.'

'What the hell is the Inter Dominion, Sarge?'

'National harness racing championship. It's a big deal. All country towns have got some claim to fame.'

Vince nodded. 'Yeah. Look at Ballarat last year, after that local nag won the Melbourne Cup.'

He slowed down and they cruised past the line of shops on both sides as the locals started to stir themselves for another day of small town life. They travelled on in silence for the next twenty minutes; the sun was starting to climb, which made for easier driving.

Eventually, as they passed a ute chugging along with a couple of relaxed dogs in the tray, Elena asked the big question. 'You must have some theories about these deaths, Doc.'

Vince shook his head. 'No idea, and I'm way past caring.'

'Not like you to go down without a fight. You seem to be just sleep-walking over the cliff.'

Vince paused to collect his thoughts. She was right, of course—he'd never been a quitter. He was from a long line of Fighting Hanrahans. 'Gotta play the game out to the end, son, even if you're gettin flogged.'

'Well, if you really want to know, I reckon both were murders and perpetrated by the same person.'

Elena whistled. 'Big statement.'

'Someone in the labour ward must have given Polly that insulin while she was delivering. So that means one of the midwives or Emu.'

'Could someone from outside have snuck in while Polly was by herself, given the injection and just disappeared again?'

'You obviously haven't spent much time in labour wards.'

Elena shrugged then nodded.

'She would only have been by herself early in the labour, and if it had been given then, she would have lost consciousness and never actually done the job,' he explained. 'The midwives usually give an injection as the baby is being born, to encourage the uterus to contract and help expel the placenta. So it's my bet it happened then.'

'Wouldn't there usually be a doctor there too?'

'Well I hit the place just after the baby was born, so it couldn't have been me, if that's what you're thinking. But Petra Smit, who was on call for the labour ward, was there for the delivery, so she could've done it as well.'

'Did Petra know Polly or Emu?'

Vince thought hard about the difficult Dr Smit. The Australian Health Regulation Agency had requested a full audit of her prescribing, but double murder was a bit different to a few extra Valium scripts.

He shook his head. 'No, Sarge, I don't think so. She's an odd girl and a bit unstable, but I can't think of any possible reason why she'd do it. Let's look at the others. Emu was at the bedside for the whole labour.'

'Motive, Doc?'

'Maybe he was angry with Polly for betraying him. And he has been a junkie.'

'Junkies are prone to kill people, are they?'

Sarcasm *again*. 'Fair call.'

'But I can tell you,' she went on, with a hint of smugness, 'that the Prof took Polly away for a dirty weekend last year and when she figured out it was courtesy of JIR, she spat the dummy and walked out.'

Vince was flabbergasted. 'I knew about the dirty weekend, but not the rest. No wonder the coppers want you in the CIU.'

She gave him a cheeky grin. 'I called Aaron last night to see if he was coming to the GreenCoast meeting next week, and he was up for a chat. He told me he'd already done his bit to stop the drilling, but that the Prof's death would rob him of the satisfaction.'

'What the hell was that about?' asked Vince, mystified.

'Apparently the Prof took Polly to Melbourne for a conference and they stayed in a posh apartment and then he plied her with champagne and, well, had his way with her—that's not actually how he put it, of course. Then when the Prof went for a swim, she found a folder that showed the place was actually owned by JIR and that they had paid for the dinner and everything.'

'Polly would've been ropable.'

Elena nodded. 'She told him that unless he reversed GreenCoast's position on the drilling, she would spill the beans on his little secret, then she stormed out and hopped on the train back home.'

'But Allan didn't back down on the drilling.'

'That's right, and after Polly died, Aaron told him that unless he reinstated the GreenCoast objection at next week's meeting, Aaron would blow the whistle himself.'

'That certainly would have been the end of Allan professionally,' Vince finally said. 'He'd put himself up there as an environmental crusader and would have had a bloody long way to fall.'

He drove on, digesting Elena's information, his mind racing through each new detail as he tried to put the jigsaw pieces together.

'So, Doc,' she said after a pause. 'Aaron Quick may have had a motive. What about the midwives?'

'They certainly all had access to syringes, needles and medications. Pat Richardson would've known Polly and Emu on and off for decades, but I just can't think of a motive. Same with Louise.'

'Rita?'

Vince's hands tightened on the steering wheel. 'According to the Partogram, Rita gave the Syntometrine injection, so—'

'—well, Doc,' Elena interrupted, 'then surely she must have given the insulin.'

'Sure, but anyone could have drawn up the insulin and taped a Syntometrine ampoule to it and either handed it to her or left it on the trolley ready to go. Rita would've just squirted the stuff in.'

Elena looked at the road ahead and nodded. 'Anyway, murder's a bit of an overreaction to infidelity, surely. Wasn't the Prof known to be a bit of a lady's man?'

'Hell has no fury like a woman scorned, Sarge.'

'Whatever, Doc, but surely Allan was the one Rita should have been gunning for, not Polly.'

'Exactly, Sherlock.'

That thought silenced them both, and it was Elena who finally broke it. 'So you figure it must have been either Rita or Aaron?'

'With accidental death due to some weird, inexplicable hypoglycaemia a distant third.'

They were nearly an hour and a half into their journey when the conversation lapsed as Vince pulled into a petrol station at Colac, a big town of over 11,000, bisected by the Princes Highway. He filled up Benny and headed off for a leak. Last year he could do the whole trip without the need. They nosed back onto the highway and were soon at cruising speed.

They travelled the next twenty kilometres without further comment before Elena again rebooted the conversation. 'Okay then, what about the Prof's death?'

'Unless, like you and every other bugger obviously thinks, I wrote that script myself, or some random punter with a pharmacopeia hacked into my computer, I have absolutely no bloody idea.'

'Do you share your room with any of the other doctors? Maybe someone else was in there for part of the day.'

Vince thumped the steering wheel. 'Shit, why didn't I think of that?' He hit a button on his mobile. 'Don't worry, Sarge, it's all blue ray speaker phone or whatever.'

'Timor Street Medical Centre, can I help you?'

'Hi Lynne. Got Elena Genovesi here too. Listen, did anyone else use my consulting room on the fifteenth of September? It was a Thursday and I was away.'

'Let me bring up the appointment list for the day.' There was a pause. 'Here it is. After you left for Ballarat, Rita used the room for a while in the morning, updating the asthma database, and Dr Smit was there briefly in the afternoon, catching up on some paperwork.'

Vince nodded vigorously. 'Thanks Lynne, see you Monday.'

'Bye Vince, bye Senior Constable.'

Vince hung up and glanced quizzically across at Elena.

'That's means your computer was probably on all day,' she said in response.

He laughed. 'Yeah, so anyone could've wondered in and written that script.'

'It would have to a person with medical knowledge though.'

'Which rules out Emu, even though he obviously hated Allan's guts,' said Vince. He reflected for a moment or two. 'But Petra could've done it.'

'And Rita Findlay obviously had the access and the knowledge.'

He couldn't accept that answer. But there were no others. 'We're just going around in bloody circles here, Sarge.'

As they drove on Vince was again assailed by a strong sense of the inevitably of his fate, then, as Benny passed a big transport full of cattle, another name weaselled its way in.

'Here's a name for you, Sarge—Jonathan Harkin. He came to the clinic for a shot just before the script was written. When I ducked out to the treatment room to get the vaccine, he could've changed the date on the computer, printed the script and sent it around to the chemist.'

When he glanced at Elena, her brows had drawn sharply together. 'But why would on earth would he do that?'

He shrugged. 'Maybe Allan was going to reverse his position and get GreenCoast to veto the drilling again.'

Elena looked sceptical. 'So Harkin murdered the Prof so the drilling could continue? Seems a bit over the top.'

'That Jupiter One strike is worth big bickies, and there's something I don't like about that little Pom.'

'Not everyone you don't like is a murderer, Doc. And I tell you what,' she added, looking at the speedo, 'you better step on it if you want to get to Melbourne today. And you've missed the Geelong bypass turn off.'

Vince had been so engrossed in the conversation he'd been crawling along at a sluggish eighty and not concentrating on the job. He sped up to just over the hundred and put on the cruise control again.

'And so,' said Elena, after a while, 'you do realise Harkin and Petra Smit are old mates, right?'

'You are full of surprises today. How the hell did you know that?'

'Come on, Doc. Don't you keep up with the goss? Suzie Smit told me all about it at Pilates. They met at the Young Liberals Club at uni. He'd just come over from England with JIR and was doing his MBA when Petra was a medical student.'

Vince fired up immediately. 'So Petra could've shown him how to use our script package or maybe done it herself. And,' he added excitedly, 'she could've given Polly the insulin on Harkin's behalf.'

Elena was still wearing her doubtful look, but Vince was up and away. 'Once Harkin realised that despite eliminating Polly's hold over Allan, he was still going to torpedo the drilling, he needed to get rid of him too.'

'But Petra Smit has got nothing to do with mining. Would she kill two people just because she was sweet on Jonathan Harkin?'

'Dunno, Sarge.' It sounded improbable when she put it like that. But …

Vince slowed as they approached Geelong—still an hour to go. He turned on the car radio and they listened to the news in silence. There were rumblings on the Korean peninsula and an update on Patrick Dangerfield's groin.

'So what's the next move?' Elena asked, obviously keen to maintain the momentum. 'Because without some evidence this is all just idle speculation.'

'Hmm.'

'And even if we can convince my guys these deaths were suspicious, you realise you'll be grilled by the Coroner and have to front up to the CIU, and it will get into the papers and—'

'If I don't find an answer, my career is rooted anyway, so bring it on.'

'But how?'

'If we could find proof Allan was being bribed by JIR, that would be something.' He shook his head. 'Otherwise … buggered if I know.'

'Could you ask Rita if we can look at his laptop? Might be something there.'

'Can't see the point, but I'll give her a ring over the weekend.'

He passed a pair of ancients crawling along in a very old Valiant and glanced at the time. Shit, after eight already and his first meeting was at nine!

'Right now,' he said, cranking up the pace, 'I need to concentrate on keeping my own bloody head above the water and playing happy families with my girls tonight.'

27

After a gruelling day of hawking himself around the CBD, Vince finally nosed Benny out of the city and onto the Eastern Freeway, then took the Bourke Road off ramp en-route to the affluent leafy suburb of Canterbury.

His meetings had been a series of suits tapping on laptops and putting him through the third degree, with lots of frowns and mutterings. Little Lachie had been his customary little Hitler-self and even Bridget Ryan had been unusually cautious, like an oncologist giving a guarded prognosis to a punter with metastatic cancer.

He turned off Prospect Hill Road through the forbidding stone and iron gates of Canterbury Ladies College, pulled into the car park and found a spot amongst the Beemers and Landcruisers, and ran up the broad flagged steps to meet the girls. He was a few minutes late ('APU Bins'). They quickly walked into the imposing Founder's Hall and ran straight into Melanie Wong, his old anaesthetist, who was standing with her daughter just inside the door. Vince had heard Melanie had recently separated from her orthopaedic surgeon husband, and by the look of her leather mini and red shoes, it seemed she was already back on the market.

'Hi gorgeous,' she said with a laugh, after inspecting his clobber. 'What's a country yokel like you doing in the wicked city?'

Vince did feel a little rustic compared to most of the Zegna-suited CLC fathers cruising the hall. He'd thrown a sports jacket into the car in the morning, but either it had shrunk or Vince had grown, because it didn't seem to meet in the middle anymore. At least his shirt was clean(ish), albeit rumpled. Compared to the twins, however, he was overdressed. They were both wearing versions of their school uniform but not as uniformly as the other students. Tessa's wrists were laced with a variety of rubber bracelets endorsing everything from 'Making Poverty History' to 'Habitats for Gorillas'. Georgie sported a new spiky orange hairstyle with matching fingernails and her school dress was as short as it could decently be.

'G'day Mel,' he responded, giving her a peck on the cheek. 'Sorry to hear about you and Johnno. Got to keep moving I'm afraid, I'm doing the absent father thing.'

She reached over and coyly popped her card into his pocket. 'We singles have to stick together, darling.'

Vince and the girls hurried off to their first appointment. They had a list of scheduled times with the various teachers and every five minutes a bell rang signifying the need to move on to the next one. The trouble was, some of those Eastern Suburb's Militant Mothers tended to cut right in, appointment or not, just like they did in their huge cars. As a result all the teachers got behind and chaos ensued. Despite their lack of education, Vince surmised, the South Warrnambool women had better manners than these High Street harridans.

The news about the girls was as bad as expected. They'd each done well in subjects they liked, which for Georgie was Lit and Theatre Studies, and for Tessa Biology and Art, but poorly at the rest.

'Why the hell are you doing accounting, Tessa, if you hate it so much?' hissed Vince after they had been severely castigated by the long-suffering teacher.

'It was Mum's idea,' she answered loudly. 'She reckons finance is the way to go, but like I just told the guy, it sucks. I want to be a DJ or maybe an actor. Didn't you hear that drama dude? He said I was gifted.'

'I want to be a marine biologist and study the seals in Byron,' added Georgia, 'and live sustainably. I'm not interested in this aspirational middle class crap.'

Great, thought Vince, *Lydia probably had them pencilled in as investment bankers or surgeons, definitely not sitting on the beach at Wategos smoking funny cigarettes and contemplating their metallic navels.*

Vince smiled at the occasional familiar face, but judging from the number of CLC parents who failed to acknowledge him as he wandered the hall, he seemed to have become invisible since his sudden departure last year. Funnily enough, back in Warrnambool, everyone said hello to him.

'Ivan the Terrible says we're just wastrels,' said Georgie, as they lined up for their last appointment. 'But we told him you would support us while we followed our dreams.'

They still want the money but not what goes with it, thought Vince. *Christ, I don't know if I'll even have a job much longer, let alone be able to afford all this!*

Finally they had an audience with the VCE coordinator, aka, 'the Gollum', a harassed odd-looking sinuous woman with large pale eyes and a serpentine body.

'The girls have attitude problems,' she coldly observed, 'are consistently late getting work in, and seem unwilling to commit themselves to the level expected at CLC.'

As Vince was earnestly promising the Gollum there would be a definite improvement next term, Tessa sabotaged his response when she caught his eye, pulled a ring off her little finger and then gazed at it longingly, as per the Lord of the Rings character.

'Omigod Bins, we did *awesome!* I totally thought the Gollum would really cut sick,' commented a relieved Georgie as they walked out to the car park.

The girls gleefully high-fived each other. 'Good job to us,' added Tessa.

'I so thought we'd get, like, kicked out.'

'Come on, girls, it was bad enough—you're really going to have to lift your game, you know,' responded Vince, suddenly mindful of his parental role. 'VCE next year, you both realise. There're a few things I need to say over dinner, so you better listen up.'

'Or you'll be off to the local high school,' added Tessa in her best Ivan the Terrible voice.

'One more strike and you're out,' added Georgie, wagging her finger sternly. They fell about laughing in the back of Benny as Vince drove out through the CLC gates.

That's exactly what Little Lachie told me last year, mused Vince, as they headed off for a feed. The girls had booked at 'The Lost Lentil', a noisy retro bar in St Kilda, featuring orange shag pile carpet, purple vinyl couches, vaguely Middle Eastern food and outrageously priced drinks.

'Isn't it awesome?' shouted Tessa. The Who thundered in the background—shades of Vince's own youth. So retro, he figured, it was part of ancient history.

'Well, it certainly is loud,' he screamed back, realising this was not the place for a stern lecture or indeed any sort of talk. There was obviously method in the twins' madness.

After over an hour of mind-numbing noise and bellowing, Vince felt like his head was about to split in half. It had been a long day and he suddenly felt very, very tired. He dropped the girls outside Ivan's stately Victorian South Yarra residence and waved to Lydia, still in her opera finery, as she opened the door, then sped off to Fitzroy where he was bunking down at his sister's place.

28

For a change Vince slept like a baby. Until seven anyway, when his three nephews discovered him on the fold-out couch in their inner-city lounge room.

'It's Uncle Bins, stacks on!'

'He's in the nuddy!'

'Na, he's got his jocks on, ya dickhead!'

The boys involved Vince in a wild pillow fight, punctuated by loud screaming and occasional howling. *Shit,* he thought, defending himself with a cushion, *how the hell can Trish and Paddy sleep through this pandemonium?* The battle finally subsided and the young protagonists turned on the TV and soon became completely absorbed by the early Saturday-morning cavalcade of noisy cartoons.

Vince eventually extricated himself, showered, dressed, and headed out into the bright morning sunshine, his ears assailed by honking horns, blaring sirens and street chatter—now all foreign sounds to a country boy. He grabbed a takeaway coffee and a pastry, then sat on a bench in the nearby park, thumbing through *The Age*, relishing the anonymity.

Returning to Trisha's place, he then woke Benny and headed back through the city, past Flinders street station, and took a left into Kings Way and a right into South Melbourne, eventually pulling up outside the Chatsworth Nursing Home, opposite the Albert Park Lake. His father, now suffering dementia, still recognised him and obediently climbed aboard for a drive to the Dandenongs. Vince liked to take old Mick, a retired farmer, out into the countryside on these rare but precious occasions.

'How are you going, Dad?' he asked as they headed off.

'Every day's a bonus son, that you don't wake up looking at that lid. What about you?'

'In a bit of strife, Dad,' Vince replied. 'Long story.'

'*Illegitimi non carborundum.* You know what that means, son?'

Vince nodded. 'Yeah Dad, I know, don't let the bastards grind you down.'

His father's deteriorating cognition saddened him profoundly—he was going to miss that sage advice.

* * *

Sunday morning he took the nephews over to the park to have a kick of the footy, resulting in another hour of shouting and mayhem as well as torn jeans and blood noses. Then he shouted the family to a long breakfast in Brunswick Street amongst the groovy bohemians. Paddy, a chippy with a ponytail and an earring, and Trish, a clinical psychologist, had lived in the area for many years and were very much creatures of the inner city.

'I'm the only one here not wearing black clothes,' said Vince, looking around. 'It's like a bloody uniform.'

Paddy laughed. 'You can take the boy out of the country but you can't take the country out of the boy. I reckon you're turning into a deadset Warrnamboolian.'

Vince sat back with his coffee, feeling as relaxed as he had for months. He always enjoyed these chilled times with Trish and Paddy and their mob, even though it emphasised what was missing in his own life, but he now felt like a stranger in Melbourne—maybe Paddy was right.

'Be nice if you came down to see Dad a bit more often, Vince,' said Trish over her smashed avocados and macchiato. 'He needs a lot of support and I can't go every day.'

Guilty as charged, thought Vince, *I've been self-absorbed in recent months.* 'Sorry, Trish,' he said. 'I've had a bit on.'

In the afternoon he drove out to Chez Ivan for a summit meeting with Lydia. He would've preferred to spend the afternoon with the twins, maybe boating on the Yarra followed by ice-cream at the Fairfield Boathouse or a trip to the MCG to watch the Cats take on the 'Pies.

'We really need to talk to those girls, Vincent,' Lydia had said on the phone that morning. 'Just as easy to meet at Ivan's, he's giving up his golf to be here.'

Vince couldn't see what Ivan had to do with it, a fact he pointed out shortly after his arrival at the palatial abode.

'You and the girls seem pretty much at home here, Lids,' remarked Vince, looking at CLC scarves on the hallstand and Lydia's walking shoes at the front door. 'You moved in or something?' he queried in jest.

'Well it seemed silly to be running two big houses,' said Lydia, looking embarrassed. 'And this is so much closer to the river for the girls' rowing.'

So that's bloody well that, thought Vince, *so much for plan A*—the anticipated reconciliation. 'What about Canterbury?'

'I'll probably lease it out, Vincent, it all depends, you know, on how things go.'

Sounds like a done deal. Who is this woman in front of me? My world is spinning out of my bloody control!

Vince and Lydia proceeded to talk the talk, as parents do, and then he read the riot act to the girls as per instructions. Unfortunately, the effect was fatally compromised when Georgie caught Vince's eye and smirked, which rapidly infected Tessa, so that by the time Vince reached his fiery ultimatum they were falling about on the couch, he himself suppressing a giggle while Lydia fumed.

He left shortly after. It was time he went home—but he no longer knew where that was.

* * *

He turned Benny to the west and started his journey in a surreal trance. As he headed along the highway, his emotions started to get the better of him. Failed husband, failed father and failed doctor. He was tired of fighting.

29

After the gruelling drive and a sleepless night, Vince rolled up the hospital tired and grumpy. On his rounds he ran into Charlie McNamee, the local Drug and Alcohol Physician. Charlie was a neat little man, apart from his large grizzly ginger beard, which dominated his face, leaving intense, but friendly green eyes as the only visible means of expression.

'G'day Charlie,' Vince said. 'Kicked any goals lately?'

Charlie had set up the local Regional Alcohol and Drug Service a few years ago in response to the escalating rate of substance abuse in the area, and it had now grown into an outpatient centre with counselling services, needle exchange, a methadone program and an inpatient detoxification unit, which was staffed by a team of dedicated nurses—'Charlies Angels'.

'Mate,' answered Charlie. 'I'm lucky if I can get my hands on the bloody ball.' Charlie was sounding flat, not his usual cheery and eternally optimistic self. 'There's lots of cheap heroin and ice around the place recently, and I've had a couple of ugly ODs. Someone must be bringing it in and using a very effective distribution network. Lots of the regulars seem to be heading back to town.'

Vince knew there was a small hard core of local users but also a drifting population who hung about if there was some stuff around and headed back up to the big smoke if they needed to do some fundraising—burgs, sex work or dealing.

'So where's it coming from?'

'Dunno, the coppers say not down the highway or off the ships in Portland, so it's a mystery. Some of the ice is being made locally but that doesn't explain it all.'

'The bikie gangs moved in yet?'

Charlie shook his head. 'Don't wish that upon us.'

'What about somewhere else along the coast?'

'The surveillance is pretty good, but anything's possible. I'm more concerned about who's doing the trafficking. Both the ODs were students, so it's my guess it's someone at Deakin. You haven't noticed anything happening out there, have you?'

Vince shrugged. 'Funnily enough, I don't actually ask the students if they're involved in the importation and distribution of illegal substances.'

'Bastard,' said Charlie, with a grin detectable only by his eyes crinkling. 'Speaking of substances, how is Aaron Quick going with the bub? I haven't seen him since he stopped coming in for his methadone. I hope he's still clean.'

'He's doing okay. His mum gives him a hand and his sister looks after the baby when he's at uni. I haven't seen too much of him lately—he's all bitter and twisted.'

'Well, hardly surprising, it's only been a month or two.'

Vince thought back to his last conversation with Emu. 'Yeah mate, but he's more angry and paranoid than sad.'

Charlie seemed a little disturbed by Vince's words, then suddenly smiled. 'Listen, Vince, change of topic. Annie's at me to get you 'round for dinner and to bring your axe. What about next Tuesday night?'

Hell, thought Vince, *I hardly know these people, why would they want me as a dinner guest?* 'Thanks, mate, I haven't touched my guitar for months, but … yeah, why not?'

They parted ways and Vince headed off to his car, feeling the need to put some heat on Emu to see what he knew about the local drug trade. And intra partum IV insulin for that matter. Maybe he *was* using again and Polly had found out?

As Vince parked Benny and walked into the clinic, he pressed his mental 'save' button and added this query to his huge pile of unanswered questions. After being away for three days, he knew there would be even more than the usual pandemonium, so he ushered his first punter into his office and quickly shut the door.

He looked across his messy desk and realised it was actually a sweet young couple, entwined together and shyly proffering a full specimen jar.

He did the test and announced the verdict, whereupon the newly-expectant parents kissed and dissolved into tears of joy. The consultation then morphed into a prolonged initial antenatal visit, with lengthy discussions about diet, scans, screening and analgesia in labour.

'Actually, Dr Hanrahan,' said the father-to-be, 'can Bec see Doc Menzies from here on? Nothing personal, but ...'

The Observer had reported the Coroner's findings regarding Polly Cotter, and Allan's death had also been covered in detail, Vince's name featuring prominently.

'Fair enough,' he said, handing over some pathology and imaging requests—*hardly worth telling them I'm benched anyway*—'Get these done and see Dr Menzies in a month.'

Next Vince got a message from the treatment room to review a wound. He headed round to find Rita removing the patient's dressing. 'Dr Vince, this is Terry, who was involved in a fight at the pub last week and sustained this nasty laceration under his eye.' It was Rita's first day back at work since Allan's death. Her face was drawn and voice subdued. 'Petra sutured it and the stitches look ready to come out.'

'Then it's her job to follow it up, Rita,' he snapped. 'Not mine.'

'I know, but I've rung her three times and Terry is sick of waiting. Maybe she's unwell or something—she was sneezing. First time I rang she was nice as pie, but just now she bit my head off.' Rita's red eyes started brimming with tears.

Vince winced. 'And now I've done the same thing. Sorry, Rit, I was way out of line.' He patted her on the shoulder. 'Not your fault.'

He inspected the wound—sutures uneven and slapdash. 'I'll get you to take 'em out, Rita. Terry, you need to be a bit quicker on your feet next time, mate.'

'Will do,' said Rita, with a faint smile. 'Oh, and I left that laptop on your bookshelf.'

'Thanks for that.' Vince had rung Rita last night and asked her to bring in Allan's MacBook Pro. He went back to his room and messaged Elena to see if she could come round after work to help him look for some answers.

My place at 8. Prawns, was the prosaic response.

His next patient was Joseph Genovesi, one of Elena's younger brothers, who'd come for a pre-employment medical for the company constructing the gas pipeline from the processing plant outside Peterborough over to Adelaide. The clinic had picked up these medicals as part of the deal with JIR.

'So given up milking cows have you, Joey?' Vince asked as he finalised the paperwork.

'You'd never make this sort of dough in the dairy, Vince,' he responded as he pulled on his boots. 'There's twelve of us locals plus a mob they chopper down from Melbourne. And they're payin' top dollar.'

'How long is the pipe going to be, mate?'

'Nearly seven hundred kilometres of fourteen inch, with a foot and a half of soil over the top. It'll cost Oceangas a shitload. And they have to compensate farmers and do land restoration after.'

'Does that pipe run all the way from the platform out at sea, Joey?'

'No, the Oceangas pipe starts at the processing plant. JIR's got a barge down here layin' the offshore gas pipe from the well underground for a kilometre inland. They also fly in about two hundred blokes to work on the barge—it's like a floating bloody factory. The whole thing's worth two hundred mill, they reckon.'

Vince whistled. 'There must be a hell of a lot of money down on that sea bed, mate.'

Joey nodded and, with that familiar, shy smile, added. 'Bloody oath, but don't tell El about me doin' it. She reckons these miners are all bastards.'

Vince laughed.

'Are you comin' down for Mum's sixtieth on Sunday?' asked Joey. 'El woulda asked you. It's gunna be a bit of a wog lunch, mate. Nonna's gunna make that biscotti you like.'

'First I've heard about it.' Elena was probably sick of inviting him to things—he'd passed on numerous other family occasions. *I wouldn't mind though*, he thought, *clean farm air, all the lovely Italian tucker, just what I need to clear my head. A few beers … couple of glasses of red … well, maybe not.*

'Thanks, Joey, I'll think about it. I'm supposed to be working.' *Funny how everyone keeps inviting me to stuff down here, you'd think they'd get the message.*

Vince called in the next punter and saw that it was 'Big Brodes', the forty-five-year-old coach of the South Warrnambool Snappers. The normally placid Brodes looked angry and was virtually pawing at the ground as if he was about to go up in the ruck against the hated cross-town rivals—the Blues.

'What's up, mate?' asked Vince. 'Your full forward done his knee again?'

'It's nothing to do with footy, Doc,' answered Brodes grimly. 'I come here to see that Smit shiela on Fridy, cos I had a flash burn in me eye and I arksed her about me prostrate test.'

Vince surreptitiously scrolled through the file—Brodes had consulted him last week over his crook back and requested a Prostate Specific Antigen blood test as an after-thought, and Vince had just handed over the referral. He found the result—shit, the PSA reading was thirty-three!

'She told me it was real high and that you shoulda rang me about it. Could be prostrate cancer, eh? Speshally since it knocked off me old man."

Bugger it, thought Vince. *How the hell did I miss that when I checked my results the next day? And how did I forget that family bloody history? And why didn't Petra give me a heads up?*

'Yeah mate, it could, although sometimes an infection will put it up. Just drop your daks, Brodes, and we'll check. It's a finger up the clacker job.'

'Shit doc,' said Brodes as Vince did the rectal examination, 'nothin against gay blokes, but I dunno what they see in that caper.'

Vince's searching finger palpated a hard, irregular enlarged prostate, and his heart sank.

'We won't know for sure until the urologist does a biopsy, but it doesn't feel too flash. Probably the big C, mate.'

By the time he talked the talk and arranged an urgent biopsy, almost an hour had elapsed. In these situations the clock stopped and the crowded waiting room suddenly became irrelevant. Amazingly, once Vince confirmed the likely diagnosis, Brodes's anger subsided and he seemed willing to do what Vince said without question. *It's probably because I'm the Snapper's doctor—football trumps everything for South Warrnambool people.*

He flattened the accelerator for the rest of the morning, then immediately strode straight to Petra's room and gave her an incandescent blast about the importance of professional communication, reinforcing his invective with numerous four letter words, finishing with: 'I don't expect you to cover my arse, Princess, but I don't expect you to drop me right in the shit either!'

She sneezed repeatedly during Vince's outburst and threw off her leather jacket, despite the unseasonable cold snap, exposing her skeletal shoulders.

'And for God's sake,' he said on his way out, 'take something for that hay fever and get some bloods done, you must be hyperthyroid or something!'

* * *

'Good *afternoon*, Rooned,' announced Shirley sarcastically as Vince hurried into the tearoom for the usual Monday lunchtime practice meeting. 'Glad you could make it, Dr Late-arse. Even Peter was on times and he only got back last night.'

The Prez was sporting a tan and looking weary. 'Welcome back, mate,' said Vince, ignoring Shirley. 'How was the holiday?'

'Great, Vince, especially for the kids, but Janine and I are both buggered. We took 'em to Seaworld, Movieworld and Waterworld.'

'Welcome back to Patient-bloody-world, Prez,' added Shirley with a laugh.

'Yes,' said Lynne, 'and Businessworld, the Happiest Kingdom of them all.'

'Just before you start, Lynne,' said Shirley, hijacking the agenda as usual, 'I've just got to fill the Prez in about Petra. Her NPS chart says she's prescribing too much benzos, champ, but she reckons it's all koshers. I've contacted AHPRA and Lynne is doing an audit and Medicare will send someone down to look into it.'

'Bit of a worry,' commented the Prez. 'Could it be just the sort of patients she sees?'

'*Maybe,* bud,' said Shirley. 'What do you think, Rooned?'

Vince just shrugged and passed no comment—it was the least of his worries.

'Okay,' said the unflappable Lynne. 'Let's get down to business—we've a lot to cover. Guess what's on top of the agenda, guys? Practice accreditation is due early next year.'

There was an audible groan from the doctors.

'But we just had those nosey buggers here!' The Prez was a notorious hater of bureaucracy.

Doesn't worry me, thought Vince. *I won't be here anyway.*

'We were last accredited two and a half years ago,' said Lynne, ignoring the whinging. 'So it's coming up again in January and I need a volunteer to lead the medical side of things.'

Vince realised she was looking at him particularly. *Why me? I get it; she obviously thinks I'm not pulling my weight. Care factor: zero.* He shook his head and looked into the middle distance.

'Okay,' said Lynne, 'I'll choose a volunteer.'

* * *

After the meeting, Vince returned to his room, still seething about Mark Brody, and realised he was more angry with himself than with Petra Smit. He was on thin enough ice as it was; he couldn't afford any more stuff ups. He just had to concentrate on the bloody job.

By the time he finished off his list and made the requisite phone calls, it was after seven. He grabbed Allan's laptop and headed for Elena's, calling in at the bottle shop for a bottle of white wine and some tonic water before a round of computer sleuthing.

30

Minutes later Vince was knocking on the door of Elena's modern North-Warrnambool townhouse. She appeared at the door, her smart sequinned red top and tailored black shorts partly concealed by an apron. *She certainly has got lovely legs*, Vince observed, following her in—he'd never really noticed before. He put the drinks on the kitchen bench, parked the laptop on the coffee table and sat back on one of the soft couches with relief.

Courtney Barnett was singing away in the background and the ambience was comfortable and relaxing. Elena's house had an open-plan living area with the kitchen flowing onto a dining space, then a sunken lounge with two leather couches and a TV. The walls were full of family photographs, and it was very neat and very Elena; homely in a way the Snapper cottage would never be.

'So,' said Elena as she opened the bottle. 'How about chilli prawns, followed by a computer science session?'

Vince tried to ignore the entrancing citrus nose of the Riesling, downed a tonic water and selected some dips and olives from the anti-pasto platter Elena had prepared.

'Sounds like a real blast, Sarge.'

Elena chopped up some fiery bullet chillies in the kitchen, tossed them in the wok along with some spring onions, garlic, ginger and coriander, and after some tossing and sizzling, added the prawns and some sauces. Within a few minutes they were sitting down to a fabulous meal.

'This is a bit of all right,' Vince commented after some serious work with the chopsticks. 'Is it Thai?'

'It's more Cambodian, really, but you're in the right ballpark.'

'Saint Charlie tells me there are lots of drugs around the place at the moment,' said Vince after another mouthful. 'Presumably you boys-in-blue are on the case. Where's it all coming from?'

'Dunno, Doc. The drug squad on St Kilda Road are sending someone down next week to check it out. They think it must be coming in by sea, but no one knows how or where.'

'Surely it can't be that hard to find out,' Vince said, 'with such an open coastline like ours. An unauthorised boat would stand out like dog's balls.'

'You'd think so.'

Twenty minutes later Vince cleared the table and Elena booted up the laptop.

'I reckon this is gunna be a colossal waste of time,' said Vince. 'Anyway I feel a little supernumerary here,' he added, putting the debris in the rubbish bin and loading the dishwasher. 'When it comes to IT, Shirley reckons I'm "useless as tits on a cow".'

'Well said, Dr Tiang,' commented Elena, laughing as she hit the first screen. 'Lucky she's not a dairy farmer,' she said, turning to him. 'What you can do is figure out the Prof's password.'

'Your guess is as good as mine.'

'At least you're around the right vintage, Doc. I'm out of my depth with the Prof's era.'

'Cheeky, but I'll let it go. Try "Rita".'

Elena shook her head.

'What about his second name, "Douglas"? No? The dog's name, "Danger"?'

More head shaking. 'Who were his heroes?'

'Gough, Luciano or Van, maybe?'

They all triggered the same negative response.

'Well, try *Moondance*, probably his favourite album.'

'That's it! See? You're not so useless after all! Let's get down to business.'

Allan's desktop came into view. Behind the columns of icons, there was the man himself, elegantly attired in plus-fours and his yellow St Andrews pullover, completing a drive.

'Trust,' Vince murmured as Elena clicked on the displayed icons one by one.

'Nothing startling here, Doc,' she commented, scrolling through a succession of PowerPoint lectures, meeting agendas and staff timetables.

'You'd think he would have a file for Abgrow, wouldn't you?' asked Vince.

'Maybe he just had it on a flash key or an external drive.'

'What about looking at his emails?' Vince suggested.

'Who's a clever boy then?' Elena opened Outlook Express.

Allan's inbox came into view. Again there were a series of routine work messages all archived into a number of predictable folders. His outbox and sent messages were no more exciting.

'Pretty scintillating stuff, Sarge. Can't you do any better than that?'

Elena motioned towards her empty wine glass. 'Tide's out, Doc.'

Vince retrieved the wine to Elena's tap-tap-tapping on the laptop, then topped up her glass.

'Okay,' she said. 'Let's see if he's emptied his rubbish recently, like a good environmentalist should.'

She opened up the trash icon. 'The usual junk we all get and some old stuff from the uni.'

'So the IT equivalent of old food wrappings and plastic bags, eh?'

'Not plastic bags, Doc. The Prof always took his Amnesty International string bag to the supermarket. Not that I saw him there much, I think Rita did most of the … Now just wait a sec, here's something more recent. He sent this the day before he died.' She highlighted an email.

Dear Jonathan.

I can't do this anymore; my conscience has resurfaced. After the GreenCoast meeting next week it will be back to the trenches and no more free lunches—excuse the mixed metaphor. No hard feelings, see you on the first tee.

Cheers, ADF

'Well there's a bit of gold,' said Elena, poker-faced as ever. 'Interesting email style with proper punctuation and correct grammar—just like a real letter.'

'Interesting!' Vince exclaimed, staring at the screen as if it had revealed the Holy Grail. 'It's bloody dynamite! This proves Allan had been on the take and that either Emu had got to him or else he'd just realised what a hypocritical bastard he was being. And he was about to reverse GreenCoast's stand on the drilling at the meeting next week. This is exactly what we've been—'

Elena put up a hand to shush him. 'Just hold your horses, Doc, there's a reply.'

WTF!!! JIR SAVED OUR ARSES WITH THAT CASH, BUT WE NEED MORE. IF YOU BLOCK THE DRILLING, NO MORE MONEY & ABGROW'S ROOTED. FS

They both stared at the screen in complete silence for a full minute, their own hard drives working overtime. 'All upper case there, Doc,' commented Elena. 'The equivalent of shouting. Bad email etiquette.'

Vince stood and began pacing the room. 'So Fletcher was worried that if the drilling stopped, the JIR funding for Abgrow would disappear.'

Elena looked unmoved. 'But why did JIR donate money to Abgrow in the first place? They aren't in the abalone business, are they?'

'Of course not, Elena, but they wanted to be seen to be helping the local community. It's Harkin's job to make them seem like nice guys.'

'I *do* know how mining companies operate.'

Vince circled the room thinking hard. 'Harkin probably asked Fletcher to do a bit of behind-the-scenes lobbying for JIR in return for the cash. It's obvious Fletch is the number one local mover and shaker.'

Elena nodded. 'And I guess the amount would have been a drop in the ocean compared to the profit from ten years pumping of natural gas.'

Vince sat again. 'Anything more there?'

Elena continued her search in the mailbox. 'Looks like a reply here from the Prof. Not so polite this time.'

Fletcher,

You know I was never happy with Jamiesons' money. Enough's enough. I will move that we discontinue that sponsoring at the AGM, as well as raise the accounting issues we discussed earlier. In short—no more money from JIR or Deakin will pull out. Surely Abgrow can fund itself. I don't mind us borrowing a few boats from them, but we need to stop dancing with the devil.

ADF

Vince leapt out of his chair again; another hand grenade! 'There it is, Sarge. Allan was having a crisis of conscience.'

'Fair enough,' said Elena, craning her head around as Vince did laps of the dining table. 'But he was on the JIR gravy train himself anyway.'

'Bit of hypocrisy there, eh, Sarge? But I never thought Allan would've supported the drilling just for the odd slap-up weekend in Melbourne and a few theatre tickets. It was all about Abgrow—that project was *so* important to him.'

She nodded. 'But why did Fletcher think the JIR money was that crucial? The Prof obviously didn't think they needed it.'

'Corporate accounting wasn't Allan's bag,' Vince responded, taking his seat again. 'Maybe Smit felt they needed the JIR cash until they established some markets and got some cash flow happening.'

He looked at the sequence of messages. 'Harkin obviously got straight onto Fletcher as soon as he heard from Allan, hoping Fletch could talk him around.'

'Sounds like the Prof's mind was made up—all that graft and corruption for nothing. JIR has already invested heavily in Jupiter One and now it looks like it's going to be curtains anyway.' Elena sat back and sipped her wine. 'Thank God.'

'But how could little GreenCoast stop a big guy like JIR? Were you gunna chain yourselves to the drill bit?'

'Funny one, Doc,' responded Elena, her jaw jutting out in defiance. 'We're part of the local Regional Stakeholders Network and they need our support for the shire to let them drill. We can veto it. And we will.'

Vince nodded. 'Trust me, Sarge, I believe you. Anything else there?'

Elena looked back at the screen. 'No more incomings or outgoings that night. I'm surprised he hadn't emptied his trash can completely. Bit slack for a professor.'

'Probably just hadn't got round to it,' answered Vince. 'He wasn't really expecting to be erased himself.' He leant over and gave her a peck on the cheek. 'Thanks, Sarge. I never thought I would say this, but … thank God for computers!'

Elena shrugged. 'Always happy to help out, Doc.' She closed the laptop and sat on the couch.

Vince noticed she looked flushed and softer somehow as she relaxed back onto the cushions, radiating a kind of 'come hither' vibe. *Surely not,* he decided, *probably just the wine.*

The moment passed and Elena quickly reverted to her business-like self. 'Amazing what you can find in people's trash.'

'Well, that was very good rubbish. I reckon we've got our man! Harkin obviously forged that script when he was in the clinic that day.'

'Whoa,' she said, holding up a hand. 'How would he know about that drug? He's a *spin* doctor not a *real* doctor.'

'That sort of info is freely available on the 'net these days,' Vince said, not in the mood for dissension. 'Easily done.'

'So you also figure Petra Smit killed Polly on Harkin's behalf. Sounds crazy to me, Doc.'

'If you have a better theory, let's hear it. I'm going to have a little chat with our Mr Harkin about some matters of mutual interest.'

Elena shook her head as she rose from the couch. 'Now just hold your horses. Surely Rita or Aaron are still more likely culprits than Jonathan Harkin. And,' she added, pointing to the laptop, 'I need to pass this information onto CID.'

'Come on, Elena, they wouldn't be interested. It's all circumstantial and we have no evidence of murder. I'm just going to shake the bugger a little and see what falls out.'

'Doc, aren't you taking this Sopranos fantasy a bit far?' said Elena with a small chuckle. 'Why don't you stick to healing the sick and let the experts catch the bad guys.'

But Vince had a full head of steam; after hours of pointless theorising, at last now he had a plan—and a chance to clear his name and save his career. And future.

31

As the week unfolded, Vince had precious little opportunity to theorise about Jonathan Harkin. Then in a flash it was Thursday, his afternoon off, and he'd promised Kieran he'd take the boy fishing—not his preferred option, but he owed the Harringtons big time. He cleared the decks and was about to make a bid for freedom when his phone rang.

'Bugger!' he said out loud, knowing these last-minute calls could lead to anything from a home visit to a long counselling session. With an impatient grunt, he picked up the phone.

'We had our GreenCoast meeting last night, Doc.' No small talk, straight to it. Typically Elena.

'So what excitement did the tree huggers get up to, Sarge?'

'Well, it was strange without Allan in the chair, and Rita wasn't there either. But there was an agenda item from the Prof regarding the JIR drilling, proposing a motion withdrawing our support for the project and calling on the Minister to immediately revoke the Jupiter One licence.'

'A posthumous addition to a meeting agenda?' Vince was missing something here. 'Allan's actually put his cue in the rack, in case you've forgotten.'

Elena gave a barely audible sigh—the equivalent of a hissy fit for anyone else—then proceeded in her usual unflappable fashion. 'Allan had emailed the item to me the day before he died but I didn't find it until yesterday morning and I tabled it last night.'

'Don't you check your emails every day?'

'It's a voluntary position, Doc,' replied Elena tersely. 'If I opened every message I receive as secretary of this and that, I'd never get anything done. I just auto-file them and wait until the next meeting is due.'

Vince frowned to himself. 'There was no sign of that message on his laptop though.'

'He sent it from Deakin that afternoon.'

It was Vince's turn to sigh. 'So what happened to the motion?'

'I was the acting chair and decided we should proceed with it. So I got a proposer and a seconder and it was passed. We've sent a letter outlining our new position to the Minister with copies to the Stakeholders Network and JIR.'

'So the cat's out of the bag,' said Vince. 'I bet Harkin will be pissed off. Allan died just one day too late.'

As soon as he hung up, his mobile rang again. With another curse, he answered impatiently. 'Hey, Vincey, how are you doing man?' It was Fletcher Smit's booming voice. 'We are having a braai tonight and we'd like you to come.'

Fletcher was not Vince's favourite person and he was definitely not in the mood for socialising, but it was a good pretext for a chat about Harkin.

'I'll be there around seven, Fletcher.'

* * *

Half an hour later Kieran and Vince loaded the tinnie on top of Benny and headed down to the river. Kieran loved fishing and seemed to have a sixth sense as to where the fish were.

'Mate, you are like a human sonar,' Vince told him.

Kieran had a marked stutter and whispered to the fish incessantly as if he could charm them into taking the bait. However, he was impatient and not happy unless the silver darlings were virtually jumping into the boat.

Not that Vince was much better.

As the boat bobbed away on the slowly moving waters, Vince could see under the bridge to the river mouth and out to the open sea. There was a big swell and heavy surf crashing onto the fine yellow sand. 'Gee, mate, I wouldn't like to be out in that sea in a little boat today.'

'N-n-no Doc, only the d-d-drilling boats could h-h-handle it.'

JIR had a couple of large motorised launches that regularly made the trip from Port Fairy out to the drilling platform off Killarney beach to fetch supplies and transport workers, and ferry various big shot management types in and out.

By six o'clock the wind was getting up and they had a reasonable bag of river perch. They gutted the fish as they went and when they got to shore, Kieran expertly scaled and filleted them. When they returned home, he presented the catch to his mother who beamed with pleasure and invited Vince to join them for 'a good feed of fish and a nice cold beer'.

'Thanks for that, Mrs H, very tempting, but you know I don't touch the demon drink and I have to go out. You two enjoy it, okay?'

'I found a heap of wet washing in your old machine in there, Dr Vince. I put it on the line and I'll press it tomorrow. Looks like you need some new clothes.'

'I appreciate it, Mrs H,' said Vince sheepishly.

Mrs Harrington elbowed Kieran in the side.

'Thanks, D-D-Doc,' he muttered. 'Can we go out again on S-S-Saturday?'

'We'll see, mate. Depends on the weather and work. I'll let you know. And Kieran, thank you for looking after Deefer for me.'

* * *

Vince had a quick shower, pulled on some clean jeans and his old Uni Blues footy jumper, then hopped into Benny and headed west along the highway. Although it was dusk, he could still see the big dunes that sheltered the network of rock pools that nestled along this wild strip of coast—home to many seabirds and different varieties of saltbush. The lights of the JIR platform sat like a watchman a few kilometres out to sea.

On the other side of the road were undulating green hills, lush volcanic plains and freshly ploughed paddocks waiting to be sown with potatoes. Black and white Friesian cattle were congregating around dairies and evening milking was just about to get underway. Vince felt that Keats et al would've had a field day describing this dreamy pastoral scene.

'This is God's own country, Vincenzo,' Allan had observed during a surfing trip in happier days. Vince had put this extravagant description down to Allan's usual hyperbole, but this evening he was inclined to believe it.

He turned off the highway a few kilometres short of his destination and wound around the back way, past the golf course and the large Nautilus Seafood shed, before eventually arriving at the Smit residence.

Fletcher's gleaming red Porsche was parked in the rear drive of the large house, which sat on a narrow strip of land between the river and the sea, and Vince pulled up alongside. He knocked on the door and Fletch greeted him with his trademark macho handshake.

'Thanks for having me over,' said Vince, extricating his hand. He then stepped to the side of the large porch and beckoned the big South African to join him. 'Fletch, how well do you know that JIR bloke Jonathan Harkin?' he asked, out of earshot of other guests. He was after anything on that man he could find.

'Not that well, my friend,' answered Fletch. 'But I'll give you the low down on him later.' He tapped his nose knowingly and steered Vince into the house.

This surprised Vince, but before he could respond they were approaching the assembled throng around the table. On the north side of the house flanking the river, there was a large timber deck leading to a jetty where Fletcher's yacht was moored. On the deck was a big table fashioned from reclaimed timbers and designer driftwood chairs.

Vince kissed Suzie, gave a cursory wave to Petra, who was watching TV and studiously avoiding his gaze, then greeted the other guests— three local couples—all lipstick, jewellery and Polos. He accepted a drink and a seat and attempted to engage in the usual pre-dinner small talk, but with limited success and even less enthusiasm. A few minutes later, Suzie called to him from the French doors, beckoning him to follow her into the kitchen. 'Please come and open that bottle of bubbly you brought, Vincey darling.'

He excused himself and went inside. Obviously Suzie wanted a chat. Vince was sure she'd opened sparkling wine before—in fact very often, and mostly French. As usual she was looking fabulous, her tiny yellow sundress contrasting with her tan, and emphasising her surprisingly firm looking bust. Maybe Shirley was right about the silicon.

'So how do you think Petra is going?' she asked casually as she handed him the bottle.

'Okay, as far as I can tell,' he answered cautiously. 'She seems to know her stuff.' *Couldn't give a stuff!* 'How is she enjoying the doctoring caper, Suzie?' he asked, wondering if Petra had told her mother about him giving her a hard time on Monday morning.

Suzie paused as she added a garnish to a huge antipasto seafood platter. 'Actually, Vince, she's thinking of giving medicine away. We always thought she would specialise, I never felt she would be *just* a country GP.'

She arranged some lemon wedges around the platter and placed some small dishes with dipping sauce in the middle. Vince was unsure whether that last remark was an oblique reference to his professional past or just her usual naiveté.

'But she tells us that, shall we say, the financial rewards are not commensurate with the long hours, further study and stress involved in specialist training.'

Stress, my arse, thought Vince, *Petra just wants to work nine to five and make a shit load of the folding stuff. Too used to the good life.*

'She's finding the work so demanding and I think it's affecting her health, don't you?' asked Suzie, obviously genuinely worried about her daughter. 'You know, losing weight and pale and tired all the time.'

'Hard for me to judge, Suzie. I only see her couple of times a week, and I don't take a lot of notice of how the registrars look, to be honest.'

'She got quite ill last year.' Suzie gave him a brief but sharp glance. 'Ended up in that clinic. That's why Fletcher wanted her to work down here this year. I would prefer her to keep up her medicine but,' she looked out to the deck, 'Fletcher makes the decisions. Anyway, she's not happy with the job, so she plans to join him in the business and help you guys out with locums from time to time.'

Lucky us, Vince thought, *can't wait to see Shirley's face when she hears this news.*

Vince carried the platter out to the table, resumed his seat, picked up his tonic water (Fletch remembered everything), chose some of the seafood, and admired the view. The sun had completely given up the ghost and the yachts on the river had faded into the darkness apart from the bobbing outlines of their masts. The conversation around the table had turned to local politics and the difficulties facing the Port Fairy Golf Club with the proposed plans to build an additional nine holes in the sand dunes.

'By the time we've satisfied the Kooris and the Department of Environment, we'll all be too old to play the bloody game anyway,' said the club president—a retired accountant from Melbourne.

'Don't tell me, Col, it's suddenly become a sacred site, has it?'

This witticism provoked a big laugh as the men downed their beers.

'That's not very PC, Duncan,' said one of the women in mock reproach.

Vince opted out of the discussion and sat back, cradling his glass and losing himself in the sounds of the water lapping against the boats in the dark and the distant crash of the surf just over the tea trees. Probably been a rough day here too, he surmised, his whole being bathed in that peaceful restfulness that the sound of the ocean always conveyed. Wouldn't like to be out in that open water in a tinny. He suddenly recalled Kieran's comments about the wild conditions and was jolted into an internal dialogue.

Those JIR boats, they can handle a huge swell. Maybe that's how all the heroin is getting in!

Now wait a minute, that's crazy, his rational mind argued, *JIR wouldn't be part of that. Could they? Would they?*

I tell you what mate, his ocean-tripping mind responded, *Harkin is just the bastard who would!*

'Vince, Vince, wakey wakey, hands off snakey.'

Fletcher's booming voice jolted Vince back to reality. 'Come out here on the stoep, Rip Van Winkle, and give us a hand with the braai.' He was wearing an apron and carrying a large tray loaded with chicken kebabs, scored calamari and marinated fish as he motioned Vince to join him out on the side deck where the state-of-the-art, turbo-charged BBQ was located.

Oh shit, not more family secrets. What is it with these people? Am I a dinner guest or a mobile family counselling service?

'Did you hear how the fourth test finished up, Vince?' asked Fletch as he fired up the black and silver beast. 'When I went to bed the Indians had only thirty-odd runs to get and a few wickets in hand, so I figured they were home and hosed.'

'Nah,' Vince said, handing him the plate. 'I haven't been following it, mate.'

'Do the Aussies good to lose from time to time anyway. My lads are in the doldrums. Hopefully we can beat the Poms over in Cape Town and then Harkin will owe me a bottle of Grange.'

He glanced up at Vince as he turned the fish over, as if to gauge his reaction to the name. 'I'd better get it off him soon though, because he'll be gone before the Test series is over.' Seeing Vince's quizzical look, he went on. 'Looks like Allan Findlay has scuppered those buggers from the grave. Apparently, he had a change of heart about JIR before he died and the drilling will have to shut down anyway. So it's goodbye to our Mr Harkin.'

Vince decided not to tell Fletcher he knew about this already and he really didn't know why. Maybe Allan's death was convenient for the big South African, too.

Fletcher picked up some tongs and turned over the kebabs, leaning towards Vince with a conspiratorial whisper. 'I hear Harkin was bloody furious when he got wind of Allan's about face. His whole career was balancing on the success of this project. Those big lads play to win, bit like the Aussie cricketers, Vincey. Would've been better for Harkin if Allan had died a bit earlier, eh?'

Fletcher winked and continued in a low voice. 'Apparently Harkin was the blue-eyed boy at JIR head office, because he performed a PR miracle to convince Allan and his Greenie mates to support Jupiter One. Now that it's all blown up in his face, he's being sent to Siberia. Well, almost,' he said with a laugh as he put the fish on the sizzling grate. 'Transferred with his tail between his legs to some new field in Canada. That'll probably suit him anyway—he used to be in the SAS and he's one of those crazy Icebergs.'

Vince knew about the Icebergs; Shirley's Gareth was one. They were a group of local men who went for a swim in the ocean at dawn each day, rain hail or shine.

Fletcher transferred the kebabs onto the warming rack, turned the fish over and tossed on the squid rings. 'You know, Vince, JIR did make a very generous donation towards Abgrow as well as lending us some boats. We're really going to struggle without that support.'

'But I thought Abgrow was humming along pretty well by itself,' said Vince, recalling Allan's enthusiasm.

Fletcher laughed and shook his head. 'The break-even point for abalone farming can be up to eight years, Vincey. Even allowing for a bit of income from selling off spat and juveniles, we need all the help we can get. Setting up the hatchery and nursery cost a shitload.' Fletcher nodded in the direction of the Abgrow complex along the coast.

'It's a blooming long process. You have to create an artificial reef with a series of plastic racks through the tanks,' he said as he turned off the BBQ, 'then you pump in sea water and micro algae flows in and attaches to the plates—that's the abalone's first tucker. After about four months when they're ten millimetres in size we'll put them in five-tonne cages out at sea for the grow out phase.'

Allan's naïve optimism must have been misguided—so much for his anticipated short-cut to riches. Still, it was hard to reconcile what Fletcher was saying with Rita's claim that Allan had told her Abgrow was already making big dollars.

'But I thought the production cycle was going to be much shorter with Polly Cotter's hybrid abalone,' said Vince. 'Allan told me that it would accelerate the whole thing.'

Fletcher nodded vigorously as he poured himself a red. A nice old Penfolds Bin 389, Vince noticed—one of his favourites.

'The grow-out is still going to take at least three years, Vincey. We have lads out there feeding them with seaweed and monitoring their health. The mesh size of the cages keeps predators out but you've still got to watch for mud worms and parasites. And now there's global warming and this bloody herpes virus to worry about!'

'Allan seemed to think abalone farming was going to be a guaranteed cash cow, Fletcher.'

Cox shook his blond mane and laughed. 'Al had stars in his eyes. When you add in the bio security costs and the collapsing price due to the Chinese competition, we'll be lucky to make a blimmin' dollar!' He nodded at the house. 'These baby abalone are more of a worry than bloody kids!'

They both looked through the window at Petra who was dozing on a large beanbag in the adjacent sitting room. Fletcher shouted something in Afrikaans, banged on the glass forcefully and then bellowed: 'Hey Petra, get yourself out here and lend a hand.'

She abruptly stood and seconds later appeared on the deck, her twitchy wide-awake demeanour suddenly restored, and with a welcoming smile she shook hands warmly with Vince.

'How are you, boss? Dad not making you do all the work, I hope?'

Any ill will regarding the Mark Brodie episode seemed to have magically evaporated. *Maybe she is bipolar,* Vince reflected.

'Sorry, Dad, must have nodded off.' She nodded towards Vince with a cheeky grin. 'These guys work me *so* hard.'

Shit, thought Vince, *I've never seen her turn on the charm like that before. The Princess certainly jumps when her old man puts the word out. That Afrikaans language always sounds so threatening, I almost bloody jumped myself.*

Fletcher unceremoniously shoved a loaded platter towards Petra. 'Make yourself useful and take those prawns into your mother.'

It was more like an order than a request and Petra visibly flinched and quickly acquiesced. Vince began to gain some insight into why Petra was like she was; she almost seemed frightened of her old man.

Fletcher watched her walk off, drained his glass and returned to his cooking. 'Anyway,' he went on, expertly transferring all the remaining food onto a large plate. 'No more Jonathan Harkin.' He raised his glass in a toast, 'and I probably won't get that Grange now, eh?'

He pulled down the BBQ lid. 'We better get this stuff onto the table, Vincey, or Suzie will be sending out a search party.'

32

After a typical foot-to-the-boards Friday, Vince grabbed Chinese takeaway on the way home and flopped in front of the TV.

Elena had called in the morning and excused herself from their usual dinner date. 'Sorry Doc, but I have to head down to the farm and do some cooking for Mum's birthday on Sunday.'

'Oh yeah, Sarge,' he responded. 'I've been officially invited to that celebration.'

'Joey, I assume,' she said with a laugh. 'I told him it would be a waste of time asking you.'

Am I that much of a bloody grouch, thought Vince? *Maybe I should go. Probably better than my current plan, which was to spend the day watching season four of 'The Wire'. And worrying.*

'Well, as it turns out, I was to be working Sunday, but Pete Menzies wants me to swap it for tomorrow, so—let me just check my social calendar—yes … I'm free.'

'You would be most welcome, as Joey's guest of course. If Mum thinks I invited you, she'll try to have us married on the spot, even though I've told her you already have a wife.'

'So I do,' said Vince. 'Apparently.'

'And don't pat yourself on the back, Doc. Any bloke with a pulse would do.'

Saturday passed in a procession of sore throats, lacerated fingers and chest pains, and Vince had no time to reflect on his discussions with Fletcher. Mercifully, the calls slowed down in the evening—lucky, because he was about to flush the phone down the loo—but instead of enjoying some much needed chill-out time, his mind promptly filled with new questions. *Fletcher had gone out of his way to downplay the short-term viability of Abgrow and also to denigrate Jonathan Harkin— why? Am I just jumping at shadows? My money's still on Harkin.*

On Sunday morning he happily handed over to the Prez and reconsidered his plans for the day. An afternoon of making small talk with a bunch of near strangers was rapidly losing its appeal. What about a run on the beach with the eager Deefer, followed by an afternoon on the couch with the cops and crooks of Baltimore?

He shook his head and said to no one in particular, 'You're always letting people down, you pathetic bastard!'

He washed his face, dragged himself out to the car and set off via the pub, where he picked up a bottle of Pizzini's Sangiovese (another favourite) and a bunch of flowers, then pointed Benny east, turned off the highway at Allansford, continued on past Cheese World and took the scenic route down the Great Ocean Road. There was very little traffic, the sun was shining and Vince felt liberated—free of the telephone, cruising through the countryside. Around him, contented looking cattle chewed on the spring pasture and the occasional passing farmer gave him the standard countryman wave of acknowledgment. Vince felt his heart rate drop and muscles soften, but his mind was still racing as the fence posts flashed past.

When he pulled up, the party was obviously in full swing. There were cars parked all over the track leading up to the house, and after finding a spot for Benny he walked around the back where there were three large outdoor tables arranged under the trees and enough food to feed an army. Joey and Tony rushed over to him and he was introduced to a large crowd of blokes as '*il nostro medico*'.

They all greeted him enthusiastically—'Hi, Doc', '*Buongiorno, Vince*' and 'G'day mate'—and tried to ply him with drinks. 'But it's a special occasion, Doc. When in Rome, eh?'—and he was surprised to find he knew most of them already.

He looked around for Elena and her mother, and waved through the window as he saw them hard at work in the kitchen. Typical country show, he thought, the men drink and make noise and the women do all the work.

'Hey, mate,' said Joey, his arm around Vince's neck. 'The Blues are gunna thrash your pussycats in the Grand Final next week. You guys are finished!'

'I don't know about that, Joey. You Carlton fans are all swagger and bullshit. Who's going to kick your goals?'

Maria rushed out and swept him up in a tearful embrace. 'Vincenzo, welcome!' She then cast off her apron and gestured to the main table. 'You come-a sit next to me!'

Elena—looking gorgeous in a sky-blue summery dress, her thick black hair cascading over shoulders, reminding Vince of a girl from a Vespa ad—laughed and went back inside to continue the cooking. She was obviously in charge of the mammoth catering operation and was coordinating the large band of nieces, aunts and neighbours.

Vince ate as much as he could possibly manage, even though Maria kept piling more and more on his plate—'Eat up, you so thin'—until he excused himself on the pretext of saying hello to Elena's grandmother, she of the macadamia and white chocolate biscotti fame.

Just as he was about to greet the old lady, the speeches started, followed by music. Maria and Luigi, resplendent in his black suit, got up and danced around the tables, accompanied by a cacophony of whistling, shouting and general yahooing.

Vince walked over and stood next to Elena, who was busily taking photos. 'Sarge,' he shouted above the din, 'time I made tracks. Thanks very much for the day, I really enjoyed it. You have a wonderful family and they are all *so* proud of you. Ciao, Elena.'

He made his farewells and beat a hasty retreat. 'Hey, Vincenzo,' Joey called out. 'Come to the Boggy Creek pub next Saturday and watch the grannie with all the boys! Big day, mate!'

As he drove back along the track, Vince felt his eyes welling with tears. This is how real families function, he told himself, they laugh and dance and love each other. What the hell has happened to mine?

33

Vince got up early the next morning, pulled on his board shorts and windcheater, and staggered outside. It was clear the only person who could get him out of this mess was himself, and he needed to apply the blowtorch.

As he opened the back door he was greeted by a gust of icy wind that almost pushed him back to the warmth of his bed. Even though it was spring, Warrnambool was experiencing a cold snap, and he kept his head down as he lifted up the red and white roller door at the front of his modest garage. Deefer appeared next to him, shaking herself, confused by his appearance so early in the morning. Vince threw his board and wetsuit into the back of the car and Deef jumped up into her usual position.

'Have to brush the cobwebs off the old board, Deef. Haven't been out for a while.'

Minutes later they pulled into the Flume car park and climbed the mound to inspect the surf. They stood there shivering in the cold darkness, surveying the heavy black water topped here and there with luminous white caps, the only sound being the occasional wave breaking—a wild crack followed by a fading, gurgling hiss.

Vince looked at the luminous dial of his watch: just after six. In theory, winter was supposed to be over and the days should be lengthening, but the heavy black blanket of night still seemed to be covering the world.

Suddenly, dawn broke. As if illuminated by a huge floodlight, the row of Norfolk pines on the eastern skyline appeared, followed by the shoreline, the beach and then the vast ocean and a burst of radial orange beams shot up in the east as the sun miraculously appeared behind the breakwater. *How good is that?* Vince smiled to himself. *This place is magic.* After standing in stunned wonderment for a few minutes, he inspected the surfing conditions.

'On shore wind, mate. All chopped up, no swell. In short—crap,' he announced to Deefer. She sat at his feet placidly, her disinterested look saying, *Tell someone who cares.*

'What about a walk on the beach instead, eh?'

It was a rhetorical question. They ambled down onto the soft yellow sand, skirting the shallows and headed back towards the surf club and the beach beyond. It was only three kilometres but it was like walking on fresh snow and their progress was slow. Deefer kept discovering irresistible smells to explore amongst the flotsam and jetsam and spent some fruitless time chasing seagulls.

It took them over a half hour to reach the main beach and for the most part they had it to themselves. There was just the odd dedicated grommet trying to find a wave, and then as they came in sight of the surf club, they could see a crew dragging a surfboat down to the water. Vince could see that it was *The Fletcher Smit.* Fletcher had been one of the club stalwarts during his time in the district, and the word on the street was that he'd made a large donation to the club for those naming rights.

A few hundred metres further along the beach, there was a small group of men, all in Speedos a la the former Prime Minister and with goggles on heads, walking in to shore through the shallows. Vince recognised them as the Icebergs—slightly insane characters who swam in the ocean all year round—and he was hoping to catch up with one Iceberg in particular. He noticed the buffed and permanently tanned trim figure of Jonathan Harkin at the back of the group as they dried off. This anticipated rendezvous had been Vince's intention all along.

'Hell, you blokes look cold,' Vince called out. 'Are you sure this is sensible for a bunch of old fellas like you?'

'Doc, it's therapeutic, keeps us out of your clutches anyway,' answered a local teacher with a smile as he draped a towel across his shoulders. Vince had to concede that point; not too many of these crazies ever seemed to get crook.

'Gidday, Vince,' said Tony Kanakis, the vet who looked after Deefer. 'You need to get down here yourself, mate.'

They all acknowledged him with a smile or a wave and Vince suddenly realised he knew the names of every one of them. *Hell*, he thought, *despite my best efforts to avoid people, I've actually made a lot of friends down here. Who'd have thought? And even though my reputation's been trashed in* The Observer, *they all still seem happy to have me as their family GP.*

He fell into step with Harkin as the Icebergs walked up the wooden steps to the path in front of the main beach car park.

'Have you time for a quick word, Jonathan?' Vince said. 'I just wanted to have a chat with you about a couple of things.'

'Sure, Vincent,' he said. 'I can give you a few minutes before I have a coffee with the guys, just jump into my car while I warm up.' He unlocked his sleek silver Beemer and pulled on a tracksuit while Vince tied Deefer to a fence.

'Okay, Vincent, fire away,' he said with a smile as Vince opened the passenger side door and sat on the comfortable leather seat. 'My cholesterol reading must be really bad to warrant this personalised attention.'

You've got to hand it to him, thought Vince, *the man certainly had charm.* 'Don't worry, it's nothing medical. It's about Allan Findlay.'

Harkin took this in his stride and responded in his customary fruity pukka accent. 'Well that certainly was a very sad business. From all reports Al was a wonderful fellow. How can I help you?'

'Well,' Vince said carefully. 'I'm puzzled by his death and trying to talk to people whom he may have confided in. I want to learn about his state of mind just before he died.'

Harkin answered promptly, with his usual bonhomie and dazzling dental display. 'We didn't have that sort of relationship, Doctor. It's not the done thing for the chaps to unburden themselves at golf. Surely people do die of asthma attacks. What's the mystery exactly?'

Vince looked for a few minutes out to sea and realised he would have to either be more explicit or just let it go. As his dad would say: *Time to have a piss or get off the bloody pot.*

He took a deep breath and dived in. 'There is a significant chance that Allan was actually murdered and I'm looking for people who may have had something against him or wanted him out of the way.' Vince looked straight at Harkin for the first time; the Englishman looked more puzzled than angry.

Can't stop now, Vince said to himself, and ploughed ahead. 'It seems to me that Allan's death came at a pretty good time for you, Jonathan. He was going to convince GreenCoast to withdraw its support for JIR and that would have meant the end to your drilling platform and just about the end for you.' He paused briefly. 'Then he died.'

Harkin's features darkened like gathering storm clouds and his voice took on an incredulous but steely edged tone. 'So, Vincent, what you are suggesting is that I heard that Allan Findlay was going to lobby his green friends to stop Jupiter One and then I killed him to save my project. Have I got it right? Or was there something I missed?'

Vince nodded and decided not to suggest Harkin might be implicated in Polly's death as well. He had the sickening premonition he was going to be shat upon from a great height. The Englishman turned around and faced him.

'Let me just tell you something, Doctor. My first instinct is to just throw you out of my fucking car. But I will allow for the fact that you are stressed and so maybe a little irrational. Anyway, what the heck? I can afford to be polite—I will be out of this shithole soon anyway.'

Harkin made a dismissive gesture toward the beach and surrounding town, gripped his steering wheel and looked out across the flat sea at the JIR drill rig visible in the distance. 'I need hardly remind you that I am a businessman, not a gangster, and we don't actually need the support of that Mickey Mouse GreenCoast outfit now anyway.'

He glanced at Vince. 'Not that it's any of your business, Dr Hanrahan, but last week I met with some important people in Melbourne, and Mr Woodright, the new Minister for the Environment told me, off the record, that our project could proceed with the full support of the government, despite any local environmental objections or pathetic local stakeholder groups. The former Minister was … well … less sympathetic, and the Premier felt it necessary to reshuffle his cabinet. James Woodright has been *very* helpful.' Harkin paused and smiled. 'Coincidentally, the Premier was at school with our CEO, oh yes, old chums. Now that we have put our infrastructure in place, a press announcement is imminent. So, Doctor, it's full steam ahead for Jupiter One, regardless of your greeny friends.'

In return for a nice contribution to the government campaign fund for the forthcoming election, Vince thought, with the feeling that he was getting out of his depth.

Harkin again turned around in his seat and leant toward Vince. From about six inches away Vince noticed that even at dawn he was cleanly shaven. However, the ubiquitous smile was absent and his eyes looked black as tar.

'I'd suggest you concentrate your efforts in your own backyard, Doctor, instead of throwing libellous allegations around. From what I hear, you've got a medical malpractice charge to defend in relation to that Cotter girl, so you've got *two* deaths on your hands. I'm now JIR Vice President for North America, and off to Canada to facilitate our new field. Bigger and better than this little fucking patch. Now, get out!'

Vince did exactly as the man suggested. Didn't have much choice really—Harkin was holding all the cards. Should've listened to Elena instead of jumping in feet first.

He gathered up Deefer and they walked off down the track, Vince confused and searching his mind for an answer, Deef happy and searching for a good place for a dump.

Vince's mind was spinning. Of course Harkin could be lying, but a call to the Environment Department should reveal whether local objections had been trumped by the politicians. And if Harkin didn't need GreenCoast's support, why would he have killed Allan? Or Polly? He was a slimy ambitious bastard and Vince knew he'd bribed Allan, but that didn't make him a murderer. And that also ruled out Petra Smit as his hired gun.

'But *someone* must have bloody well done it,' he said aloud. 'Someone who really, *really* needed that drilling to continue.' Back to bloody square one again!

As he got to the car, Vince could hear his mobile singing. By the time he opened the door, the sound had stopped. He grabbed the phone, hit the missed call button and Elena answered immediately.

'Vince, thank God you're there. I'm around at Aaron Quick's place. The baby is missing! Can you come over?'

34

Vince quickly dropped Deefer at home, pulled on his tracksuit, then headed to Emu's place in the town's east opposite the racetrack. There were a couple of vehicles out front, including Elena's work car, so Vince parked in front of the neighbour's house, walked quickly up the drive and knocked loudly. Elena opened the door and motioned him back out again.

'What's the story, Sarge?'

'I was in the shower when I got a frantic call from Aaron's mum.'

'Why does she have your number?'

She smiled ruefully. 'I gave it to Aaron after Polly died, but now the whole family regard me as their personal copper. Anyway, I got dressed and came straight around—Aaron is saying nothing, but maybe he'll speak to you.'

Vince knocked on the front door again and Mrs Quick let them in. 'Thank Heavens you're here, Doctor,' she said. 'Aaron is in a real bad way; he's in shock. Who coulda done such a terrible thing?'

Emu was slumped on a couch, a cigarette dangling from his pale fingers, seemingly half asleep, his rhythmic loud breathing punctuated by frequent sobs. Gabrielle was sitting with him. Elena continued her investigation in the bedroom.

'So what happened, Emu?' Vince said, putting his bag down amongst the nappies and toys on the grubby carpet.

The youth slowly turned his head towards Vince. 'Indy's gone.

Those bastards have … She's gone, can't you bloody see?' His voice was strained and flat.

He lay back on the couch and lapsed back into a pathetic torpor.

'Who's taken her, mate? Who do you mean?'

Emu looked at Vince through his tears for at least a minute and then closed his eyes. Silence.

Vince tried again. 'Can you tell me exactly what happened, Emu? Was there anyone here last night, mate?'

No response. After a further few minutes staring blankly at the wall behind Vince, Emu stirred himself, and sat forward. 'There was no one bloody here, Doc. I've tole the coppers already. I put Indy down at about ten and I woke up about six-thirty to have a piss and looked into her room, and she wasn't fucken there.'

He shook his head and slumped back onto the couch.

'Well,' said Elena, coming back into the living room. 'I need to go back to the station, speak to the boss and get the wheels in motion to find Indy. I promise you, Aaron, we will leave no stone unturned. If you hear anything, you know where to find me.'

Vince walked out with Elena and they stopped to talk at the front gate. 'What do you reckon the deal is here, Sarge?'

She frowned as she stood there in her working gear, black hair neatly tied back under her police cap, and Vince had a sudden naughty thought about women in uniform. *Where the hell did that come from?* He pushed it away and they both looked across the road at some horses doing track work.

'Don't know, Doc. Nothing else was taken, just the blanket from her cot, but no bottles, nappies or other clothes.'

'Any sign of forced entry?'

'No, but Aaron said he never locks the back door anyway and the neighbours didn't hear anything.' She lowered her voice. 'You don't think he might have done away with her himself, do you, Doc? He's pretty messed up and he might've found it all a bit much.'

Vince shook his head. 'Sarge, anything's possible, but I don't think that he would or *could* do that. He really loves Indy; I think he sees her as a continuation of Polly. And he just looks so devastated in there … unless he's a really great actor, I think his story rings true.'

On the other hand, Emu could have honed those acting skills with a similar performance in the labour ward last month.

'You don't think he could be using again, Doc? That would change things.'

Surely not; he's got too much to lose. 'No, I'm pretty sure he's clean. I certainly bloody hope so.'

'But who would sneak in Emu's back door in the early hours and steal a sleeping baby?'

'Dunno, Sarge, that's why we have the police.'

Elena winced as she pulled out her car keys. 'Ouch. Thanks, Doc. Better get moving on this.'

'Let me know when you find Indy and I'll have a look at her.'

* * *

Vince darted home, had a shower and a quick breakfast, did a brief dash around the wards and headed for the salt mines. His mobile registered a message as he walked into the surgery. *'Ivan the Tool wants us 2 see a shrink cos of our non-violent protest—Ghandi and Mandala xx'*

Bugger, thought Vince, *just what I need!* He had a vision of the two of them staging a sit-in at the front of Ivan's house and chaining themselves to the Jag. He quickly messaged them back telling them to behave themselves and made a mental note to ring Lydia to find out what the hell was going on.

The waiting room was full and there was the usual sense of barely controlled chaos in the air. His first patient was Big Brodes. This time Vince *had* done his homework and discussed things with the urologist. The multi-core prostate biopsy showed there was cancer in most of the cores and the histology showed an aggressive tumour.

'It's a nasty one, mate, but the scans show no sign of spread outside the prostate and the lymph glands look okay too. So Mr Widgeratne reckons you've a big chance for a cure.'

He then walked Brodes through the treatment options—always a complex discussion with prostate cancer—and after a long talk the big man decided to go down to Melbourne for the robotic radical prostatectomy.

'At least with a robot doc, you know it hasn't been out on the piss the night before! Anyway, Vince, thanks for takin' the time to explain it all.'

Thirty-five minutes! *What was that all about,* thought Vince, *compassion or guilt? Anyway, maybe I've dodged a bullet, too.*

He struggled through the rest of the session, with the spectre of the missing Indigo hovering. *I should've realised Emu wasn't up to the fatherhood task, probably self-bloody-evident.* At lunchtime he rang Emu's place and his mother answered.

'Any news about Indigo, Mrs Quick?'

'No we haven't heard nothing yet.'

'How's Emu?'

'He's still asleep, Doctor. He must be real tired.'

Vince grabbed a coffee and went to the archived patient records room to hunt up an old file he needed for an insurance report. As he was putting the folder back he noticed Rita Findlay's old hard copy file next to it and something made him pull it out. A quick perusal revealed her failure to conceive all those years ago hadn't been due to her endometriosis at all; she'd been ovulating and her Fallopian tubes were patent. Puzzled, Vince quickly scanned through the infertility specialist's letters and discovered a bombshell—Allan had a complete absence of sperm!

He went straight to the treatment room where Rita was stocking the vaccine fridge. 'Rit, sorry to be snooping and all that,' he said, file in hand, 'but did Allan know he was infertile?'

She shrugged, arms outstretched and open palms pointing to the heavens. 'He was such a vain man and I knew he wouldn't cope with the humiliation of donor insemination, so I told him the problem was with me.' She paused, eyes filling. 'You see, Vincenzo, despite it all, I really loved him.'

Vince walked back to his room, shaking his head. So much for the 'jealous infertile wife' theory! Thank God. But if not Rita, and not Harkin, then bloody well who?

He found a message on his desk from Shirley. *Get your sorry arse into the conference room, Rooned, powwow bout big issue. Sandwyches.*

Wouldn't mind some small issues for a change, he thought. He found the others already there, mowing steadily through the lunch. 'Grab a plate, Vince,' said Lynne, 'before Dr Menzies eats it all.'

'Okay people,' said Shirley. 'Lynne done an audit on Dr Smit's benzo prescribing and it's nearly all *Xanax,* and it's mostly for old codgers who don't even take the stuff or punters she's invented and put into Medical Manager.'

'She must be getting all those scripts dispensed and taking the stuff herself.'

'*Der,* Rooned!'

'Maybe she's got panic disorder or is bipolar and uses it to calm herself,' he added.

'Get real, champ! She's obviously hooked on the gear.'

'Either way,' said Pete patiently, 'I've discussed it with the Board and we need to talk to her.'

Shirley picked up the phone. 'Sharon, could you ask Dr Smit to step in here please?' She then mimicked a handpass to the Prez, who pretended to drop the ball.

After several minutes, Petra Smit sauntered in and languidly sat down. The Prez shut the door.

'Petra, we've done an audit of your prescribing and you've been doing multiple scripts for Xanax illegally. AHPRA have suspended your registration and you'll be hearing from the police. The Medical Board has an advisory service for doctors with health or drug problems and naturally we would be happy to help—'

She jumped up, eyes blazing and face pinched and pale. 'I'm not going to listen to this bullshit any longer! You people have no idea what I've been through and you've been out to get me from day one!' She kicked the door open and walked straight past the startled receptionist and waiting patients, through the front entrance and disappeared.

* * *

The afternoon held a procession of sick punters, phone calls, anxious punters, more phone calls and just plain whinging punters. *Bloody hell,* Vince thought, *I'm so over this stuff!* As he eventually shut the door behind the last one, his desk phone rang again. 'What is it?' he shouted.

'Settle, Doc, it's only me,' answered Elena in her usual placid fashion. 'You're wound up like a spring.'

'This is nothing, Sarge, you should've seen me in my prime. I used to be really wired.'

'Spare me. Anyway, Indigo's turned up. Can you come and check her out?'

Vince suddenly saw red. *Give me a break!* 'Elena, I am not on call for the bloody Victoria Police twenty-four-seven. I actually have a day job.' Once he'd established that the baby seemed okay, he arranged to meet them at the hospital in twenty minutes.

He eventually arrived to find Emu clutching Indy and pacing up and down in the corridor outside the Emergency Department. Elena was sitting quietly on one of the waiting-area benches and she gave Vince a quick rundown on the story while Emu kept walking.

Apparently old Boxer Holten, the octogenarian funeral director, had received a ring on his doorbell just before six. Since his wife died, Boxer had lived in a flat on the premises and although the office always closed at five, there was another entrance off a small porch with a night bell for after-hours emergency calls.

Boxer opened the door to find no one there. Damn kids, he thought, about to shut the door, when he noticed a small bundle on the concrete floor of the porch, in the corner away from the light. He looked more closely and was shocked to find that it was a baby, fast asleep, dummy in situ, and wrapped in an old-fashioned woollen checked blanket. He picked the baby up and rang his daughter, who came round and took care of her while he contacted the police, then returned to his omelette. After fifty years in the business, nothing surprised Boxer.

Emu, Indigo, Elena and Vince went through the security door into the ED and Vince did a careful examination of Indy in the Paediatric Assessment Room. 'She seems fine, mate,' he told Emu. 'She's obviously been fed and changed and seems none the worse after her ordeal.'

Emu said nothing. He picked up Indigo and headed for the door.

'Just hang on, Aaron. Now that we know she's all right, there's something I want to talk to you about,' said Elena. She sat down and handed Vince a buff coloured document in a plastic sheath. 'Mr Holten said this was pinned to Indy's jacket.'

Vince pulled out the form and recognised it straight away. 'It's a death certificate,' he said reluctantly, 'just the undertaker's copy. It's filled in too—in very primitive block letters, except the date is for the thirtieth of September, which isn't till next week, and in the cause of death section there's just a series of question marks. And it's ... well it's all Indy's details on here, Emu ... you really don't need to see this, mate.'

Emu gave Indy to Elena, snatched the document from Vince's hands and quickly read it. The colour drained from his face and was replaced by a crazy-eyed pallor. 'Bastards,' he said vehemently, dropping it to the floor.

'What bastards, Aaron?' said Elena gently. 'Do you know who did this?'

Emu stared vacantly at the Thomas the Tank Engine wallpaper for a full minute, then took a deep breath. 'I don't know nothin' about it,' he said, speaking very slowly. 'I tole you that this morning. It must just be sickos who think this shit is funny. So why don't you just find 'em? That's your job, isn't it?' He seized Indy from Elena and lurched through the ED doors and out into the night.

'Sarge, are you sure you should let him go?' Vince said, jumping to his feet as they watched the doors swinging. 'Is it safe for Indy to be under Emu's care in this state?'

'It's okay, Doc,' responded Elena with a tinge of annoyance. 'His mum and sister are in the car park waiting to pick them up and they're staying at Gabrielle's house for a few days. Community Services have a Child Protection Worker on her way, and Aaron is coming in at nine in the morning to talk to the Detective Sergeant at the CIU.'

For the first time ever, Vince detected a small crack in Elena's detached objectivity. There was a slight tremor in her voice and she looked almost fragile. Instinctively, he gave her a hug and she softened and leant into his embrace, but then he immediately stepped back and the window closed.

'Sorry, mate,' Vince said. 'I know you've had a hard day at the office. Never mind me, I just open my mouth to change feet.'

They simultaneously glanced around at the soft toys, bright colours and wacky wallpaper of the Paediatric Assessment Room and laughed at the incongruity of their surroundings.

'Doc, let's go somewhere and talk. This stuff is spiralling out of control and we need to get on top of it.'

'What about my surgery?' Vince looked at his watch—quarter to eight. 'No one will be there. We can send for pizza.'

35

Vince ushered Elena through the front door of the clinic and went to disarm the alarm, only to find that it had not been set.

'Well, well, well, if it's not Batman and Robin,' called Shirley as she peered at the intruders through the open door of her consulting room. 'This an after-hours consultation? Or are you helping the police with their enquiries? How are you, Inspector Mona?'

Christ, Vince thought, *wouldn't you know it—the boss still here!* Shirley had dubbed Elena 'Mona', due to her customary half smile and placid temperament.

'Fine thanks, Dr Tiang,' answered Elena. 'And you? Good. If you'll excuse me, I might just pop into the loo.'

Vince sat on one of the waiting room chairs. 'Baby Indigo was found this evening, Shirl—fit and well, but it's all very bizarre and we need to talk it through.'

'A debrief, eh?' responded Shirley, winking lewdly. 'Plenty of couches here for unloading your rocks.'

'You mean getting your rocks *off,* Shirl.'

'Whatever you say, Rooned.'

Vince sighed; he was too tired for Shirley's mischief making. 'Now just behave yourself, maybe you can help. Indy was dumped outside Holtens and she had this pinned to her clothes.'

He handed the document over and Shirley put on her glasses to inspect it.

'Just leave it in the plastic sleeve please,' added Elena as she came back into the waiting room. 'We'll be fingerprinting it later.'

'Message received, Constable,' answered Shirley with a salute.

The cleaners were vacuuming Vince's room so they went through to the tearoom. He rang the pizza shop and put the kettle on while Elena sat and Shirley studied the certificate.

'It's a warning to Emu Quick,' she commented. 'Like … do as we say by the end of next week or the baby dies.'

'He looked terrified,' said Vince, filling the coffee plunger. 'Some-one's really got the hooks into him.'

Shirley touched her head and tapped her feet. 'These one's for danc-ing, this one's for thinking; it's not that hard, is it? Once a junkie, always a junkie. It's got to be about drugs. Maybe Emu owes money to some pushers or something. He's probably just a little prawn and maybe he's doing some subcontracting and they found out.'

Vince and Elena both nodded; what else could it be?

'I hope you've taken that baby off him, Sergeant Mona,' Shirley said. 'Give her to some poor infertile girl—quicker than IVF, eh? They shouldn't let these druggies have kids. Should sterilise 'em all.'

'Why are you such a hard arse about drugs, Shirley?' asked Vince. He knew her daughter had died in her twenties; maybe it had been drug related.

Her only response was a shrug.

'And Aaron's been clean,' Elena told her. 'And he is Indy's father.'

'*Is* he and *is* he?' said Shirley with a laugh that set her earrings jan-gling.

Vince was now sure Emu was using again. He was on the nod yes-terday and his pupils were smaller than you'd expect in a dark room, but he decided to keep that to himself, otherwise the social workers would take Indy away from Emu and Vince didn't want this to happen. Not yet anyway.

'Speaking of druggies, Princess Petra has been a real naughty girl.'

'We know that, Shirley.'

'There's more, champ—steak knives, too. An AHPRA dude rang me today and said that one of the Senior Constable's mates at the Drug Squad had called him and—'

'Sounds like a game of Chinese whispers,' said Vince with a grin.

'You being racist again, Dr Hanrahan?' responded Shirley tersely. Elena looked worried.

'Relax, Sergeant,' said Shirley with a laugh. 'Just joshin'. Anyways, they did a test on her wee wee and guess what—coke!'

'Coke!' exclaimed Vince. 'Who'd have thought?'

'We're not talking fizzy drinks here, PC Mona.'

Elena smiled and nodded. 'I get the picture, Dr Tiang.'

'The Princess told the coppers she's been a regular user since she was a student. Started snorting coke at posh parties in Melbourne and then got a taste for it.'

'Were there any benzodiazepines in the specimen?'

She nodded with the usual noisy result. 'Apparently the Princess only takes the benzos for the post cocaine crashes and our peth and morph when she's hanging out.'

'Cocaine,' said Vince. 'That explains her mood and energy swings and sneezing and bloody noses, and the dysfunctional relationship she has with her father. Well, well, well.'

'Her father!' exclaimed Shirley. 'Shut up your ears, Inspector Mona, bit of patient confidences here.' Elena nodded and ducked out into the hallway.

'That man is a bully, Rooned,' Shirley said. 'Suzie is shits scared of him.'

I'm not surprised to hear that. 'Has he been knocking her around ?'

'Either that or she's been walking into a lot of doors, mate. That bastard is probably what's messed Petra up!'

'Why didn't you tell me about this before?'

'Nothing to do with you, champ. Doctor-patient stuff. I told Suzie to leave him, but no dices. You know how it is, that weird victim-abuser dependence thing.'

'So where's Petra now? Is she still in jail?

'She's been charged and is out on bails and going into rehab next week.'

'Let's hope it works for her, Shirley. Sounds like she'll need a heap of counselling, too.'

'Rehab never helps,' scoffed Shirley. 'Lock 'em up and throw out the key!' With that parting shot, she summoned Elena back in and walked off to her room, raucously singing: 'The Needle and the Damage Done.'

* * *

The pizzas arrived and Elena and Vince attacked them with gusto.

'This is hitting the spot, Doc,' commented Elena after a few minutes of refuelling. 'Although with this gooey base, it wouldn't make the cut in Lygon Street, let alone Italy.'

Vince shrugged and kept munching.

'So,' he said eventually, sitting back to allow his upper digestive tract a fighting chance. 'What do you reckon, Sarge?'

'Let's look at the facts, Doc. Aaron's been an IV drug user in the past. He alleges that Indy was stolen from his house overnight and claims he knows nothing about who and why. She turns up with a partially-completed death certificate attached and a projected date of death. Aaron's behaviour suggests he knows who might have done it and he's obviously very frightened.'

Vince nodded.

'We have to assume that whoever took the baby wants Emu to cooperate in some way or Indy will die.'

Scary, but true. 'Maybe Shirley is on the money after all, Sarge.'

'Some drug connection would seem very likely.'

'And all this extra heroin about the place must have something to do with it surely?'

Elena looked unimpressed. 'I can't imagine Aaron has the resources to import heroin and set up a trafficking network, Doc.'

'Nor is he the sort of evil bastard who would. If Emu's involved, to quote Shirley, he must be just a prawn in a bigger game.'

'We'll have to leave all that to the experts. Bit out of my league.'

Suddenly Vince remembered the disastrous start to his day; seemed like weeks ago. 'Speaking of being out of your league, I had my chat with Mr Harkin this morning and got towelled up good and proper.' He gave her a rundown of the conversation and the conclusion he'd reached.

'I did advise you to hold your fire, Doc,' responded Elena, with a hint of I-told-you-so. 'I can easily check his story out. But if the Minister has ignored our objection, we'll have to change our tactics.'

She really is a true believer. 'You Greenies going take to the streets and man the barricades, Sarge?'

'We'll see. GreenCoast may have to apply for a Supreme Court injunction. Anyway, it looks like Harkin's off the list of potential murderers.'

'Sure, but he's on top of my list of drug importers.' He told her about his theory, triggered off by the chance remark from Keiran Harrington, about the drilling platform boats potentially being used to bring drugs in.

'But Harkin's leaving town, isn't he?' asked Elena. 'He could hardly hand a drug importing scheme over to his successor. Surely not even the multinational resource companies are that corrupt?'

Vince picked up another piece of pizza; it was getting cold, a bit like his leads. 'He's probably got a trusted lieutenant or two. I don't see him actually doing the deed himself anyway. More the mastermind and profit distributor. He could still pull the strings from wherever he goes.'

He wiped his hands on a tea towel. 'Time for you to chat with your colleagues in the drug squad.'

She shook her head. 'We don't have a shred of evidence, only a half-baked hunch. The CID will investigate the kidnapping and the certificate, but the rest is pure speculation.'

They sat in silence for a few minutes, staring at the detritus of their feast. 'And Doc, you still haven't found your murderer.'

There was a knock at the door and Shirley popped her head through. 'Not interrupting anything, am I, kids?'

She looked at the containers. 'Pizzas on the Run, eh? I could eat the crutches of a low flying duck, but that stuff's crap! Anyway, I'm off—like a new bride's nightie. Hooroo!'

After Shirley's departure Vince turned off all the lights and set the alarm, and he and Elena headed out in silence to Vince's car—they had talked themselves into a standstill. He nosed Benny back up the hill and pulled into the hospital car park.

'I'll just wait with my lights up until you're in your car, Sarge.'

'What's with the chivalry, Doc?' she asked with a laugh. 'I'm a big girl now.'

What indeed? thought Vince. *Six months ago I wouldn't have bothered.*

'Before you go, Elena, there's something I want to tell you.'

She looked over expectantly.

'You asked me once what happened back in Melbourne and I owe you an explanation.' She nodded, and he took a deep breath. 'I had a first-time pregnant patient with a breech presentation, usually an automatic Caesar, and she fixed me with her baby blues and asked if I would deliver her vaginally. Sure, I said, no probs.' *Big fucking hero.*

Vince paused, breathing hard. 'On the night I got the call, Lydia and I were at a dinner party, a few grogs on board.' He rubbed his temples to ease the throbbing. 'The patient laboured away and dilated up then started pushing, and the … the baby's head got stuck.' He paused again. 'I tried with forceps, but the patient started haemorrhaging and I couldn't stop it, then she bled like stink and used up all her clotting factors.' He stared at Elena, *through* her. 'Her blood pressure plummeted and she … she arrested and we couldn't get her going.' His voice dropped to a whisper. 'She … she died.' He looked away, his voice breaking. 'So did the baby.' He paused. 'It was a boy—a perfect little boy.'

He put his lights up and motioned Elena towards her car. She opened her mouth and closed it again and quietly got out, her cheeks wet with tears.

Vince experienced a sudden wave of nausea. He exhaled slowly, fighting off that bitter memory, and drove slowly down across the railway line into South Warrnambool, his mind defaulting to an edgy stream of consciousness born of tiredness and anxiety, his 'Kerouac stage', as Sarah used to call it.

Elena was right—I've been obsessed about Harkin and all for nothing—who cares whether he's a drug importer? Not the bloody Medical Board. As Dad would say, 'Son, you're still up shit creek in a barbed-wire canoe.' Okay, back to the main game. Let's think—Emu, well he couldn't have killed Allan anyway, could he? No way he could've have written that script. So that just leaves Rita. But she knew Allan couldn't have been the father and she wouldn't have killed him just because he was having an affair with Polly—she was the latest of many. What about Fletcher Smit? Seemingly a bad, bad man. Allan was going to oppose the JIR funding and raise irregularities in the books at the forthcoming Abgrow AGM. Fletcher knew Abrow needed that money, so he needed JIR to hang around—but was that enough reason to eliminate his mate and business partner? Surely not. Maybe the two deaths weren't connected ...

When he eventually collapsed into bed, Vince's thoughts were still spinning like a carousel. As he fell asleep there was a pair of horses that just kept coming around. One had Little Lachie sitting in the saddle, using Vince's stethoscope as a whip, and the other was ridden by a gasping Allan, screaming out for Propranolol.

36

Next morning, Vince felt like he hadn't slept at all. Exhausted. He struggled through the day and eventually made it home and collapsed on his couch, then cursed as his mobile disturbed his reverie. He glanced at the screen. *Bloody Lydia!*

'I really don't know what will become of them. Your pep talk was an abject failure—if anything they're even worse!' Vince winced and moved the phone further away from his ear. 'Ivan says they need counselling before it's too late. They've introduced this ridiculous ban on homework and refuse to even make their beds. And as for those ludicrous belly button rings, what were you thinking, Vincent? I've made sure they had blood tests. Who knows what they might have picked up? I want you to tell them to make the most of their opportunities ...'

'Yada, yada, yada,' Vince muttered as he tuned out and started flicking through the newspaper.

' ... need to put their heads down ... start acting responsibly ... on the Friday night train ... Hopefully this work experience down there will make them see sense ...'

Work experience, he mused, *that's not till* ... he glanced at the date on the sports page—*shit, it must be next bloody week!* Tessa was to spend the time with the park ranger at Tower Hill—a local extinct volcanic crater teaming with flora and fauna, while Georgie did time at Waves FM, learning to operate the panel and presenting some music programs.

Lydia eventually ran out of steam, so Vince dutifully promised to pick up the girls on Friday then promptly hung up. Apparently they were all now firmly ensconced at Ivan's South Yarra residence, and although Tessa loyally described it as 'way OTT', Georgie's comment was, 'it's, like, totes amazeballs, Bins: four bathrooms and a tennis court.'

Vince looked around his own modest abode, realising he would have to tidy up the Snapper house over the weekend and do a big supermarket shop. He sat at the kitchen table, wrote a list and stuck it to the fridge. A start at least.

He then had a quick shower, pulled on some clean clothes, grabbed his guitar and headed off to Charlie McNamee's house out on the Hopkins. He didn't have his heart in the idea but, as he told Shirley when asking for directions, he felt obligated. 'Letting St Charlie down,' she'd agreed, 'be like shooting Bambi.'

Charlie's wife Annie, a petite blond high-school music teacher, and a gaggle of small children, welcomed Vince at the door. While the roast lamb was cooking he was inveigled into a game of hidey around the garden and thoroughly enjoyed the mindless mayhem and hysterical screaming. After the lovely dinner he sat back and experienced an odd sensation of bodily stillness and mental quiet.

Despite his protestations, Vince was forced to drag out his guitar— badly in need of a tune—and accompanied Annie as she sang some bluesy ballads, with Charlie howling away on the harp. The meditative effect of the twelve-bar blues progressing rhythmically towards its satisfying resolution each cycle was like a balm for Vince's troubled soul, and in a flash it was midnight. As he drove back home across the river he was aware of a rare feeling of contentment.

The following day, Vince rose at sparrow's fart, went into work and attacked his mountain of paperwork. Amongst the pile he recognised an envelope—the Coroner's office! With his heart in his mouth he ripped it open. Bugger! An exhumation and an inquest. Not unexpected, but the reality of it chilled him to the bone; Little Lachie and the Board wouldn't be far behind. It was all closing in.

Vince shut his eyes, took a deep breath, slowly let it out and tried to still his mind. He opened his eyes again, glanced at his list and concentrated completely on the day's punters. The day flew past, and at mid—afternoon he was interrupted by his desk phone ringing.

'It's Senior Constable Genovesi, Doctor. She says it's *urgent*.' There was a trace of sarcasm in the receptionist's voice.

'Put her through, Sharon.'

Elena's voice was insistent but unmistakably stressed—unprecedented. 'Sorry to ring your work number, Doc, but you didn't answer your mobile. Aaron Quick's been brought into ED by the ambos. Yeah, OD. Gabrielle called them. She came round to drop Indy off and he was unconscious on the couch.'

Vince shuddered. 'What's Darren saying?' His mate, Darren Gallus, an experienced Emergency Physician, was in charge of the ED.

'He told me it was heroin and he gave Aaron that reversing stuff. Lucky Gabrielle came when she did or he probably wouldn't have made it. Another thing, Doc,' she added, 'I was talking to Gab Quick at the hospital. Do you realise she works for the company that cleans your surgery? It wouldn't be hard for her to print out a script if a computer was left on.'

'Good work, Sarge,' Vince said, his mind starting to wind up again. 'I have noticed Gab amongst the crew, and she and Emu are very close.'

* * *

By the time he got to the hospital, Emu had been transferred to the Intensive Care Unit under the care of Danny Nguyen. Vince pulled the curtains around, dragged up a chair and moved his head close to Emu's tousled dreadies. His thin face was even more sallow than usual.

'You're lucky to be still around, mate. I thought you were straight these days. Aren't you supposed to be on the 'done?'

Emu turned and stared at Vince for a few minutes before he responded in a hoarse whisper. 'I knew I had to stay clean, Doc, but I thought, like, one taste won't hurt.'

Vince let out an exasperated sigh. 'Emu, I don't know whether a junkie is an appropriate person to be caring for a small child, and it's my job to notify Community Services. They've already received one report from the coppers. Maybe it's time Indy had a proper family to live with.'

Emu sat up like he'd been given another dose of Narcan. 'You wouldn't do that, Doc. I've been lookin' after her real good. She's mine.' He turned his head and stared at the wall.

'Emu, we don't even know if you really are her father, do we?'

Emu spun back and faced Vince. 'That's all bullshit. Polly and me knew it couldn't be Findlay. You know when she had that bleedin'? The scan showed she was already knocked up when they done the job. We just strung him along a bit, to teach the old bastard a lesson.'

'What sort of lesson, mate?'

'Well, Doc,' he said with a sneer, 'when Polly told him she didn't know who the father was, he got all fired up and said he'd find out. He told her that if the baby was his, they would move to Port Fairy and live happily ever bloody after.' There was considerable venom in Emu's voice.

'And what if the baby wasn't his?'

'Bastard said if that he wasn't the father, he wanted nothin' to do with it. Findlay just wanted a kid to carry on the family name,' Emu added. 'He didn't really care about Polly at all. She was just a side issue.'

More like a bit on the side, Vince thought. 'How did she feel about that, Emu?'

'What d'ya reckon, Doc? She hated his guts.'

'But they still had to work together, mate.'

Emu smiled. 'She was nice as pie at work. We wanted to keep him bloody guessin'.'

Was that just mischief making or what?

'When you brought Indigo in for her shots, you said, "Findlay knew what he had to do." You didn't blackmail him after Polly died, did you, mate? Like, I'll say nothing about you fathering this baby, Professor—for a price.'

'I'm not a bloody criminal, Doc,' Emu said ambiguously, with as much dignity as he could muster in a backless white gown with a drip in his arm. 'Anyway, the old prick figured it out for himself. When he came round to see Indy, he wanted to see her baby book, and he just looked in it and did this stupid laugh and said he couldn't be the father.'

What's that about? Anyway, another theory down the drain—what now? He instinctively felt Emu held the key to it all, and Vince needed some leverage. Again, he leant close to the young man's ear, so close he could see the row of holes from where an array of hardware had been removed.

'Emu, here's the thing. Someone killed Polly and someone killed Allan Findlay. You were in the labour ward with Polly and you had the opportunity. You also hated Allan and you could have got your sister access to his medical records at the clinic.'

A low chuckle emanated from under the tousled dreadies. 'Geez, Doc, you must be desperate. Gab's dyslexic, can't even read let alone use a bloody computer.'

Fair enough, thought Vince, *another idea evaporated.* 'You're still suspect number one, smartarse, so I think I'll have a little chat to the coppers about you, mate, and—'

Emu rolled over and sat up in one movement, almost knocking Vince off his chair. 'Listen, Doc, I wish I had killed one of 'em, but I fucken didn't. And I didn't kill the other one,' he paused as tears welled up in his bloodshot eyes, 'but I bloody well might have.' He fell back again, exhausted by the effort.

'What are you talking about, Emu?' asked Vince, a little more gently.

Silence.

'There is a shitload of heroin about the place, Emu, and I reckon you know all about it. If you don't start giving me some answers, mate, you will lose your daughter *and* face murder charges.'

Nothing.

Vince rose and looked around the ICU: monitors beeping and lights blazing. 'Well, you won't get much sleep here. You've got the whole night to think about it—bit late to ring CSV now. I'll come back in the morning and we'll have another chat. Sleep well, sweet prince.'

* * *

Vince called back at the clinic on his way home from the hospital and was surprised to find the lights still on and a smart-looking young woman sitting in the waiting room. Someone must be working late. As he walked to his room he encountered Shirley and the Prez escorting an equally smart-looking young man out of Shirley's room.

'What are you guys doing?' he asked Shirley as Pete farewelled the bloke and beckoned the woman in.

'Just a bit of interviewing, Rooned,' she responded sheepishly. 'We have to plan for next year. Petra's gone and you …'

'Hell, Shirl,' interrupted Vince, 'I haven't been given the arse yet!

He strode to his room and slammed the door.

Vince started his computer and brought up Polly's file. She'd come in on the eleventh of December thinking she might be pregnant, and with some light vaginal bleeding. The pregnancy test was positive and she thought the first day of her last period was around the thirtieth of October, giving a due date of the sixth of August, meaning she should have been six weeks. The bleeding had stopped and her cervix was closed, so Vince had arranged a blood test and an ultrasound. So, Polly must have then realised that she was with Allan around the time of conception and told him about the pregnancy that night. He looked back at the file. The scan the next day confirmed things were okay, but gave her gestation as ten weeks with a due date of July tenth, so she was actually four weeks further on than she thought and already pregnant at the time of her weekend with Allan.

He sat at his desk, thinking hard. Despite the previous morning's paperwork blitz, a new pile was already forming on his desk. Sitting on top were a number of Maternal and Child Health booklets, waiting for him to record details of vaccinations. He grabbed one and flipped open the front page. There was the baby's name, mother's name, and date and place of birth. And—the baby's blood group!

Next he located Indigo's file; her blood group was AB positive. Then he looked up to see if Allan's group was in his history. He ran down through the various cholesterol levels and sputum culture results. There it was: O negative. So that's how Allan figured it out. Oh well, goodbye to the paternity motive for both Allan and Emu.

That only left drugs.

A few pieces of the jigsaw were joining up in Vince's head, but he needed to see what the whole picture looked like. And he had an idea how.

<h1 style="text-align:center">37</h1>

The next morning Vince received an early call from Danny. 'Ox, that kid's in a spot of bother.'

'I thought he was going okay,' Vince said. 'I figured you'd kick him out of the unit and into the wards today.'

'Oh yeah,' said Danny with a wry laugh. 'He got away with the overdose, all right, but I've just got his path back. He's both Hep B and Hep C positive, and by the look of his liver function tests he's already got significant parenchymal liver damage and is in hepatic failure. Too far gone for drug treatment.'

'No surprises there, Danny. Emu's been an IV drug user for years.' Vince cast his mind back to Emu's file at the clinic. 'I think we knew he was positive for Hep C.'

'So did you do the PCR to see if he had an active infection?'

Vince laughed. 'Settle down, mate, that result was ten years ago. Way before my time.'

'I'm guessing no one tested his viral load or genotype either. Really Vince, you GPs need to be more ...'

'Just back off there, Daniel,' cut in Vince. Louder than he meant. 'I told Emu he needed follow up, but you can only lead a junkie to water ...'

Danny nodded. 'Fair enough. Anyway he's obviously had active Hepatitis for ages. I did a fibroscan and his liver is already cirrhotic.'

'I thought it took decades for Hepatitis C to cause cirrhosis. Emu's only twenty-nine.'

'Usually does,' replied Danny. 'But co-infection with Hepatitis B accelerates the inflammatory process.'

'What about the new Hep C wonder drugs?' Even Vince had heard about this breakthrough from Shirley during one of his tutorials. Instead of the old-fashioned interferon treatment, which was very user unfriendly and mostly ineffective, there was a new medication—one tablet daily for twelve weeks with an almost cure.

'Emu's in advanced liver failure, Vince. Too far gone for drug treatment. And it looks like he might have a hepatoma.'

'Poor bugger,' said Vince. This meant liver cancer, a recognised complication of Hepatitis C.

'I'm planning a biopsy in case he gets a shot at a transplant.'

'What about his HIV status?'

'Still to come. I might let you tell him the results, Ox. You GPs have those special communication skills.'

'Gee, thanks, mate. I'm on my way to have a little chat to him now.'

* * *

'You can piss off,' Emu said as soon as Vince walked into the ward. He pointed to his bed card. 'Doctor Danny is my guy and I've got nothin' to say to you.'

He looked a bit more composed than last night. Mentally that was. Physically he looked wrecked—his jaundiced cheeks almost meeting behind his nose. He was in a single room in the general medical ward.

'I just came to say congratulations, Emu—you've hit the jackpot. Hep B positive and Hep C positive. You're moving right through the hepatitis alphabet. It doesn't look good, mate.'

This news put a small dent in Emu's defiant attitude. 'That doesn't mean jackshit. Bulk people are hep positive and they're just carriers and lots of 'em never get the bloody thing.'

Vince sat and held out some pathology printouts. 'Seeing as you're an expert Hepatologist, let me show you something. Do liver function tests mean anything to you, Professor? Some people do clear the virus but others don't. Their liver gets scarred to buggery, shrinks from a football down to a meat pie, and they develop liver failure. And then they die.' He pointed at the results. 'Looking at these numbers, matey, I'd say sooner rather than later.'

'What about them new Hep C tablets?' Emu struggled into a sitting position. 'The government's payin' for them now.'

'Too late, Emu, too late.'

'You'd spin any crap to get me to talk, Doc. You're just tryin' to get yourself off the bloody hook.'

Truer words never spoken. Time to lay it on the line. 'Just read my lips, sunshine. Your only chance is a liver transplant and most people die before their number comes up. So much for looking after your daughter, so much for protecting your own arse, and so much for covering for these pricks. If you don't believe me, ask Dr Nguyen. You've got nothing to lose, mate.'

Emu sank back into the bed and closed his eyes. After a few minutes he opened them again, but with a distant look. 'I can't tell you much, Doc,' he said softly, 'and that's the bloody truth. Since Polly died I've been clean, but I needed money for rent and all that formula and nappies and shit for Indy. So I started to deal a little around the campus.'

At last! 'So where is the stuff coming from?'

Emu's voice dropped to a scared whisper. 'All's I know is what I had to do. I meet this dude every Thursday night at the back of the skateboarding ramp behind the Bayview pub.'

'Who's the guy?'

'Dunno—he keeps his motorbike helmet on. I hand over the money and he gives me the gear plus my cut, then jumps on his big hog and pisses off up the road.' He nodded to the west.

'Except the last time, he gave you a little bonus, did he Emu?'

'Like I said, it was just a taste.'

'Ice?'

'No, I keep right away from that shit, Doc. I got fucked up on ice before. It was smack.'

'And what about the day Indy was snatched—you'd had some then, hadn't you?'

After a few minutes of mental struggle, Emu looked like a defeated man. 'I knew what would happen with Indy if I started using again. But those bastards wanted me to do more and more dealing, and I said no way. So they gave me some H for free, but it must have been cut with some other shit, 'cos it completely messed me up and when I woke, Indy was gone.' He paused for a minute, exhausted. 'When I got her back I said I would do anythin' they wanted and the guy gave some more, as … as like a reward.' He looked desperately around the ward. 'And now look where I am.'

'Giving a hot shot to a clean junkie like you was a kiss of death. Maybe you'd passed your use by date, eh, Emu? Now's your big chance to be a good guy. You're going to help us find these mongrels and bust them.'

Emu suddenly sparked up. 'Like hell I am! I'd rather take my chance with a buggered liver. I tole you—I don't even know who they are. I just do the business and ask no questions. Find someone else to do your dirty work.'

There is no one else. Vince looked around the ward, at the nurses and the patients in their beds. *This medical caper is all I know and this wasted junkie is all I've got.* No choice. Time to put the screws on.

He looked at his watch. 'Ah, just after eight. CSV will be open in half an hour. By midday Indy will be in State care, you'll be in *here,* and those bastards will still be out *there.*'

38

Vince walked out of the ward, disgusted with himself for being such a bastard, but hoping his bastardry had done the job. The morning was getting on, so he raced around the wards and finished up at the Day Stay Unit to put in a drip for a patient who was having chemotherapy. As he was leaving the ward, he got a page from the hospital switchboard—a patient on ward six wanted to talk to him.

'Yes!' Vince said out loud, punching the air as he turned and raced up the stairs again. After another ten valuable minutes with the noticeably failing Emu, he shot out of the hospital like a rocket. Time for action! He jumped in the car and grabbed his mobile. 'Elena, it's me, what are you doing tonight?'

'I'm pretty free on Thursday nights. What did you have in mind?'

'I've been talking to Emu. He's been dealing again and Thursday nights are his pick up and drop off nights. I need someone with a fast car to help me catch the bad guys.'

'Gee, Doc, you know how to make a girl feel special.'

Vince told Elena about his conversation with Emu, leaving out the bits that could be interpreted as unprofessional or even illegal.

'Now, wait a minute,' she said. 'I need to tell the boss and CIU and maybe the drug squad need to be involved, not a junior uniformed copper and a middle-aged GP. Who do you think we are, Special Ops?'

Vince was not in the mood for objections. He even let the 'middle-aged' crack go.

'Elena, listen, if you call in the cavalry, these bastards will smell a rat and the whole deal will be blown. Emu's okay tonight but by next week he may get cold feet or even be cold all over. As they say in the classics, baby—tonight's the night.'

There was a long pause over the line. 'You're not trained for this sort of thing, Doc. Better to leave it to the experts.'

'If things look like they're getting out of hand, we can call for reinforcements from your uniforms—what else do they do Thursday nights? Add up traffic fines? We just park behind the pub, then after Emu does his deal, we wait till we hear a motorbike engine go past and then follow him and—voila!'

She still sounded unconvinced. 'And what if the guy spots us?'

'Come on, Sarge. You must know how to follow in a discreet fashion. Didn't they teach you anything at that academy?'

* * *

'I must be out of my mind doing this', whispered Elena exactly twelve hours later. They were sitting in a canary yellow Leyland P76 behind the Bayview Hotel, a large ugly brick construction exemplifying the worst of sixties' design and notorious as a place to score drugs.

'Where did you get this barge anyway?' Vince murmured, dragging his eyes away. 'It's hardly inconspicuous, stands out like dog's balls in a snowstorm.'

The P76 was a large, ugly sedan that had gained a modest cult following in the seventies for reasons unknown even to the aficionados.

'I borrowed it from my brother—in-law, he's a P76 tragic,' she hissed. 'Mum's got my Honda. Did you want me to come in the patrol car with lights and sirens?'

Vince glanced around the car park. 'Fair call. Now don't forget, if anyone comes past we need to do some heavy duty canoodling and make it look like we mean it. These drug people know the real thing when they see it.'

He looked at Elena. It was a warm evening and her low-cut top revealed a considerable amount of cleavage. Vince forced his gaze away and focused instead on the steering wheel. He was reminded of the Jerry Seinfeld comment: 'Looking at cleavage is like looking at the sun—you don't stare at it. It's too risky.'

Elena certainly looks the part—the sexy young lover. Actually, maybe that's what she is.

They had dropped the reluctant and declining Emu near the front of the pub and Vince hoped like hell he would last the distance. Danny Nguyen had given him shots of steroid and anti-emetics and run in some IV fluids to keep him upright long enough to close the deal—not that Danny actually knew what the deal was. 'Just trust me, mate,' was all Vince had told him. Danny had the impression Emu was visiting Indy and Vince left it at that.

They sat in the dark, both uncertain and apprehensive.

'Emu looks terrible, Doc,' Elena finally said. 'Isn't this a bit cruel?'

'There's nothing more we can do for poor Emu; he's on his way out, so he might as well take these buggers with him.' *And he just might just save my skin too.*

'But won't his contact wonder what's wrong with him?'

'He never looks too flash at the best of times, Sarge, and believe me, Emu's health is the last thing this bloke will be worrying about.'

Suddenly a couple slowly cruised past in a ute, maybe planning on a spot of amorous parking too. Vince pounced on Elena and pulled her face to his, the first touch tentative before she returned the kiss, her lips wet, her tongue searching as she pushed her breasts against him. Not to be outdone in the 'method acting' stakes, Vince renewed his efforts and wriggled his legs around to allow room for the sudden increase in pressure in the front of his jeans.

Scarcely realising their performance had segued into the genuine article, he slid his hand up the front of Elena's top and under her bra as she pulled down his fly and turned that pressure rise into a near explosion. At that second they both heard the sound of a highly powered motorbike throb into action, and in an instant it shot past, trailing dust and vanishing into the night.

Elena extricated herself, readjusted her clothes, turned on the ignition, and the big car wheeled around and headed back out onto the road. They anxiously scanned in both directions.

Vince's mobile phone started ringing from deep inside his jacket and he fumbled in the pocket with a curse and turned it off.

'It's gone left,' he shouted. 'I can't see it, but it sounds like its headed west!'

'I couldn't see where it went,' responded Elena as they sped up the highway in pursuit and were soon on the main coastal road out of town. Suddenly they caught a glimpse of single taillight way up ahead, and Elena fell back enough to keep in touch.

They travelled across the Merri River bridge, through Dennington and past the cheese factory on to the highway. The lights from the off-shore JIR platform were visible as they tailed the bike for the next fifteen kilometres, travelling well inside the speed limit.

'Looks like just a law-abiding respectable biker,' Elena commented. 'Probably just going to visit his old mum in Port Fairy.'

'I certainly hope not,' said Vince. 'Talk about *bikus interruptus*.'

'Hmm,' she said softly, looking straight ahead. 'I hope we haven't jumped the gun, Doc.'

Jesus, Vince thought, *I almost jumped the bloody gun myself!*

The motorbike continued on up to Tower Hill, an extinct volcano, and then took a left off the highway at Killarney towards the beach. They followed him down Mahoney's Road between a series of dark paddocks towards a group of large steel sheds, gleaming silver in the moonlight, the ocean visible and audible just beyond. Elena stopped twenty-five metres short of the complex, which loomed in front of them like an array of massive aircraft hangers.

'Well, well, well,' murmured Vince as the motorcyclist switched off his engine. 'All roads lead to Rome.' The guy dismounted and disappeared around the far side of the nearest building.

'Is there something you're not telling me, Doc?' asked Elena.

'Let's go,' Vince said urgently, leaping out of the car. 'Time to rock and roll!'

'This is madness, we can't just go in there,' she responded, swinging open her door. 'We have no warrant, no back up, we …'

But Vince was already walking quickly towards the path that ran alongside the sheer metal wall, and he could hear Elena in hot pursuit. When he glanced over his shoulder, she was punching in a message on her mobile phone.

Seconds later she caught up with him and they crept along the path. There was no outside lighting and the blackness was blanket-heavy. A small window, weakly lit by an internal light, revealed a big sliding door on the side of the building. The only sound was the low rumble of a small motor and the occasional crash of the surf.

Vince nodded toward the door. 'He must have gone in there,' he whispered. 'There's no other entrance.'

Elena carefully scanned the area with a small Maglite. 'Hey, Doc,' she muttered, briefly illuminating the ground around them. 'Do up your fly.'

Vince followed her advice, then gave the door a gentle push. It slid open surprisingly easily. He felt Elena pressing up close right behind him. Thirty minutes before, that intimacy would have made his heart race, but it was already belting away like a badly tuned lawnmower. She then slipped past him, taking the lead as they stepped inside.

They had a brief glimpse of a huge network of tanks, pools and pumps, but a second later everything went black; Vince could see nothing and all he could hear was the thunderous sound of rushing water. Elena switched on her torch again and it cut an arc through the black, exposed eerie slices of silver metal and dark wetness. They crept slowly across the concrete floor, hands on the wall to guide them towards the front of the building.

Brightness exploded around them, lightning-bolt harsh. Temporarily blinded, Vince took a step back. Engines revved, raging growls that shook every part of him.

He blinked rapidly, and as his sight came into focus, huge lights were on all over the building and a figure stood no more than five metres away, holding a large flashlight and a gun.

Fletcher Smit.

Two forklifts sped towards them, herding them back into a corner of the building where a large open trap door awaited. Wet blackness beyond.

'We were expecting you, Dr Hanrahan,' said Fletcher. 'But the presence of Senior Constable Genovesi is a surprise. Shame your visit will be so short. We don't want any of your lads in blue to spoil the treat I have arranged, so we will dispense with the niceties.' His lips drew into a snarl. 'I know you both like the water, so I have arranged a late-night dip in our seawater holding tank. Very cold and very full.'

They were backed right up to the opening and the forks were forcing them closer to the edge. Elena stepped forward, shielding Vince. 'You don't have to do this, Smit,' she said, tone conciliatory but firm. 'Let's just talk.'

Fletcher laughed and motioned the drivers onwards.

'Come on, Fletch!' Vince shouted in desperation. 'At least let Elena go. She knows nothing about …'

Vince snapped his head toward the unmistakable sound of car engines outside, followed by slamming doors. Fletcher turned and ran to the entrance as his henchmen leapt from their machines and followed … where they all ran into a carload of Warrnambool's finest.

39

The crowd was down for a Friday night. Vince guessed the punters might've been scared away by the news of the arrest of the restaurant's owner. Double murder and drug trafficking could certainly be enough to put you off your green curry.

However, Elena and Vince had seen no reason to change their habit of almost a year—Fletcher Smit was safely behind bars and Vince had suddenly rediscovered his appetite.

'So, Doc,' said Elena, as she poured herself another glass of cabernet. 'Did you know that last night's pursuit was going to end at Fletcher's door? And if so, why on earth didn't you tell me?'

Vince leant back in his chair. 'It was really a process of elimination, Sarge. I figured that, apart from Rita, he was the only person Allan had confided in about his concerns about the amount of money going through Abgrow's books. It was all in those emails you found.' He raised his glass in a toast to Elena. 'Trouble was, I found it just about impossible to believe myself, let alone try to convince you.'

'Yeah, Fletcher Smit—pillar of society, Chairman of the Warrnambool Chamber of Commerce, Life Member of the Surf Club ...'

'Not to mention serial abuser and psychopath,' added Vince quietly, leaning forward. 'I got a call from Shirley's husband Gareth this morning. He'd been talking to one of his shrink mates at the Melbourne Clinic and apparently Petra had a lengthy spell there last year with PTSD and substance issues. So maybe Fletcher was knocking her around, too.'

Elena looked disgusted. 'What a failed human being that man is.'

'Course that information didn't come from me, Sarge,' said Vince.

Elena nodded. 'And Petra Smit was in the labour ward during Polly's labour and in your consulting room the day Allan's prescription was issued. So she had the opportunity and means to commit both murders. Obvious, looking back.'

Vince murmured his agreement. 'Exactly, but as Shirl always says, the best instrument in medicine is the retrospectoscope.'

'Same in policing, Doc,' she responded with a laugh.

'I should've picked Petra for a cocaine user too, especially the way she acted at work.'

'Just shows that drug abuse can occur right across the socio-economic spectrum, eh Doc?'

'You sound like a sociologist, Sarge, but yes, from Braybrook all the way to Brighton. Now there's one less in Warrnambool,' he said sadly.

Emu had lapsed into fulminating liver failure in the early hours of the morning and died en-route to Melbourne for a transplant. Vince's prognosis, although exaggerated, had proven correct. Indy was in the safe care of Gabrielle and Grandma and would probably stay there.

Vince still felt puzzled as he expertly seized some bok choy with his chopsticks. 'I figured Fletcher was our villain, but I still don't understand the whole drug smuggling process. Fletcher was bringing in heroin and trafficking it via users like Emu, okay? What did that have to do with JIR?'

'Fletcher was using the Abgrow boats that go out to the abalone tanks in the ocean to pick up the drugs from ships further out to sea—probably North Korean or Chinese, then bringing them back to the abalone nursery and distributing from there.' Elena added some chilli sauce to her stir-fry and took a bite. 'He needed JIR, because with all their craft going back and forward to the drilling platform, his own boats could cruise around unnoticed.' She leant forward. 'And *that* information didn't come from *me.*'

They ate in silence for a few minutes.

'That's why he needed to eliminate any opposition to the drilling.'

'Correct. He also needed Abgrow as a laundry for the drug money, and when Allan discovered that the sums didn't add up, Fletcher realised he had to go before he could raise it at the AGM.'

Vince nodded. 'It was when Fletch told me there was very little money coming in that I first smelled a rat—it just didn't ring true.'

Elena poured herself another glass of red and topped up Vince's water. 'But why Polly, Doc? What threat was she?'

Vince thought back to his last conversation with Emu. Pointless to keep any secrets now. 'Emu told me Polly was really shitty when he got back on the gear and she discovered he was dealing as well. She said she'd leave him if he didn't give it away, tell you guys too and blow the whistle on the whole network.'

Elena looked surprised. 'So Polly's death was all about drugs, not paternity or mining. Emu must have told his contact that Polly was on to them.'

Vince nodded. 'He virtually signed her death warrant.'

'Well he didn't have much choice really, Doc. Either he kept dealing and Polly shopped him or he backed off and hoped those guys would leave him alone.'

'Emu was very naïve in some ways,' said Vince. 'I reckon it was only when they snatched Indigo that he realised they had definitely killed Polly.'

They both fell quiet, Vince exhausted with all that talking.

Suddenly the twins appeared behind Elena like apparitions from a dream.

'Georgie! Tessa! What are you guys doing here?' Vince exclaimed, dropping a mussel on his lap. 'You're not coming till next week!'

The girls reeled back in mock indignation, hands on hips and lips pursed—perfect caricatures of their mother.

'What a crap welcome for his lovely daughters, don't you think, PC?' said Georgie. 'Friday, the thirtieth—it's not that hard, buddy. We waited at that old station for over an hour, and then walked all the way here to find you out on a date.'

'Yeah, we were alone in the dark,' put in Tessa, milking the abandoned waif angle vigorously as she pinched a prawn from Vince's plate, then picked his phone up from the table and tried to turn it on. 'Dead as.'

'I'm sorry, girls, I thought your mum meant next Friday. I was going to charge my phone last night, but I left my charger at home and,' he glanced at Elena. 'I got, ah, well caught up.'

They raised their eyebrows.

'Sure,' said Tessa.

'As you do,' added Georgie.

Vince had a sudden terrible thought. 'Probably no need to mention this to your mother, girls. She'll kill me.'

'What evs,' said Georgie.

'Maybe not, Bins,' said Tessa. 'But it'll cost you.'

A sudden thought hit Vince like a thunderbolt. *Why should I give a bugger what Lydia thinks anymore, anyway?* The real estate agent had told him on Monday that the Snapper house was back on the market and he had a good mind to make an offer.

A waitress arrived with the takeaways the girls had ordered and Vince escorted them out with copious apologies and put them in a taxi. 'Catch you later, PC Elena,' called Georgie. 'We'll turn the bed down for you!'

When Vince came back, he and Elena concentrated on eating for a while.

'So Fletcher got Petra to murder them both,' Elena said after a few minutes. 'Talk about a dutiful daughter, Doc. I guess killing people was her role in the family business just because she had access to the appropriate drugs.'

'Yeah. Plus I reckon Fletcher was drip-feeding her habit too, so he really had her cornered.'

'What a bastard!' Elena exclaimed, with considerable vehemence. First time Vince had ever heard her swear. Maybe she was loosening up.

'Exactly, Sarge.'

Listen to me, Vince thought, *I'm hardly Father of the Year either.* In fact all through this sorry business, fatherhood itself had taking a bit of a beating. Himself, Fletcher, Allan and of course Emu. The old Queen base run thudded in his mind: *'Boom boom boom boom, Another One Bites the Dust.'*

Elena suddenly sat forward. 'Doc, why didn't you warn me last night about what we were heading into, so I could've organised some cover?

I broke every rule in policing and the Senior Sergeant is ropable!'

Vince's initial cheeky smile disappeared when he saw the look on her face. 'I'm really sorry about that. I kept it to myself because I needed to lean on Emu and he would've clammed up if coppers were involved.'

Elena shook her head vigorously. 'But if I hadn't texted work just before we went in there, my guys wouldn't have come at all. Then what?'

'Yeah, I know, but I just wanted to keep it simple. I didn't think Fletcher would actually try to knock us off. Stupid, I guess.'

Vince shrugged; it had been crazy and dangerous, but he'd been desperate. He'd needed to flush Fletcher out.

'How did you exclude Rita? Being unable to have a baby could just about send you round the bend.'

Vince glanced at Elena to see if he could discern any hint of the personal on the other sides of those deep ocular mirrors.

'Till yesterday, I had still had her as a contender, but Emu told me that Allan couldn't have been Indigo's father, the timing was all wrong, and Allan had eventually worked that out too. But what Allan didn't know, and Rita did, was that biology ruled him right out of the paternity stakes anyway.'

Elena frowned.

'You didn't hear this from me either, mate,' whispered Vince, 'but he was firing blanks.'

Elena digested all this and then smiled. 'I'll bet it wasn't for want of trying, Doc. The Prof certainly had a wandering eye.'

Nothing wrong with a bit of wandering, Vince thought, as he gazed at that beguiling smile as if for the first time. He took a deep breath, tipped his tonic into the water jug and poured them each a big glass of red.

Elena looked worried. 'Are you sure that's a good idea?'

Vince put his hand on hers, proffered his glass for a toast, safe in the knowledge that he was in the clear. At last.

'Trust me, I *am* a doctor.'

About the Author

Bill Bateman practised medicine for twenty-five years on Victoria's rugged south-west coast, before moving with his family to the city. Currently he works at an inner suburban GP practice and a drop-in clinic for the homeless. He was the author of a fortnightly (hopefully funny) column in *The Australian Doctor*, a national medical magazine, and now turns his pen to novel writing. The characters and setting of *Hard Labour* will appear in Bill's future books.

www.ingramcontent.com/pod-product-compliance
Lightning Source LLC
Chambersburg PA
CBHW050519190726

48284CB00003B/869